GIRL ON FIRE

GIRL ON FIRE

CHERIE DAWN HAAS

Copyright © 2016 Cherie Dawn Haas
Title page art by Dwayne Haas
All rights reserved.
ISBN-13: 9780692751879
ISBN-10: 0692751874

Dedicated to my mother, Darla Wipfel

And to my tribal sisters

CONTENTS

ACKNOWLEDGMENTS

"So, what made you get into fire dancing?"

This is the most common question I'm asked when someone finds out that I am a fire eater.

The personal experiences in my life that led me to writing this story are due to unlikely circumstances. My mom and dad introduced me to dance classes when I was about three years old, and high school introduced me to depression when I was about fifteen. In my healthier twenties, an office colleague said to me one Friday, "Hey, I'm going to someone's house tomorrow morning to take a belly dance class from her. It's only five dollars. You should come."

I went, and it changed my life in the most amazing ways.

My experiences in the tribal belly dance community were nothing short of amazing, and there are many people to thank for that. This includes, but is not limited to, the dancers and musicians of Gaiananda, Keshvar Project, Tree of Life World Music, the Cinnamon Sisters, Mayan Ruins, and the tribe of fire and belly dancers that I called family, Dante's Gypsy Circus: Andi Clemons, Laura Hughes, Danielle Kuntz, Sadi Pushing

Daisys, Britney Bogard, Master Pokes, and Megan Clark Strabley. We had a lot of fun pushing others (and ourselves) outside of their comfort zones.

By taking care of my sons, my mom, Darla Wipfel and my stepdad, Carrel Wipfel, gave me countless hours to attend or teach dance classes and workshop weekends, to go to performances (others' and my own), and, if I'm going to be honest, sometimes even to sleep in the next day after my performances.

Shawn Daniel Buckenmeyer (rest in peace), Chuck Heffner, Heather Lea Hitson, Laura Hughes, Renee Miller, and McKenzie Graham bravely read this book in its earliest, messiest stages. Each of them contributed in some way, giving me friendly advice or encouragement as well as nitty-gritty copyedits.

My "main" editor, Lauren Bailey, believed in this enough to truly be a part of it and encourage me with her sometimes brutally honest feedback. How grateful am I that this process that began as a business arrangement turned into a friendship. She's fucking brilliant, and I'm a lucky girl to have met her.

Brianna Scharstein so wonderfully designed the cover art. She was enthusiastic from the beginning and came up with so many creative ideas for how to approach the cover of this, my first novel. I hope we can work together again in the future.

Other friends also continuously supported this project with their feedback and advice, or by simply asking how it was coming along, thereby keeping me accountable and motivated: Kevin Moran, Jamie Markle, Brian Klems, Chuck Sambuchino, Paul Miller, Michele Zeh, Sue Smith, Larry Brown, and Carol Rothenberger.

My husband and number one supporter, Dwayne Haas, has been my makeup artist, music selector, costuming department, fire safety, and all-around better half. His encouragement continues to drive me. I simply can't say enough about how amazing he is.

My sons, Dylan Haas and Aaron Haas, have inspired me to be the best example I can be. My hope is that they will find their own creative path and run it as hard as they can without letting anything stop them, even if they grow up and have two children who *often* fight with each other. Just stay focused, boys. If I can do it, you can, too.

Chapter 1

NICE TRY

It wasn't the first time I held a razor blade, but as I sat on the floor in my room, it felt like a foreign object. My window's gray curtains were pulled back, showing a few stars and a sliver of the moon. "God's thumbnail" is what I once heard it called.

When I heard steps coming down the hall, I set the razor down quickly behind me on the floor and picked up a nearby book. With a brief tap on my bedroom door, my mom peeked inside. I expected her to tell me to turn down my radio.

"Going to bed. Your dad's staying up a little longer to finish watching the game. Turn down your radio. I told your dad to be quiet so you can go to sleep, too." She winked at me, and I smiled back with my mouth, knowing that I couldn't smile with my eyes, not now.

"Everything okay?" she asked as she paused in the doorway.

I shrugged as I used the remote to turn the music down. "I guess." I hated lying to her.

"Let me know if you need to talk. I love you."

"Love you, too, Mom."

She shut the door, and I looked at my hands, holding the book that I would never finish. My nails were short and clean, my fingers long. I stretched my right hand, seeing the tendons and veins move under my smooth skin, then reached back to pick up the blade.

I knew it would shock my parents. To help me cope with what they believed was normal teen angst, they encouraged me to stay in the dance classes that were as much a part of my upbringing as watching early-morning cartoons. They tried their best, but there was only so much they could do.

I poised the razor above my wrist. I knew that I needed to cut it up the length of my arm and not across, like some amateurs did. I wasn't an idiot, after all.

This act would stupefy the dance school. I taught classes to third- and fourth-grade girls. Ballet, tap, jazz—all paid for by the bourgeoisie parents who would come to silently judge others—I mean, watch the classes and recitals.

My own dance teacher would likely mimic the guilt of my fellow high school students, though I knew she didn't really like me, especially after seeing my latest hairstyle. *"Summer, we can't have someone with purple hair teaching our children,"* she said to me last week. *"The parents are paying good money for these classes."* As if my hair color had anything to do with my teaching ability. She had to know that dance was my only outlet. I attended every single class that was offered, taught extra shifts when possible, and practiced relentlessly at home. The dance studio was the only place where I fit in.

I held my breath and pressed the razor, making a speck of blood appear on my arm. Now set in motion, I felt removed from this life force, like it wasn't my blood, wasn't my arm.

The high school talent show producer, who denied me a spot in the culminating show of this, my senior year, would surely feel the same guilt as well. I auditioned yesterday. I was rejected today. My modern dance choreography, it turned out, was too "abstract," and they were looking for acts that were more "peppy." The cheerleaders. I got it. My style is not what the audience was paying five dollars a pop to come see.

And I could envision my high school classmates—the ones who afterward would say they knew me—grieving and saying things like, "She was so sweet/different/quiet," while they were maybe thinking, *I should've done something/said something/stood up for her.* They'd likely find out tomorrow when I wasn't at school, not that they would normally notice when I was absent.

The speck on my arm grew, creating what could have been a red teardrop sliding down my skin. I knew that I didn't have all night. Dad would be turning off the television before long. I wondered if he, too, would pop in to say good night. I wiped the blood off on my pajama pants before it hit the gray carpet.

When they found out, my few dear friends would get it. They would be surprised perhaps only by the method I chose. They saw our classmates making fun of me each day because my skin was so assaulted with acne that I could have been the face of a pharmaceutical cure for pimples. The "before" picture, of course.

Beyond my complexion, I thought I was at least average looking. My hair had darkened from sun-kissed blonde to what was described as an unflattering "dishwater blonde" in the teen magazines that I would read in my room. I tried to wear makeup, but it felt so fake. Not to mention that once, going to school with eye shadow and liner, one of the football players saw me, and as my pink-lipsticked mouth began to form a smile when our eyes actually met, he said, "Nice try. Makeup doesn't help." His friends laughed with contempt. I sank with a fleeting combination of bafflement, hatred, and lastly, self-pity. I hated them. I hated me.

Aside from my so-so face, my weight and build were average. Although I was healthy and slim, I never could understand why my thighs looked so incredibly huge when I sat down. I attributed it to being a dancer and having a lot of muscle. In reality, it was just genetics.

Between my hormones and the stress of becoming a teen, the acne never really ceased, no matter what dermatological wonders the doctors would experiment with on my face. Creams, pills, popping blackheads under their magnifying glasses—it all ended in frustration for me as well as for my parents, who were paying for the treatments.

I was given demeaning nicknames and was ridiculed relentlessly by the "preps," the kids who were somehow popular despite how nasty they could be to other people. The teasing was enough to make me feel worthless, and I couldn't see that all this was temporary. With high school graduation beyond the foreseeable future, I just wanted to die.

It seemed as though I could not walk down the hallway without someone calling me a random, insulting name other than my given name of Summer Kayes: "Summer the Bummer" and "Dumber Summer" had become popular alternatives, as meaningless as they were. I looked forward to each class because it meant that my peers would have to be quiet, although they were talented at finding ways to pass harassing notes to me that said things like, "Why are you so ugly?" I wasn't a model by any means, but even if I were an ugly human being, you would think that they would at least take pity and not rub it in.

One of them, ironically, was a boy who had been greatly burned in a house fire. After he healed, his face was left scarred. It was a landscape of wrinkled skin that was whiter than the rest of his body, since the grafted skin had been transplanted from his buttocks. I remember the uncaring look in his eyes as his best friends would ridicule me for my acne. His silence had almost the same effect as their insults. He would feel the guilt, too, I was sure.

Maybe, I thought, *when I go through with this, then they'll stop being mean to others.* They would see how hurtful their comments were. The show producer would realize that cheerleaders weren't the only ones who deserved to perform. My dance teacher would convince others that being unique was a good thing. And at the same time, I would be free from it all, and I would be able to dance in the afterlife without all this pain.

I took my last full-lung inhale, drove the razor into a deep line down my arm, and started to cry quietly as I lay down on the floor, my emotional pain driving any physical pain from my awareness. What had I done?

"If she tends to it well, there shouldn't be a scar. You're lucky you got her in here quickly."

"Thank you, Doctor." I heard my mom's voice before I opened my eyes. "We'll get her healed up and get her enrolled in some counseling so we can figure out what brought this on. I don't know what we could've done to prevent it."

"She'll definitely need some therapy. You may, too, to be honest. This is never easy on a family. I'll give you some references before you leave. Good day." I heard footsteps leaving the room, then blinked my eyes a few times.

"I'm sorry," I said.

"We love you," my mom said. "Rest. It'll all be okay." I think she was saying this more for herself than for me, but I took comfort in her words. Help had come.

"Am I in trouble?"

"You're not in trouble."

"I'm sorry."

"I'm just glad you're still with us. We'll work through this. Get you help, homeschool, whatever it takes. You have a lot of life ahead of you yet, Summer. A lot of life."

FIVE YEARS LATER

Chapter 2

BODY ADORNMENT

"Sorry. I think I just pulled your hair."

"Is that going to cost me extra?" I asked.

The body piercer at Permanent Productions responded with a pleasantly surprised smile.

We didn't say much, and the experience felt sacred; together, we were performing an ancient practice. The music floated from the front room to the small piercing studio that was likely once a bedroom, where I perched on a table similar to one you would find in a doctor's office. The artwork on the walls portrayed mysterious people of various ethnicities who had an array of cultural piercings. I sat, sweating, wanting to say something, wanting there to be silence. Adrian Weldge practiced his craft with ease and precision. Just prior to each of my two new ear piercings, both in my left ear, he quietly said, "Take a breath." I felt the sharp but brief pain, and then he said, "That was it." I don't remember if I started breathing again, but I can tell you that I didn't pass out, and I must have inhaled at some point because I noticed that he smelled like sandalwood.

Adrian had short, dark hair and was covered in tattoos. Piercings decorated his body in visible places that, until then, I didn't know could be pierced, and I found that I was simultaneously curious and aroused.

He was about as tall as I was, so when he stood in front of me the first time we met, we were eye to eye. He was slim and dressed in a black V-neck T-shirt, fitted black jeans, and black combat boots. He was cute. So cute, in fact, that I returned just two weeks later, a glutton for punishment.

This was not my first trip to a tattoo parlor. I got my first ink when I turned eighteen, practically before the smoke on the birthday candles had time to dissipate. But other than it being a celebration of my age, I found that tattoos were a great way to distract others from the subtle scars of my acne and what my parents referred to as my "accident." By that time, the scars had faded, for the most part, from their peak in high school, but I still cringed when I saw my reflection in certain lighting that highlighted the unevenness on my cheeks. In a way, the tattoos enabled me to show that I had control over my own body. *I'll tell you what to look like,* I wanted to say to my skin.

In addition to my desire to be near Adrian again, there was something about the space at Permanent Productions, too, which pulled me back. It was more than just a tattoo parlor; it was a place where people sat through pain and discomfort, sometimes bleeding, to brand their bodies with symbols that meant something, or everything.

I had hid my earliest tattoos from my parents, perhaps out of respect and maybe just a healthy little dose of fear. It turned out that the fear wasn't unwarranted, as my preferred choices for self-expression were less than celebrated by my mom and dad. They saw it as continued "rebellion," and to my dismay, it seemed as though every drop of ink pushed them further away.

A woman on my own path, I returned to Permanent Productions several weeks later. As I swung the door open, the small set of bells that hung on a tapestry rope from the doorknob rang softly, and I let the door shut gently behind me. My feet stepped onto the well-worn carpet, which needed to be replaced, and I could hear the dentistry-like sound of a tattoo needle buzzing in the background. The place was a brick two-story home, and the parlor took up the first floor. The living room, which was now a lobby, was comfortable; wood floors and mustard-yellow walls made you feel at ease even though you were likely to be pricked with needles if you were there. A counter lined one wall and displayed large silver jewelry pieces along with binders full of colorful and exotic tattoo drawings, and an antique cash register sat on the counter. A radio played the punk music of the Dead Kennedys just loud enough to take one's mind off the potential pain they were likely about to experience. Vintage posters decorated the walls. Tacked into the drywall near the door, nestled in between an Ed Hardy–inspired sign that said "No crybabies" and a print of Norman Rockwell's *Tattoo Artist*, was an ordinary sheet of computer paper. It announced:

Tribal Belly Dance Classes @ Dance Mecca
Let the spirit of this feminine dance move your body.
Let it move your soul.
Beginners welcome.

Without thinking, I tore a strip of paper from the bottom and held it in my hand, staring at the website it listed and momentarily forgetting where I was or why I was there.

"You're back." Adrian had come out into the parlor toward me. "How's everything healing?" he asked over the music.

"Just fine, thanks. I was actually thinking about getting a couple more piercings, like my nose and belly button," I said as I slipped the paper strip into my patchwork purse. Just saying *belly button* made me blush. I was single, and I will admit that I was hopeful. He was cute, like I said.

He held my eyes with his as he said, "I have an opening in fifteen minutes. Can you stick around until then?"

"No problem."

"Excellent." He smiled. "Why don't you check out the jewelry? Rhiannon here can show it to you."

He waved toward a young woman at the jewelry counter, then nodded to a guy sitting on the couch and told him, "I'm ready for you now, man. Come on back." With another subtle smile at me, he disappeared from the lobby with his other client.

I approached the glass counter, which held belly and nose rings, gauged studs for expanding earlobes, and spikes that could be dermatologically inserted just about anywhere on the human body. The woman was lighting a stick of incense. She had perfectly manicured dreadlocks and piercing blue eyes.

"You want a belly ring and a nose ring?" Rhiannon asked. Her voice was like a melody.

"I do. What's a good size?" I said, hoping to sound like I knew what I was talking about. I thought my voice sounded rough in comparison to hers.

"You should go with an eighteen-gauge for the nose," she said slowly, considering the choices before us. "This little silver mushroom cap is a good option for you, I think. And for the belly button, we have these." She pointed to a tray that held an impressive variety of rings, studs, and dangling pieces from which I could choose. I noticed that her hands were decorated with intricate henna tattoos. Trying not to stare at them, I studied the different colors and shapes of the body jewelry, trying to see if one spoke to me.

"Let me see your belly button," she said. "The shape of it'll actually help determine which jewelry you should start with, but we'll probably go with a fourteen-gauge for it either way."

I was not expecting to lift my shirt in public, but we were alone in the lobby by then. I sucked in my stomach like a good American girl and pulled up the middle of my T-shirt so that we could both see, as strange as it seemed, what shape my belly button was. Just then, Adrian walked back out to the lobby with his newly pierced customer, who was wiping a single tear from the corner of his eye. I wondered what he must have had done in the back room.

"Hmmm . . . I think you should probably go with one of the smaller rings," Rhiannon was saying, her face level with my waist. I blushed slightly as Adrian glanced at us and then rang his customer up for the bill. I dropped my shirt and then settled on the silver mushroom cap for my nose and a silver ring with an amber ball to hold the ring in place for my navel piercing.

"Thanks so much for your help with these," I told Rhiannon. "By the way, I dig your hair. I've always wanted dreadlocks."

"You could totally dread your hair," Rhiannon replied as she ran a slender hand over her locks. "It's a pain in the ass, especially at first, but it can be done."

"Really?" I was curious. I had considered it but thought it would be impossible for me to have them without hair extensions.

"Sure. Go for it, sister," she said. "You'd look good with dreads."

"Oh, thank you," I said, looking down. I was still learning how to accept a compliment.

Adrian had finished taking care of his customer, who walked out the door with at least one more hole in his body than he had walked in with. "You ready now?" he asked me.

"She's all set," Rhiannon told him. And with that, I walked with Adrian back to the piercing room. I was nervous, but more relaxed this time, as everything was familiar, including Adrian. This round was similar to the first: a religious experience. We exchanged few words, and I said a little prayer in hopes that the pain would be here and gone quickly.

"I'm going to put my finger in your nose," he said, breaking the silence.

"Shouldn't you at least take me to dinner first?" I asked jokingly. He stepped back, looked at me for a moment, and smiled.

"Here it comes." He put one finger on the inside of my left nostril, then guided the needle through my skin. It was over in a moment. My eyes watered from the sting, no matter how much I willed them to stay dry. *Be a big girl,* I thought. *You asked for this.*

"You doing all right?" he asked as I wiped at my eyes with the back of my hand, leaving a thin streak of black eyeliner on my skin. I wiped under my eyes again quickly to try to fix any makeup that had gotten smeared.

"Yeah, I'm good," I said.

"Excellent. Now lie back on the table."

I did as he said, feeling my stomach sink toward my back as I lay flat, instinctively folding my hands over my stomach. I didn't want to see the needle go into my skin for the belly ring, and so I stared at the ceiling, which had a blown-up Calvin and Hobbes cartoon pinned to it. Instead of reading the word balloons in search of humor, I closed my eyes, and with nothing to look at, my other senses heightened and I noticed that Adrian was so close to me that I could feel his breath on my stomach.

"I'll need you to move your hands so that I can work," he said. I moved them up to my chest and folded my fingers, trying to remember to breathe as he gave me the belly ring. It was not unpleasant.

"You did well once again," he said. "All done."

With the piercings in place, he held his hand out to help me get down from the table. "You feel okay?" he asked.

"I do," I said simply. I looked at my belly ring, feeling a powerful sense of superiority over my body, and adjusted my shirt so that my belly was covered.

He nodded his head, seeming content to have yet another satisfied customer, and opened the door for me. "After you," he said.

Once I was back in the lobby, Rhiannon rung me up. I felt liberated as I signed the credit card receipt. "Thank you," I said to Rhiannon.

"Thank you, dear," she replied casually. "See you around."

Chapter 3

THE LANGUAGE OF DANCE

Dance Mecca was housed in a former church that had been established in the 1850s. The sanctuary was lined with mirrors on the back wall, and two of the walls had large stained-glass windows that told of stories and people from long ago. The ceiling had gothic arches, and a pipe organ still rested behind what used to be the pulpit. The floors were hardwood, and I could tell that they had had many miles walked and danced upon them. The boards were scuffed from years of use and had been sanded down to a smooth finish, presumably to exorcise the floor of any potential splinters.

I acclimated to the space as I took in the tapestries that hung in the doorways and the large, textured sitting pillows on rugs with patterns that hinted of Morocco.

Above the mirrors in the back were notecards with strange words written on them in large letters: *Arabic Hip Twist*, *Mayas*, *Egyptian Half Turns*, and so on.

"You can sign in here," said a voice behind me. I turned, and a woman in her midfifties stood next to a display counter that had a notebook and pen laying next to a candle. The woman had a pierced nose and dark dreadlocks, which she wore in a large braid that hung down her slender back. I could tell just from her presence that she was more than a teacher. "Are you new here? I don't think we've met."

"Yes. I mean no. I mean, not yet," I fumbled over my words, wanting to make a good impression but probably looking like a fool. "I'm new here. This is my first class. We haven't met. I saw your flyer at Permanent Productions a few weeks ago."

"Oh good! It's working then! We've been hanging those up all over the place. I'm Miranda Foster, the owner and, I hope, your new belly dance teacher. Just fill out this form since you're new, and after class you can decide if you want to sign up for the session and pay then. Sound good?"

"Sounds fair to me, thank you," I said.

With our business finished, she switched gears. "What's your name?"

"Summer. Summer Kayes."

"Who are you?"

"I, uh, I work at the library, and I went to school . . ."

"No, I didn't ask what you do for a living or what your history is. Who are you? What do you love?"

"I love dance." The answer came easily.

"Then you'll fit right in. We'll get to know each other better, I'm sure. For now, slip off your shoes and come stretch. Let's dance."

She walked onto the dance floor and began stretching in front of the mirrors. Others had come into the studio for class as well, putting their purses down next to the pillows and filling in the empty spaces on the studio floor. I removed my shoes, feeling as though I were leaving all my baggage with them. The bare floor felt cool beneath my feet as I padded over to find a spot. I took a deep breath, raised my arms over my head, and stretched my body as tall as I could, listening to the sounds of my fellow dancers saying hello to one another over the music that had started. Suddenly, a familiar, sing-song voice was saying hello to me.

"Could it be you?"

I opened my eyes and dropped my arms to my sides. "It is me. Is it *you*?" I replied with a mysterious grin.

"Yes, it's me." Rhiannon smiled from ear to ear. "Is this your first class?"

"It is," I said. "I actually saw the flyer at your work. Are you new here, too?"

"No, actually, I've taken classes here practically since the doors opened. But Miranda's always adding new moves, so I like to make sure I learn them all. I just love it."

"All right, ladies, let's come together in a circle and begin," Miranda said to the class. I smiled at Rhiannon, thrilled that I already found a familiar face in this foreign territory.

I felt at peace when I was at Dance Mecca. Although the names and specific movements were alien to me, it was like my body was waking up from a long, deep sleep, newly injected with passion for simply moving to music with intention. Through the classes, Miranda showed me how to stand in the correct posture to protect my lower back as I learned more advanced movements down the road. She taught me how to scoop my hips upward, downward, and in figure eights, how to move my arms in a snakelike way, and how to begin training my abdominal muscles as a primer for the ultimate move: the belly roll.

She encouraged me, and I felt confident after learning a few moves. "You're a natural at this. I can tell you've always been a dancer," she said. I needed those words of support, as this was such a new arena for me. But it was true—I could feel that my muscles understood the movements more than my brain did at the time. I let my body take over and tried not to overanalyze the new terms or choreography; I wanted to enjoy the natural motions of this ancient art form. I felt like my feminine unconscious,

---

passed down from generations of women before me, was enough to guide my hips, belly, shoulders, and hands. It felt intuitive.

These movements and this vocabulary became the foundation for a new language: that of tribal belly dance. At the studio, Miranda showed me some of her costuming, which included brightly colored skirts reminiscent of Flamenco dancers and interesting belts made of textured fabric, cowrie shells, intricate beading, and coins from other countries. I learned that tribal was earthy, spiritual, and could be flirty. Everything about it captured my curiosity.

Every Sunday, I drove thirty minutes to Dance Mecca for a meditative hour with other women whose company I enjoyed, even though I barely knew them. There was an openness, a welcoming vibe in this space. *Everyone here is equal*, the atmosphere said. *Find yourself; express yourself; share your beauty.* I learned how to feel the earth (or at least the floorboards, during class) under the different parts of my feet. To move each part of my body—arms, elbows, wrists, and fingers—with intention. To make eye contact with other human beings, and to hold it for a breath, or five.

To us students, Miranda was a mentor, a den mother, a driver of creativity and concord. Although she certainly belonged at Dance Mecca, she didn't seem like the average Midwesterner. One day she spent half of the class teaching us about adornment with flowers, jewelry, and makeup. She had been showing us how she used an eyeliner pencil to draw intricate designs next to her eyes, and as the other students got up and left, I sat next to Miranda to practice applying makeup in the classroom wall mirror. "How did you get here?" I asked her out of curiosity. As she held the pencil in her hand, she stopped looking at her own eyes in the reflection and turned to me. She seemed to be gauging how much to tell me about her path.

"I studied theatrical dance at another studio. We danced to Broadway show tunes. I just did it for fun, because I wasn't interested in acting and

I can't carry a tune in a bucket, as they say. I stayed afterward one day to take a yoga class, and I met a girl who was a belly dancer."

"And the rest is history?" I offered.

"You could say that. I went to as many workshops as I could afford to, traveled to dance festivals within a day's drive to study with other teachers, and learned a lot—about belly dance, about teaching, and, I hate to admit it, how not to be." She broke our gaze and looked at the eyeliner pencil in her hand. "Let's just say that not everyone in this community is as 'centered' as they may claim to be. I hope that you, dear, make many wonderful friends, as I know you probably have. Hold them tight, and listen to your intuition. Sometimes there's a broken stair." Miranda looked at me, smiled maternally, and brushed my hair away from my face.

"What do you mean by a broken stair?" I asked.

"It's just a saying. Sometimes a stairway can seem completely safe, and you wouldn't think to question the steps. But sometimes there's a step that looks just fine, as sturdy and solid as the rest, but when you step on it, you quickly learn that it's broken, and you fall." She put her hand under my chin, lifting it gently. "Close your eyes."

I closed them and stayed still as I felt the eyeliner pencil touch the sides of my own eyes. When she let go of my face, she said, "Take a look."

I opened my eyes and looked into the mirror. Intricate black swirls extended beyond my blue eyes. I smiled and looked down, honored with this pretty gift she had given me.

She lifted my chin again, saying, "You'll do well. But lower your gaze for no one."

"You ladies still here?" Rhiannon had walked into the room, breaking the spell. "I was waiting outside, but my ride is late and it's starting to rain."

"Come on in, Rhiannon," Miranda said as she tucked her eyeliner pencil in a beaded makeup pouch. "I actually need to head out, but you're welcome to stay here. Just make sure you lock the door when you leave. You don't need a ride, do you? I mean, is someone coming?"

"Oh yeah, he'll be here," Rhiannon answered with a nod.

"I can keep you company," I said to her. "I'm free for the moment."

"Cool. Thank you," she said.

"Well, girls, I'll see you at the next class then," Miranda said with a wave. "Namaste!"

Rhiannon and I stood in place for a moment as Miranda's energy dissipated from the room. "Want to have a seat?" Rhiannon asked me as she sat down on one of the oversize pillows.

"Sure. Is your ride okay?" I asked.

"Yeah, it's my boyfriend. He should be here anytime. I just wish it wasn't raining."

"Did your dreads get wet? Is it okay if they do?"

"Yes, and yes," she said, running her hands over the locks. "I just have to make sure that I get them totally dry. Didn't you say you always wanted dreads?"

"Oh my God, yes. And more so now than ever. Yours are so pretty."

"I can show you how to dread your hair sometime if you like," she offered. "You have good energy, and I like that. You buy the coffee, and I'll help you with your first dreads."

"How sweet of you! Yes! Let's do it!" I replied.

"What are you doing next weekend? Maybe we can get started next Saturday after class. You can come over to my place."

"Consider it a date!" I told her. I liked Rhiannon and decided to take a leap at a possible new friendship. I had recently graduated from college, and it seemed like most of my friends had suddenly spread out, like seeds that had been blown from a dandelion with a gust of wind. Marriage, new jobs, and adult responsibilities pulled us away from the life of study halls and parties that had been our common thread. The only exception was a close friend of mine named Morgan, who stayed local and single with me.

Suddenly the studio door opened, and before us stood Adrian.

"Hey, babe. Sorry I'm late," he said to Rhiannon as she stood up and gathered her purse and water bottle. "I got a last-minute appointment."

"It's fine. You've got skills that pay the bills," she said. They leaned in to kiss each other, and as they parted I unintentionally cleared my throat. I stood and picked up my belongings, feeling awkward and disappointed to see that he was the "boyfriend."

"Hey, I know you," Adrian said to me. "Taking classes here, I see."

"Yeah," I answered. I felt so lame.

"Let's leave together, and I'll lock up behind us," Rhiannon said. We walked to the door and I waved what felt like a flappy hand at the couple, all the while wishing that I was the one getting into his car.

"See you soon, Summer!" Rhiannon said sweetly as she locked the door behind her.

Adrian gave me a nod and said, "Later, Summer."

I returned the nod quickly as the drizzle started to dampen my clothes. As I walked away, I turned back and saw that he was still watching me.

Chapter 4

NEW EXPERIENCES

"Welcome to my humble abode," Rhiannon said as I walked into her apartment a week later. Her small living room barely fit the little amount of furniture she had. A kitchenette was off to the side, separated by a string of hippie beads.

"Have a seat on the floor, if you don't mind," she said. "It'll be easier to do your hair there than on the couch."

While she turned on a mellow dance station that she was streaming online, I sat cross-legged on the floor, taking in the eclectic decorations that reminded me of my own decor. Nothing matched, in that everything came from different stores or brands, but it all fit well together. Mismatched frames hung on the walls; some of them held paintings, some drawings, and a couple were empty, showing only the wall behind them. A tapestry that displayed henna designs hung on one wall. A gray, long-haired cat was curled up in a rocking chair. When I sat on an Indian-inspired rug with Rhiannon, the kitty lazily lifted its head to look at me, then stood, stretched, meowed, and laid down to face the other way. Incense was burning next to a few candles of various sizes and colors on the well-worn coffee table, on which also sat a small bowl of smooth stones with a whimsically drawn note that said: *Help yourself.*

"What are these?" I asked, touching the stones.

"They're earth stones. The pink ones are rose quartz, and the green ones are called peridot. Together, they encourage the energy that helps you open yourself to new experiences. Have one, or two, or three."

I looked at them cautiously. They were glossy in their smoothness and varied in shapes and sizes. I picked up one at a time as Rhiannon got settled on the floor close to me.

"This one's interesting," I said, holding a rose quartz that was the size of a nickel. "It reminds me of fire, the way the little white lines run through it. They're like tiny flames."

"Sounds like it chose you. Take it. Keep it."

"Thank you." I put it safely in my pocket as she began explaining the process of dreading my hair.

"The first thing you want to do is decide how fat you want your dreads to be," Rhiannon instructed. "You might want to start with smaller ones, because they tend to grow thicker over time."

"How does that happen?"

"Normally, your hair would shed and fall out, like a few strands a day. But when it's dreaded, it's locked all together."

"Makes sense." I accepted this new knowledge without wanting to turn back.

"Put a rubber band around what will become your dread, then twist that section of hair, and just start backcombing." *Seems simple enough,* I thought. As she and I twisted and backcombed, sectioned, twisted, and combed some more, I asked Rhiannon about her job at Permanent Productions.

"Do you like working there?"

"It's cool. Adrian hooked me up with the job after we started dating about a year ago. They pretty much let me work when I want or need to, and I get a great discount on body jewelry. I get to meet a lot of interesting people, but you'd also be surprised by how many men show up for ink and then back out."

"No kidding," I said, feeling a pang from the fact that Adrian had been dating Rhiannon for so long. *I probably don't have a chance at all,* I thought. "What's the craziest tattoo you've ever seen come out of there?"

"Well, I don't see them all because I'm at the front desk. The craziest one I laid eyes on was on this guy's face. I swear to God, it said 'Fuck off.' I was afraid to ring him up and take his money!"

"That's not so bad," I said, trying to keep a straight face. "I would totally get 'Fuck off' tattooed on my face." I smiled, feeling closer to Rhiannon already.

"Oh yeah. I can really see that happening. You're a little bit of a smartass, aren't you? I like that. By the way, I'm not pulling your hair or anything, am I?"

What does that mean? I thought. *Did Adrian tell her about my comment when I was with him getting pierced? I'll play it cool.* "No, not at all. Thanks for asking, though."

"So where do you work, Summer?"

"I actually just scored a job at the library downtown," I said. "I'm hoping to go back to college eventually and get a master's in library science. I graduated with a degree in English lit this year."

"A scholar, huh?" She smiled at me. "So you live around here, I assume?"

"I do. I have a little apartment near the Beanery."

"I know the Beanery. Cool little coffee shop."

"But the coffee is terrible. You have to get the tea, or anything other than the coffee."

"So very true," Rhiannon said. "Although everyone gets the coffee anyway."

"It's not bad if you drink it with a ton of cream. And a ton of sugar. And some cinnamon . . ."

"And some cocoa . . ." We laughed; she was so easy to get along with.

"Tell me, what made you want to start taking the belly dance classes, other than just seeing the flyer?"

"Well, long story short, dance is in my blood." It felt so serendipitous to be here with my new friend that I momentarily forgot about my hiatus from dance. I hadn't so much as tapped my toe since the, um, incident.

"Tell me more about it," she said.

"It was always my outlet. I've taken classes all my life, but I never quite fit in with the other girls, ya know?" I felt myself opening up just talking about dance again. "I was always the odd one out, especially in my late teens, when I began expressing my individuality, as they say. In my senior year, my teacher told me that the school's parents didn't want their girls learning ballet from someone with purple hair and tattoos. Ballet, tap, jazz, modern, hip hop—I loved it all. What's your drug of choice?" I asked.

"Tribal belly dance, all the way," she said. "It's earthy. Spiritual. Sensual. Communal. I love it."

"I love it, too, already," I said.

"Stand up and look in the mirror. Tell me what you think."

When I saw my reflection, my hand raised automatically to touch my "new" hair. There were several locks, each about as thick as my pinky finger. I loved the way they looked.

She stood next to me and said, "Cool?"

"Cool," I said. "Thank you so much."

"You're welcome," she said, lighting a new stick of incense. "Now, sit back down and I'll show you how to do this so you can start working on them, too. Let me tell you, if they didn't before, guys will dig the shit out of your hair now."

"How so?" I asked. I wasn't sure what it was like to have guys dig me very much.

"They just love them. Adrian tells me all the time. He's the best."

There it was again. The pang. Surely this is just a crush, but every time I heard her say his name, it was like a needle pricking my skin, a reminder that even if he was interested in me, he was unavailable. And not just unavailable, but tangled in a relationship with someone whom I was quickly coming to respect and adore. I could only hide my selfish inner reaction with a friendly, and truly genuine, outer smile.

"You're all finished, dear," Rhiannon said to me as she ran her hands over my dreads. "You don't regret it, do you?"

"I try to live without regrets." I smiled. "For the most part. Thank you, thank you, thank you for helping me get started with these dreadies."

"You're welcome. Always. Hey—want to come to one of my performances?" Rhiannon asked. "The house tribe, Hypnosis Dance, has a show at Dance Mecca Friday night. The cover's only five dollars. I'm going to dance a special number."

"Of course!" I said.

"Good. Meet me here again? Miranda will probably mention it in class because everyone's invited. They're a lot of fun, and attending is a great way to support the community and to practice all those moves you've been learning."

"Sounds amazing," I said, excited about hanging out with her again. "It's another date!"

Happy with my baby dreadlocks, I left Rhiannon's apartment with renewed energy. Something had shifted, but I wasn't quite sure what. I was excited about the prospect of continuing to learn a brand new movement art. It seemed exotic, mysterious, and yet attainable. And with my dreads and adorning piercings, I felt like my outside appearance more closely matched my inside, my spirit. I knew that with a glance, others would be able to look at me and see what kind of person I was. To me, the dreads especially symbolized a loving person, and however that conception may have come to be, I embraced it. I went through a lot of hurt from dealing with bullies in my teen years, and all I had left was to attempt to reflect the positive things that I could find in myself and others. It became my mission.

The next several days I did little but go to work and then come home to tend to my dreads each evening. They were coming along nicely. While I twisted, backcombed, and tightened them up, I would watch television or just listen to music, thinking about how my life had changed, and fantasizing about Adrian.

Chapter 5

WHAT'S A HAFLA?

Friday nights are charged with electricity. Take that baseline anticipation for a great night and combine it with the opportunity to join a group of friends specifically to dance, and you'll understand my version of heaven. When I arrived at Rhiannon's as we had planned, she was almost unrecognizable—her hair had intricately carved beads woven throughout her blonde locks, and colorful flowers were tucked in her hair as well. She was in full tribal gear. It was a tapestry of earth-toned colors, various fabrics of silk and cotton, layers of skirts and veils, and strings of foreign coins that were tarnished with age. I could have stared at her much longer than I did, but I forced myself to blink when my eyes started to dry out. I put my keys into my pocket and felt the rose quartz that she had given me. It was warm from being so close to my skin, and its symbol of new experiences spoke to me as I looked at Rhiannon's ensemble.

Suddenly Adrian walked out from the kitchenette. "Pretty cool, huh?" he said, seeing my reaction to the costuming.

"She looks amazing," I responded. Then I spoke to Rhiannon directly, saying, "You look amazing." I was wearing a simple skirt that brushed my ankles and a tank top that I planned to tie around my waist when it was time to dance with the others. My dreads were pulled back into a low ponytail, and although they were beautiful on their own, they seemed naked compared to Rhiannon's, which were decorated with the beads, flowers, and feathers. Even her makeup looked professionally done, while I had just put on some eyeliner and lipstick, which was my version of "getting ready to go out." I hoped that Adrian wasn't comparing me with his girlfriend. Then I thought, *Why would he, anyway?*

"This is going to be a fun hafla," Rhiannon sang as she gracefully spun, the air lifting her heavy skirt in small waves at her calves.

"What's a hafla?" I asked.

"It's what we're having tonight. It's like a party, but it's so much more than just hanging out. There'll be musicians there who play Middle Eastern music, and we'll all dance together. For some haflas, the students can perform on a small stage with their teachers to share what they've learned from their class sessions, and then the floor is open to everyone. It's a supportive environment: there's no competition; no one's judging anyone about anything. It's just about sharing our joy. Tonight is more of a professional show, although there'll be about an hour of open floor time."

"That sounds terrible," I said sarcastically.

"It is," Adrian said, picking up on my humor. "For hours I have to sit and watch belly dancers. It's really rough."

"Life is hard, I know. Thanks for tolerating it, Adrian." Rhiannon winked as she took her keys from a hook next to the front door. "Let's head out."

As we drove to Dance Mecca in Adrian's car, I naively asked what kind of role men played in this world that was so new to me. I was curious what Adrian himself would be doing there, besides watching. "Do guys dance at all at a hafla?"

"Well, there are definitely men in the community," Rhiannon answered. "But they don't usually dance, at least in the sense that we belly dance. You're more likely to see them playing drums or other instruments. Guitar, flute, tambourine."

"And cowbell. Always the cowbell," Adrian said.

"He's being an ass. No one plays the cowbell," Rhiannon said, shaking her head and laughing.

"And you play the drum, as opposed to the cowbell?" I asked.

"Actually, no," Adrian said. "I'm just an enabler."

"Don't let him fool you," Rhiannon said. "He's everything to me, and I wouldn't be the performer I am without him."

"Yeah? How so?" I was curious, as Rhiannon seemed independent. I could not imagine how Adrian, adorable as he was, could uphold this high role with which he had just been labeled.

"Finding recorded songs to dance to that we haven't used before, researching costuming ideas and helping me make them, doing my makeup for me when it's tricky and takes a more steady hand . . . you name it. He rubs my feet at the end of the night, makes me coffee in the morning . . ."

"And everything in between," Adrian said with a hint of naughtiness.

"Oh, all right, mister humility. But seriously, Summer, he pushes me further."

I nodded thoughtfully and looked out the window, feeling as though I had peeked into an intimate part of their relationship. Although I still found him attractive, I tried to put to bed the idea that he and I might ever become an item.

When we arrived at Dance Mecca we went inside together, although Rhiannon and Adrian were quickly distracted by saying hi to their friends. I wandered off on my own, looking for other familiar faces. On the stage, which was only about a foot off the floor where the pulpit would have stood, a woman rehearsed, captivating my attention. She was petite and slender, with wavy brown hair that fell down her back to her waist. She was dressed in tribal gear similar to Rhiannon's. Her movements were full of grace as she spun in a circle, stopped abruptly, and then allowed only her eyes to move across the room, until they met mine. Rhiannon apparently noticed me watching her. "That's Audrey Wood, the creativity director of Hypnosis. She teaches here and is one of the most talented dancers you'll ever see—belly dance or otherwise. Let me introduce you."

Audrey stepped off the stage, and Rhiannon got her attention by shimmying her hips and making her coin belt rattle with sound. Giggling, they hugged each other, and Rhiannon introduced us as promised.

"Audrey, this is Summer. Summer, Audrey."

"Nice to meet you," she said.

"The pleasure is mine," I replied.

"Are you new around here?"

"I just started taking classes. This place is amazing. I love the energy here."

Audrey nodded her head in agreement and said, "I gotta go get ready for everything to start. Hope to see you again soon!"

Throughout the evening, I watched various small groups perform on the stage, including Hypnosis Dance. I could see how they came up with their name, as the entire audience was clearly hypnotized by the movements they created together, moving as one to the sounds of the band. Rhiannon's performance was mesmerizing as well, and from the joy I saw in her eyes, she apparently loved the art form. During the open dance, I ventured onto the floor and practiced some of the tribal combinations that I had been learning in Miranda's classes. I laughed with the other dancers when one of us would make a mistake or do a move wrong, and by the end of the night, I felt confident when it was my turn to lead the dancers throughout a song. We spun, we turned, we twisted, and we celebrated a perfect Friday night.

It was during a slower song that I saw Adrian watching me. I was dancing alone, as most everyone was, lost in my headspace as I let the music carry my limbs without a thought from my conscious self. Perhaps that's why I was surprised. Unsure of how long he had been watching me,

I paused for perhaps only a second, not letting the distraction interrupt me from the song. I continued on as though he wasn't there, or perhaps exactly as if he was there. My chest lifted a little higher, my knees bent a little lower to center my balance, and my abs tightened as if they, too, realized on their own that they were being noticed by an outsider. Every time I turned, I saw from the corner of my eye that he was watching still, and it fueled my movements. *Even if we never talk about this,* I thought, *I could dance in front of him forever.*

I continued to explore this mysterious art form. All my former training seemed to have prepared me for it, including the smallest details and isolations of the movements, from holding my body still and using only my eyes to draw attention to a hand gesture, to rolling the muscles of my belly in waves of modestly sensual undulation to the music. And for the first time, I could do something new with my dance—not just practice it at home but also perhaps perform for an audience that consisted of more than the parents of the youth on stage, like when I was an assistant teacher. This possibility drove me to a new level of perfectionism, and so after the first two months of religiously taking classes at the studio and practicing the moves and combinations at home, I was able to perform on the very same stage where I first saw Audrey. Each class session ended with a hafla, where we students performed for our peers and Hypnosis performed a set for us. When they did so, it felt as though they were setting an example for us in a guiding way. They were tight as a group, and even off the stage they gave off a family vibe. I admired it from afar, wondering what it would be like to be part of a group of people who I could dance with, practice with, perform with, and befriend. I was making friends at the studio, at least, and loving the experience. It was the epitome of a supportive environment. Perhaps this was one of the reasons that I found solace in this open and loving community of dancers and musicians.

At the end of every class and at the beginning of every hafla, Miranda would lead everyone in a nondenominational prayer that gave our dance great meaning. At a time in my life when I was not religious, I found spirituality there. Mind you, I was the kind of girl who would still bow her head when someone was praying, but I had grown away from church as an institution, as people sometimes do when they develop new thoughts on religion. But this prayer felt sacred, and I honored it. It went like this: "We come together to rejoice through music and dance. We respect the spirit in each other and offer gratitude for this time to make joy. Namaste."

Participating in the motions that went with the words solidified their meaning. This mentally prepared us to make magic together. All the while, I continued to admire Audrey from afar as she assisted Miranda during some of our classes. It seemed like Audrey would pay extra attention to my movements, taking the time to correct me when my head was turned the wrong way or if I was missing a hip bump on a certain count of music. I thanked her each time, appreciating the level of detail she was holding me accountable for. Other than these corrections, we spoke little, only acknowledging each other with an extended moment of eye contact that no one else would likely notice.

From the beginning I noticed that I had a smaller waist than many of the other dancers. It was something that I had been trained to notice throughout my life as a woman in American culture, to compare myself to others. And while I didn't feel the need to judge them, it was hard not to at least notice our physical differences. This awareness may not have come as a surprise to anyone, but the lack of acknowledgment about it likely would. The other women seemed so comfortable with their round bellies, proudly wearing crop tops or just sport bras during class, not at all self-conscious about their bodies. This empowered me to embrace my own body in a new way and to appreciate my healthy bones and muscles, and even the roundness of my belly. I forgot about the flaws that were so much a part of how I used to define myself. It was easy to do, seeing these women compliment each other endlessly. *I could get used to this,* I thought.

When it was my class's turn to share on stage what we had learned from our lessons, I took my place among my peers. We were an eclectic group of women varied in age and size. I was on the average side of the age spectrum; there were a couple of older and younger students, but most were in our early to midtwenties. I think we did well, considering that we had been studying tribal belly dance for only a couple of months. We sort of moved in sync, and no one fell off the stage or threw up with nerves. So, while it was not a professional set that would have video crews flying in to film for mass production, it was entertaining to our audience—no one threw tomatoes, and everyone clapped for us—and I thought it was gratifying. It satisfied my desire to dance for an audience and to share this art that had carried me through life up to this point. The applause gave me an unexpected adrenaline rush as well. The sounds of clapping, hoots, and whistles were a gift from those watching, and I came to crave it. My new self had been born, and I was about to discover yet another outlet for expression.

Chapter 6

ISN'T POI SOMETHING YOU EAT?

"Are you planning on taking the poi classes that are coming up?" Miranda asked me. It was my second hafla, and the sanctuary was dim, the dancers were mingling, and the musicians were still on stage fiddling around with their instruments.

"Poi? What's that?" I responded. The studio often held classes that were focused on movement arts other than tribal belly dance, but I was so consumed with learning the basics of this that I had ignored the flyers and class announcements for anything that didn't include the word *tribal*.

Miranda answered by holding up a pair of what she called "practice poi," which were basically balls of newspaper the size of an orange, each covered with fabric and tied to a string that was almost as long as her arm. She stepped a few feet away and began swinging them around in different patterns in time with the music. I thought it was cool and entertaining. Miranda finished, came over, and said to me, "Some people like to use glow poi. They change colors with LED lights. When you get really good at this, you can do it with fire!"

Fire? It was like a light switch flipped in my head. *I have to do this,* I thought. I wanted to do it. I wanted to spin fire. My pulse beat faster at the thought of it.

I signed up for the two-hour workshop that Miranda had told me about, which took place just a couple of weeks later. A skinny girl with very light blonde, messy hair taught the class. She was a couple of years younger than I was. Her name was Leslie Hayes, and she was one talented poi spinner. On the day of the workshop, Leslie and Miranda had welcomed everyone to come to Dance Mecca early so they could teach the students how to make their own sets of practice poi. This was typical of the type of generous community that tribal belly dance and poi spinning generated. In that single afternoon, Leslie taught me and several others the basics.

"With one in each hand, start swinging them in a forward motion, careful to watch your planes," Leslie instructed us.

"Our planes?" I asked, thinking of aircrafts.

"Yes, they're called vertical planes. You want the poi to swing up and down in a vertical line for now, like the trunk of a pine tree."

Right. Planes, lines, trunks. Looking around, I saw that we students were equal in our ability to keep the planes straight, and only occasionally went wonky with the poi and hit ourselves softly with one of them. The names of the poi tricks were more linguistically familiar than those I had first seen on the walls of Dance Mecca. They described tricks such as "chase the sun," "helicopter," and "butterfly." It was still humbling. Every time I started to feel confident about a new move that she taught us, I would inevitably smack my body with a poi head. But with nothing to lose, I continued on, laughing at my clumsy swings.

At the end of class, Leslie gave us her phone number and e-mail address so we could keep in touch and ask questions if we needed help.

Simply put, spinning poi was fun. Once I went home, I continued to practice every day, even if it was just for a few minutes. I studied my notes and bruised my arms with moves gone wrong. Even so, I kept spinning. That is the trick, I learned; anyone can get to the point where they can spin fire and be totally awesome, but they just have to keep practicing.

Spinners have to lose their ego each step of the way, every time they begin to learn a new move. Once they do that, they are free.

I watched videos of those who had been practicing for years, and this toxic line of thought would creep into my mind: *You'll never be that good,* it whispered. I was dismayed. I closed my laptop and dug in my purse for Leslie's phone number. She picked up on the second ring.

"Hello?"

"Hey, Leslie. This is Summer, from your poi class."

"Summer! How are you? Are you still spinning?"

"Yes, as a matter of fact, I am . . . but I'm getting frustrated. I was watching some videos online, and I just don't know how I'll ever be as good as people like you, ya know? Have you ever felt like this?"

"At first, for sure. But listen, one of the number one rules of poi spinning is that you cannot compare yourself to others. Say it. Repeat it. 'I will not compare myself to others.'" Her tone was sweet, but firm.

"I will not compare myself to others."

"Good girl. Now quit watching videos of people spinning poi, and spin your own poi! Do; don't watch."

"You're totally right," I said. "I will not compare myself to others. Do; don't watch."

"Yes. If you listen to this advice, you won't have anything holding you back."

The type of negative self-talk that I was hearing is something that all dancers and artists allow to cross their minds at some point. I was lucky, though. I would have been more fortunate if I had had this guidance when I was in high school, for example, when I was embedded in a culture of "who's better than whom." Now I was free, and a feeling of lightness quieted the voice that so many have heard.

Two hours of class time during the first poi workshop was not enough to satisfy me. In fact, it was just enough to make me crave more. Soon after that initial introduction, Miranda hosted an eight-week class session taught by Leslie, who followed each poi class with a hula-hooping class. We students were lucky. Leslie lived an hour north of Cincinnati and was kind enough to drive to the studio to continue teaching the classes. There were no other poi teachers in the area because it was such an underground hobby.

Leslie earned my respect from the beginning. As I spent more time around her, I learned that she was an incredible performer with every prop she touched, and she was a skilled teacher, too. She gave her business card to me after class one day. It featured a burlesque-type silhouette of her with a hoop, wearing shorts that just barely covered her ass cheeks. I, being modest and not yet keen on the variety of girls that I would come to meet in this underground culture, blushed and acted cool and nonchalant about it.

Typical to this community, Leslie openly shared her knowledge and her skills beyond studio time. In addition to the class that I paid for, she invited me and the other students to come jam at her house anytime. I took her up on that a couple of times but could not justify the drive to do it often. If only we had lived closer to each other, things might have been different.

On one of the few occasions at Leslie's house, she suggested that I learn fire arts safety, for when I was ready to begin dancing with fire poi. "It's good to know," she told me, "and even if you're not spinning fire yet, you'll be able to safety for someone who is." This made sense to me, so the next time I went, I dressed as instructed: 100 percent cotton clothing, nothing too baggy, none of the dangly bits that belly dancers are known to don. We stood in her backyard as she explained the different types of fuel that fire artists use, and how to put the flames out.

"Now, I'm going to set myself on fire, and you're going to put me out," she said, and before I knew it, she took a torch, dipped it in a can of fuel, covered the can, and walked away from it. She then lit the torch and lightly dragged it up her leg. I watched in disbelief. I started toward her, even though I was reluctant to get close. But before I was within reach, she calmly bent down and ran her hand over the fire, extinguishing it with her hand. "You'll learn how to do that, too."

I was scared, but there were untamable factors driving the fear out of my conscious reach. I knew that through the flames, I would be able to truly redefine myself and give my soul a new, fierce beginning.

"Have you ever seen fire poi, Summer?" Leslie asked.

"No, I've only heard about it, and I've seen a couple of videos." I wasn't going to admit the hours that I let slip by as I devoured one video after another of fire spinners from all over the world.

"Okay, tell you what. I'll light up first, explain what I'm doing and why, and then you can give it a go."

I nodded my head and watched her prepare her fire poi by dipping them in her fuel and then setting them on fire.

The moving light cast by her poi continued to highlight her face, the ground, and her body in varying patterns as she swung them all over. It seemed like there was no rhyme or reason to her intricate movements, but I knew better. Keeping the poi from tangling was difficult, and yet she made it seem so very simple. At one point, she swung her arms forward as the poi spun backward in small circles, creating this seemingly impossible perfect shape of a round flower, complete with petals that were far from delicate. The entire time, she had this look of serenity, even as her body was surrounded by flame. I wanted it, although I couldn't yet define was "it" was.

I continued spinning my practice poi, which began to come easily to me. As classes went on, I noticed with as much humility as possible that I picked it up more quickly than the other students who were learning at the same time. I practiced faithfully, and poi just became my thing. I loved the serenity that came with putting all my focus into the prop, the repetitive moves that took discipline to master, and the dance aspect of it. I felt like the poi were extensions of my arms, and as I swung them in large, arcing circles, I felt like my wings were opening. They just needed room to spread.

My apartment had two bedrooms: one where I slept, and the other that was mostly empty except for some still-packed boxes from when I moved out of my parents' house. I decided to make the extra bedroom into my dance space, where I could practice my newfound hobbies. The double closet door conveniently had mirrors from top to bottom, so I was able to critique my own movements and make adjustments as needed. The space was empty and undecorated, but it was mine, and I loved that the room now had a purpose.

The first time I used it as a practice space, I turned on a light from the hallway and flipped off the dance room's overhead light to try to emanate some ambiance. In the dimness, I turned on some music that I had bought from Dance Mecca's house CD collection, for students to use when they practiced at home. I sat in the middle of the floor, closed my eyes, and let my chest rise and fall with my breath. I guess you could say that I was symbolically baptizing the space and setting my intentions for it. My shoulders started swaying naturally to the music, and then I let my elbows begin leading; then my hands took over, and the movement was led by my shoulders, elbows, and hands, rather than my mind. Before I knew it, I was dancing, but without thinking about what move I was going to do next. It was like my muscle memory had taken over, raising me to my feet and spinning me in slow pirouettes and with leg extensions into the air, and then falling into the simple belly dance movements that I had learned, my hips falling into figure eights in time to the music.

I would not be able to tell you how long this went on, except that I know the CD had about forty-five minutes of songs on it. When the music ended and my CD-player clicked off, I opened my eyes completely, letting them adjust to the reality of the walls, the hall light, and finally, the mirrors before me. Looking into the reflection, I knew that this was a new version of me. The girl whose eyes I met in the reflection had rediscovered herself, found the community in which she belongs, and she was ready to try just about anything.

I had told myself that I would wait to start spinning fire until I had practiced with regular poi for a year. It seemed like a logical timeline, and although my excitement was stirred at the idea of using fire, I wanted to make sure I was absolutely ready before experimenting with the real deal. I used fabric sets or the kind that glow in the dark and change colors with LED lights, but before long I was ready to take it up a notch. Four months after my first poi class, I felt ready to light up for the first time.

"You're doing what?!" my college friend Morgan said when I called and invited her over, with the brief and unexpected explanation that I was going to start fire dancing. Morgan had an easy laugh that sometimes ended with a smoker's cough, then a shake of her head. Inconvenienced at worst, it was not enough to make her think about quitting, and smoking was part of her normal appearance. My accessories included things like feather earrings and colorful bracelets, while Morgan's were comprised of simple silver jewelry dotted with onyx stones, and a cigarette. I found it ironic that she so often needed a lighter. Other than this frequent oversight, she had her shit together. I admired this about her, too, and had kept a lighter handy just for her throughout our semesters together.

We had stayed in touch since graduating, and I was dying to share this with her. She had taken on a full-time job at a textbook warehouse, so she often had to work overtime. This discovery of mine felt too big to try to convey in our brief calls.

"They're called poi, and they're wicks on metal links, and you spin them around," I tried to explain on the phone. "You simply have to be here. I don't want to do it for the first time without you."

"But how did you even find out about this stuff?"

"Well, it's a long story, but I started taking belly dance lessons at this place called Dance Mecca, and then I found out about poi spinning. Oh, and I dreadlocked my hair! Just come. You have to be here."

"You dreadlocked your hair?! Dang, girl. We need to see each other more often. I miss you! Why didn't you tell me about it sooner?"

"We've both been busy. Just come, please."

"I'll be there. But I want to know everything!"

Leslie had agreed to drive to my place and walk me through my "virgin burn." She and Morgan arrived at my apartment, where we set up in the communal yard. Music was playing from my open car in the parking lot next to the green space. Leslie went over the details with Morgan and me about how to be a safety for someone spinning fire poi, especially to help put me out if I caught on fire. It was not a duty to be taken lightly.

"Will I get burned?" I asked with hesitation, thinking the answer must probably be negative or else other people would not be doing this.

"It's not a matter of *if* you'll get burned," Leslie said. "It's a matter of *when*, and how bad."

Morgan's eyes grew wide. I took a deep breath.

I gently dipped the fresh, yellow wicks into the can of fuel that would become as important to my being as water is to the body. Tiny bubbles rose as each pocket of air in the wicks was filled with the liquid. I was nervous, but I had read up on the safety of spinning fire poi and felt well prepared.

I lifted the poi, now heavy with fuel, and shook off the excess fluid so that it would not go flying with fire once I lit them. The music—a nice, mellow beat —coming from my open car windows—was loud enough to dance to, but not so loud that any of my neighbors would complain. It was a Friday night, with a full moon brightly lighting the yard.

With the wicks soaked and ready to go, I gently held the leather straps that made up the handles of the poi set, which were attached to the wicks with a steel ball chain that was almost as long as my arms. "Do you have a lighter?" Morgan asked. I nodded toward my duffel bag. She found it, flicked it on, and held it just under the wick. The sound of the fire was much louder than she and I had anticipated, and the flames licked at my hands. Leslie smiled. There was only one thing left to do: spin.

I was shocked at how intense the flames were as they passed by my head with each swing of my arms and flick of my wrists. The fire made a rushing sound, similar to the roar of its opposite earth element, water, when it rushes through a gulley. I could no longer hear the music, or the neighbors and my friends talking casually as I moved. My mind let go of everything as I fell into a groove. Focusing on only the poi themselves, I concentrated on my hands, wrists, and arms. When I felt bold enough, I attempted to do some simple tricks, such as crossing the poi in front of me, one wick over the other, and back again. I fell into a rhythm with them, feeling a brief flash of warmth at times but never feeling in danger. The poi fell in beats, heartbeats of a sort, which pulled me into a trance.

It was such an adrenaline rush. I spun the poi wicks in their circular planes, creating light and moving shadows around my body as I turned, paused, and found my art within the heat of the flames. I ventured to try a move that, although was simple to do, looked impressive. It involved wrapping the poi chains around each hand one time, shortening the length of them. Once I wrapped them, I lifted my shoulders back and brought both poi into small circles, bringing the fire in a line from my belt, up to my chest, under my chin, and then back down to my belt. In class it was called the buzzsaw.

In class I nailed it.

When practicing at home with my glow poi, I nailed it.

But this time, perhaps because the weight of the poi was different with the fuel they had soaked up, or perhaps because the chains were longer than I realized, one of the poi heads smacked me under the chin. I coughed, tasting the white gas and seeing only black smoke. For a moment, everything was silent.

"It's out! It's out now," Morgan said. Suddenly she was patting my face as she checked me over.

"Drop your poi!" Leslie commanded.

I let them drop to the ground and stepped away as she put out the remaining flames. They looked too unassuming, laying there with their dying light.

I was so embarrassed. Here I was doing so great, or at least I thought, and I completely fucked it up.

"Morgan, that was nicely done," Leslie said. "You okay, Summer?"

"Yes." I brushed my fingertips over the tender skin of my chin and throat and tried not to cry. *Keep it together, girl,* I told myself, realizing it was mostly my ego that was hurt. "Morgan, how did you know what to do?"

"I don't even know. I just grabbed that towel, or whatever, out of Leslie's hands and ran at you. The fire was small, and it went out so quick. Thank God. Let me have a look."

I raised my chin, and Leslie said, "Oh yeah, the old chain burn. Damn, it'll get you every time. The fire might not be so bad, unless your clothes catch or something. But the bolts and metal parts of the poi get so hot. You have a nice little stencil mark on your neck from the bolt, but it should heal."

"Just wear a scarf, maybe, if you don't want anyone to see it," Morgan said as she stared at me. "You're officially a badass now."

"Call me a badass when I've stopped shaking. I don't feel like one right now."

"You *are* a badass," Leslie said. "You'll be even more of a badass as you work on this. Try not to let it stop you from lighting up again. Shit like this happens. You're new. Be more careful next time, and I'm sure you'll be fine."

I made Leslie's advice my mantra for the rest of the evening. After they had left, I put my poi gear away, took a shower to wash the soot from my skin, and went to bed, hoping to put this behind me quickly, before I had a chance to let it scare me off. With my head on my pillow, I stared out the window, my hands twisting a lock of my hair as I tried to sleep. Sometimes that period when our brains are turned off to the world as much as possible erases the pain, the embarrassment, the mistakes of the day before. The earth keeps spinning slowly, leaving in its wake our pasts. But sleep was not coming easily. How could I go on in this journey that I had begun, knowing that there was the real possibility of physical danger? This was so different from when I had intentionally hurt myself as a teenager. Then, I wanted to die. I didn't think I had anything to live for because my foreseeable future included only dead ends. No pun intended.

With dance back in my life, I had *something*. And with fire, I had so much more. I had passion.

Lying there, I watched the moon make its way across the sky. *I'm not dead yet,* I thought. I kicked the blanket off my body and sat up, putting my feet on the floor. The carpet was soft, and I grabbed it with my toes, then put pressure on the balls of my feet, stretching the arches. I rolled my ankles in circles, then said out loud, "Fuck it." I stood up and walked into my dance space, lit a candle so that the shock of electric lightbulbs wouldn't dilate my eyes too quickly, turned on some music, and I danced. I don't know if this makes sense, but my dance was like a person who was separate from myself. I mean, I don't want to sound schizophrenic, but I felt like I didn't want to let the dance down. I owed it to this entity—this other form of my *self*. It had gotten me this far. And here I was, introducing dance to fire. What kind of friend was I? But maybe the dance wants the fire. It *does*, I realized. I will let the flames woo the movements that are already coming from me. I will marry them.

Chapter 7

A BELLY DANCE TROUPE THAT DOES FIRE, TOO

"Can I get a little help taking off this T-shirt?"

"You're such a perv," Rhiannon was saying to another woman in between classes at Dance Mecca. I knew from hearing her name here and there that she was Rosie Hart.

"What? It's a caption. It's supposed to be catchy!"

"You're hopeless," Rhiannon said as she stretched.

I stepped closer to finally introduce myself. Rosie had a gorgeous, full figure, long black hair, and a kind but strong presence. Tattoos dotted her tan skin. She seemed approachable, and I was curious (if not downright nosey) about the conversation she and Rhiannon were having.

"A caption for what?" I asked Rosie with a smile. "I'm Summer Kayes, by the way."

"Rosie. It's nice to meet you, sugar! This is for a Robert Downey Junior fan club poster. They post an image of Robert on their site once a month, and then you enter your caption to win prizes."

I raised an eyebrow, not sure if this girl was pulling one over on me or if she was actually serious. "Really? Robert Downey Junior, huh? Can I ask why?"

"Oh, here we go." Rhiannon rolled her eyes. "Rosie, you can fill her in so she knows right away what a weirdo you are. I gotta jet, since class is about to start."

"Ta-ta, Rhiannon!" Rosie said. She then continued, putting her hand on my arm in sincerity. "Robert is just funny, and sweet, and I love his smile, and I love that he's been through so much but has come out on top. I love his movies, his face. Just look at him!" She crinkled her nose and held up her phone, displaying the poster image for which she was submitting her caption. It was a black-and-white photo of the actor from the waist up. If he was wearing anything below the waist, I could not tell, and he was pulling up the side of his white T-shirt with a bored/sexy look on his face.

I shook my head just enough to show that yes, I thought this was over the top, but that I would not judge Rosie negatively for it. *To each her own,* I thought. "Well, at least you're into something you care about. Have you ever met him?"

"No, but I hope to one day. It's hard since we're nearly in 'fly-over' country. I'm sure I'd need to get to LA or something. I went there once for a national competition when I was a stripper, but it's too expensive to just go for fun. Anyway, that's enough about me. What about you? What's your story? What are you passionate about?"

"Fire." I didn't so much as blink as I said the word that came out before my brain had a chance to stop it. But I knew it was accurate. At the same time that I answered about myself, I felt like I wanted to know more about her—I had never met someone who was actually a stripper before, and I had a feeling that there was more to her than met the eye.

"Hmmmm," she said as she slipped off her socks and shoes for class. "Nice. I like that. Well, Summer Kayes, until we meet again."

"Later, tater," I replied and removed my sandals. I adjusted the scarf that I had draped around my neck. It had become a staple of my outfits since the fire poi had left a mark on my skin. We approached the dance floor and found spaces to sit and stretch with the class as we prepared for the following hour of yoga-like dance.

The music was playing a foreign rhythm during the end of a hafla, and the dancers of Hypnosis were on the stage, swaying their hips in a single motion. They were a tapestry of colors in their bright skirts, which were layered with dark hip scarves, and tops that revealed the intricate movements of their bodies, their arms decorated with aged jewelry, their faces adorned with perfect eyeliner and lashes that I could see from my seat in the audience. I couldn't take my eyes off them so I leaned to the side and whispered to Rhiannon, "What does it take to be able to dance with them?"

She leaned in to me, also still watching, and said, "Luck. Fate. Kismet. Or apparently something I don't have because I've always wanted to be a part of it. The turnover, if you will, is really low. They rarely hold auditions."

"The stars have to be aligned, huh?" I said.

"Precisely."

We continued to watch, entranced by the music and the dancers, until the song came to an end and they bowed, exiting the stage only to be embraced with praise from the students.

"Is this the only group around?" I asked Rhiannon as we stood up to mingle and get drinks.

"Yes," she said. "I've never heard of another one, around here anyway. I'm sure that you could find a group in any major city, at least. I've been to workshops in St. Louis and Chicago, where other troupes host a weekend and I take their classes. They're a lot of fun."

"You know what would be a lot of fun?" I asked, looking around to see if anyone else was in earshot. I saw Adrian talking to one of the drummers and thought, *I can think of a few things that I won't say out loud.* Then

I shook my head to dissipate the idea and said to Rhiannon—my *friend*, I reminded myself—"If we started our own group." I could see the gears turning in Rhiannon's mind, and so I continued with momentum. "If we start something, we can make it different. A belly dance troupe that does fire, too. Maybe Rosie will want in, even. Between the three of us, we can start something. We can start our own tribe. What's the worst that could happen?"

"That's quite a lot to take in, but my heart says yes. Absolutely yes," she added. "Let's grab Rosie and tell her. I've known her forever, and I bet she'll be in. She has a wild streak, after all."

Rhiannon walked away to find Rosie, and I stood there, in my own headspace, wondering what I had just started and where we would go from here. As quickly as the idea came to my mind, I began to wonder, *What in the hell was I thinking? Where we will perform? What will we perform?* It was the famous roller coaster that artists experience. I was strapped in for the ride, so I just let it take me forward because there was no turning back.

Suddenly I felt awkward just standing there by myself, so I looked around, and when I saw that Rhiannon had found Rosie, I walked over to them.

"She's in!" Rhiannon said.

"Hell yeah, I'm in," Rosie said, giving me a hug. "What a perfect idea! I've fucked around with fire a little. At the bar, I used to serve this drink called a Flaming Dragon to my customers, and I would run my fingers through the flames. It drove them nuts, which meant it drove my tips higher." She gave us a wink.

"Well, that sounds delightful," I said, thrilled that she was in with us. "It's official then. I guess now the only thing we need to do is make it happen."

In the beginning, Miranda kindly allowed the three of us to quietly practice together on the stage even while a class was in session on the nearby dance floor. It was fun and convenient, but we quickly realized that we needed more time and the ability to talk about troupe-related business. We were taking it seriously, after all.

We started meeting at Rosie's house, which was another good space. It held a tranquil energy, we were happy there, and it felt comfortable, like a second home. Rosie owned a one-story cabin that sat on several acres of wooded land just outside the city. She had inherited it from her grandparents, and although it contained her relatively contemporary belongings, it still held the same warmth that a grandparent's home does. The living room was large with high ceilings and had limited furniture: a small couch and a single rocking chair. This made it ideal for our rehearsals, as we had enough room to practice inside when needed. Although, we often took advantage of the warm weather and danced barefoot on the deck that was attached to the back of the cabin. Of course, we always practiced with our fire tools outside.

Artwork decorated Rosie's walls: prints of Hindu gods and goddesses, abstract landscape paintings that she had created while studying art in college, and bookshelves full of nonfiction books, including one small but prominent section devoted to Robert Downey Junior biographies. A yoga mat rested in the corner of the room, rolled up next to a stack of DVDs featuring belly dance and yoga lessons. The entire home had Rosie written all over it, and I felt like I had known her for years after spending just moments taking in the cabin. There was just one thing missing, I thought. *Morgan.*

"You know, if we're going to do this professionally, we should have an actual, dedicated fire safety person for our practices and shows," Rosie pointed out one day.

"You mean someone to watch a group of women belly dance with fire, and not take his eyes off them? Oh, that sounds terrible. But I'll take one for the team. I'll do it," Adrian jokingly volunteered.

"Oh, you poor thing." I gave him my flirtiest frown, appreciating his comment—on behalf of everyone, of course. "You know, my friend Morgan would probably be totally into this. She's pretty excited about my fire dancing, and actually curious enough about tribal dance to start taking lessons with me beginning with the next session."

"Can you trust her?" Rosie asked. "We need someone that has quick reflexes, understands the nature of the dangers we're dealing with, can hold back drunks from the audience, and who's not afraid of fire."

"And can stay sober for a night while we're performing," added Rhiannon, looking at Adrian with a sarcastic grin. "We'll probably be in any kind of atmosphere. I'm hoping, anyway, to be at festivals, clubs . . . anywhere we can get stage time."

I was taken aback by the barrage of questions *If they can trust me, they should understand that they can trust someone I'd suggest,* I thought. "She was there when I lit up my fire poi for the first time, so yes, we can trust her," I ventured to say. "She's totally cool, and she said she wants to learn everything, too."

"Okay, so she was there, and she's cool. But is she willing to put out a fire on another human being, risking her own safety?" Rhiannon asked.

"*Fuck.* Yes, okay?" I had no choice but to tell them about the accident I had. "She already proved it." I pulled the scarf off my neck and showed them the healing burn mark from the poi's hardware. With a little TLC, a lot of aloe, and a few weeks' time, it was finally beginning to calm.

"What the hell happened?" Rosie said as she moved closer to me, putting her hand on my shoulder.

"Been there, done that," said Rhiannon. "You all right? It probably could've been a lot worse."

"I'll be fine. I was doing a buzzsaw with my poi. It was my first fire spin. I got the first burn out of the way, that's all. So there. Is she in or not?"

They agreed and I thought, *'Nough said then.*

Chapter 8

SPINDERELLA

"Omagod, yes, that sounds so cool!" Morgan had just the reaction I thought she would when I invited her to join the group and be a fire safety.

"Really? You're in?" I knew she would say yes, and was thrilled that she agreed so quickly.

"Hell yeah. When do you need me?"

"I'll pick you up on my way to Rosie's at 6:00," I told her.

That evening, we walked into the cabin together. I introduced her to Rosie, Rhiannon, and Adrian in one fell swoop. "Everybody, this is Morgan. Morgan, this is everybody."

"Morgan, welcome to the tribe!" Rhiannon said as she offered a hug. I could tell that Morgan felt shy since she was the newest person in this unexpected circle of friends, so I offered some kind words about her.

"This girl is a mad music mixer, guys," I said. "She used to cut songs and mix them up for the parties we went to together in college."

"Maybe we should call you 'Spindarella,'" Rosie said as she came over to welcome Morgan with a hug as well.

"Call me anything but late for dinner," Morgan said as she put her purse down.

"Let's go on out back and get started, guys, and we can show Morgan how to put out the fire on our tools," Rosie answered.

We shuffled outside, carrying our fire gear bags and drinks, to set up and practice in the backyard.

"Anybody have a light?" Morgan asked as she pulled out a cigarette.

"Yes and no," I answered.

"What she means is that we can't smoke near the fuel," Rhiannon winked at Morgan, giving her the first rule of fire arts. "The gas we use is highly flammable, so we take as many precautions as we can, like keeping it covered and at a safe distance away from the audience and the fire tools that are lit."

"Don't worry, though—it's simple when you get down to it," Rosie added. "Keep open flame away from the fuel. That's the most important rule of safety."

"Safety third!" Adrian hollered.

"Oh, behave," Rosie said to him, looking at the rest of us with a smile in her eyes.

He looked at me without anyone noticing and winked. My heart fluttered.

As Rosie practiced with her tools, Rhiannon and I taught Morgan how to extinguish them. The timing for each fire prop had to be just right because if the fuel was gone, then the fire would begin burning the actual wicks and we would have to replace them sooner. If there was too much fuel still on the wicks, then the fire was more difficult to put out.

Practices continued each week, and as she became more comfortable, Morgan began contributing during the meetings by sharing her ideas about costuming, music, and the ultimate goal of the group: performing.

Chapter 9

FIVE YEARS AGO

"Have I ever told you all how much I love you?" Rosie said during a practice night at her place as we took a break from our fire tools to rest on the back patio. "I mean it. I'm just so glad we're in this together."

"Me, too," I agreed. "I can't imagine where I'd be if it weren't for all of this, and all of you." The sun was sinking below the horizon, reminding me of the same shades and spectrum that moments ago I was spinning through the air with my fire poi. It was quiet except for our voices and the sound of a pair of owls calling to each other in the distance.

"Shit, I'd just be working more hours," said Morgan. "Can I see your lighter, Summer?" I handed it to her as Rhiannon spoke up.

"It's crazy, you know. I never would have dreamed that I'd be a part of something like this. Ten years ago—heck, five years ago—I was in such a different place."

"Let's hear it," Rosie prompted her. "Everyone. Where were you, let's say, five years ago? Morgan, you go first."

"Five years ago, let's see"—Morgan exhaled a puff of smoke—"I was a senior in high school. I had just taken the same job that I have now, in a warehouse. It started out as a part-time position, and I took it because it paid well and I could use the money to help pay for my college classes and stuff. I kind of hated working there because some of the guys were perverts and would get on my nerves. And trust me, it only takes one of those types to make your day miserable. But I gave it right back to them, and they eventually realized they weren't ever going to get in my pants, and they came to respect me. I had to put up with a lot of shit from them. You'd think that kind of stuff, the 'sweetie pies,' and the 'nice ass' comments were things that people have evolved out of doing by this day and age, but nope. Not in that environment. They see you as a piece of meat until you prove otherwise."

"Weren't you ever able to get away from it?" Rhiannon asked. "I mean, if you went to college. I just assume that that means a free ride to success, or at least a job that you really like."

"You would think, and maybe for some people it is," she said.

"What did you study? Maybe it's not too late to go into that field," Rosie said optimistically.

"My major was philosophy, and I minored in art," Morgan answered with one eyebrow arched. "Technically, I should be robbing liquor stores for a living. Hell, I've already been in jail, so it seems about right."

Rhiannon and Rosie looked at me for an explanation. I could see it in both of their faces: *Your friend has been in jail? This is who you bring to join our group?*

"I almost forgot about that," I said, trying to bridge my friends. "At least you went to jail for a good thing, and not for actually robbing a liquor store."

Morgan continued to explain. "Yeah, it was when I was a senior in high school; fortunately it was *after* I landed my job. I was out with some of my older friends one night at a party and they were drinking. A lot. I had only had like one Bud Light and that was hours before it was time for us to get in the car and actually go home. So before we got in the car, I convinced the driver to give me her keys and let me drive them home.

We didn't have cab money, and there was no way I was going to call my parents or anything like that. We got pulled over when I didn't use a turn signal."

"You went to jail for not using a turn signal?" Rosie asked.

"No, I went to jail for one night because I was driving a vehicle without a license. The cop didn't care about the fact that I kept someone from driving drunk. Well, maybe he cared about that, but it didn't stop him from taking me in to 'teach me a lesson' about the kind of people I hang out with."

I laughed to myself a little. "Well, I'm not sure if it taught you a lesson or not, by the looks of our group."

Everyone laughed with me and we held our drinks up in cheers. Rosie slipped off her sandals and sat down on the patio step. "I was still stripping for a living five years ago. I made a killing, working nights at this nice little club called The Office. My manager was decent, and the DJs were good to me. To get good songs, you'd have to share some of your tips with them. Otherwise, they'd play stuff that you just couldn't dance to. Well, couldn't *strip* to at least." She laughed. "I had so much fun putting together my acts. Each one had a theme, where I would dress a certain part and tease the audience. I did more than just get up there and take off my clothes. Even the women tipped me, because everybody loves titties. And if you don't, you're an asshole. You know what I'm saying?"

"You must've had a reason to start in the first place," I said, wondering how a woman makes the conscious choice to take such a difficult job, or, at least, what *I* would consider to be difficult.

"Well, I had dropped out of high school and moved out of my parents' house because I hated them. They were trying to tell me what to do all the time, and I didn't want to have it. I knew what I wanted. I thought I knew what I was doing, so I left. Working at the club was the only way I could pay the rent on my efficiency while I got my GED."

"Do you still talk to your parents?" Morgan asked, putting her cigarette out on the bottom of her boot.

"We're on good terms now. Once I really got my shit together, we reconciled. I earned my high school diploma, quit working at The Office, and found the job I still have now."

"Which is?" Morgan asked.

"I work at the counter at Your Party Starts Here. It's the liquor store you never robbed," she teased Morgan affectionately. "It doesn't pay as well as stripping did, and I'm living paycheck to paycheck, but I get to keep my clothes on and the hours are better. I'm putting away a little money so that, I don't know, maybe one day I'll get to go to college, too. Maybe be something or someone one day."

"Is there anything specific you'd study, or do you know what direction you'll go in?" I asked.

"I haven't gotten that far yet. I love to dance, so maybe I could get a degree in something that involves movement arts, or even on the other side like physical therapy to help others recover and be able to move, period. I figure I have time to narrow it down, and as long as I have some kind of degree, I can get away from a register."

"You'll be able to do it," Morgan said to her. "I can tell just from the time I've known you that you'll get where you want to go, where you're meant to be."

"Thanks, sugar," Rosie said to her. She took a drink and said, "That's the plan."

In the pause of our conversation, I realized that either Rhiannon or I would go next. She spoke up first.

"I'll go next." She smiled sadly at Rosie.

"You really don't have to," Rosie said.

"It's only fair. I'll play," Rhiannon said. She was leaning against the patio railing and looking down at her nails. "Five years ago I was pregnant. 'Baby daddy' was nowhere to be found. It was a one-night stand.

Not that I did that a lot, but it happened." The rest of us waited silently for her to answer the question that none of us wanted to ask. "My parents talked me into having an abortion. It was hell. It was fucking hell. But I didn't feel like I had a choice. Ironic, now, I know. I went through counseling, and I still go to a support group once in a while, when I feel like I need it. Or, if I feel like it needs me, ya know. I stayed in school, finished what I started, and then got an apartment in the same building where Rosie was. That's how we met originally, and then we signed up for the tribal belly dance classes together as a way to try to have some good, clean fun. The rest is history."

"We've come a long way," Rosie said to her.

"Yes, we have," Rhiannon said. "And then I met Adrian through a mutual friend we had. It was one of those setups where the friend just knew that we would be a great couple, and he wasn't too off track. There are some things about Adrian that I'm not a total fan of, but we've worked through a lot, just like you have to in any relationship. When we first started dating, I was a jealous lover. I couldn't stand the thought of him even looking at another woman, even if she was in a movie. It was extreme, I realize now, but I guess he just came at a time when I was very vulnerable, and I needed him. I needed someone. But I would be with him even if it wasn't for his friendship through that time of my life, when I was still healing. I guess I'm still healing. Probably always will be. But I love him."

She pulled her hair back behind her shoulders and looked at me. "Summer, looks like you're the only one left. Five years ago. Let's hear it."

"First, I'm sorry for what you've been through," I told her, stepping forward and putting my arms around her. "I can't even imagine."

"Thank you. It's okay. It'll be okay. You can't go back in the past and change things. All you can do is keep moving forward, trying to do your best with what you have. Taking dance classes has been my salvation, to tell you the truth. It's healing."

I know all about that, I thought. I was feeling so heavy with empathy for each of my friends that I didn't want to go into my dark history from just five years ago. I only wanted to hear more about Rosie's stripper days, high-five Morgan for not taking shit from her co-workers, and, especially, to comfort Rhiannon. So I figured I would save my rock-bottom story for another time. "I understand that, about the dance classes. I've always lived for dance. It's my breath. Five years ago, I was teaching classes as well, to third-graders at a small academy in the rich part of town. I didn't fit in with the other teachers though. They were from the area, and they were spoiled and stuck up. The families who sent their kids there were upper class, and so I didn't connect with them, either. I only went there because it was such a great school. They would compete and go to conventions. I thought I could've gone somewhere with them."

"What happened then? Do you still go there at all?" Rosie asked.

"I got fired," I said with a frown.

"You got fired from teaching third-graders how to dance?" Rhiannon chuckled. "What the hell did you do?"

I had to laugh at myself at this point. It did sound hilarious. "I was just myself. Purple hair. Enough to scare the parents, I guess."

"Well, they didn't deserve you," Rosie said. "If they were so worried about your looks, let them have some crappy teacher who wears her hair in a bun. You could probably move better than any tight-ass . . ."

"Hold the phone, girl," I said, laughing at how sincerely she was defending me from people she didn't know. "It's fine now. They let me go. I moved on. I found you guys."

"Cry two tears in a bucket, mother fuck it," Morgan said as she shook her head.

"Exactly," I nodded, glad that, for the moment at least, I had only shared a sliver of my own painful history. "Now, let's set some shit on fire and dance."

Chapter 10

WE NEED A NAME

During one of these early meetings at Rosie's, I met Phoenix Fleming, a usually shirtless twenty-year-old with long brown hair, who had drifted into this newborn group through Rhiannon. He used a seven-foot-long staff that had fire wicks on both ends and earned a living as a personal trainer. He had a Johnny Depp-like quality of mysterious sexiness, and he used it when he worked with his fire staff by making eye contact with each of us as we watched him and his beautifully fluid movements. There was only one thing about him that I couldn't quite get past—he didn't believe in wearing deodorant of any kind. It may not have been an issue except he was so physical in everything he did. No one else said anything about it, so I rolled with it. And so as much as I loved watching him at practices, I was only interested in being his friend.

Adrian was usually at practice, too, as he was a staple presence when Rhiannon was around. He contributed with honest and constructive criticism. He quickly became adept at being a fire safety for anyone who was fire dancing and was diligent about his duty. Rhiannon used fire poi, and Rosie danced with a fire fan, which was similar to a Chinese fan in nature but was bigger, made of black metal, and had five spikes that were a foot long sticking straight out, tipped with wicks, where the fire resided when lit. Rosie's background as a stripper had strengthened her performance skills; she danced with a mature sensuality that I had yet to develop.

There was a lot of room for sexual innuendos ("nice staff, Phoenix" and "my balls are hot" were just a couple of prop jokes that never got old), and everyone in the group was pretty damn attractive—and flirty. We were having fun with each other, but we needed to get serious about our tribe.

"We need a name!" I announced at one of our earliest co-ed meetings.

"I've been thinking about that, too," Rhiannon said, "and I've come up with something that I wanted to throw out there." She continued when everyone looked open to the idea. "What do you think about Peace, Love, and Fire?"

Rosie's face scrunched up, and Morgan looked thoughtful.

"It's nice, but it doesn't sound as professional as it should," Rosie said. "Our name might be the first impression that we give some people, like if they're looking for something like our group online."

"I think she's right, Rhiannon," Morgan added softly.

I began writing notes as they talked, jotting down words that I liked and thought would sound more accurate.

"I like it," Rhiannon said. "Peace, Love, and Fire. I think it expresses our individual and group missions of peace in general, our love for life, and of course, fire itself."

"What about this: Noir Arts of the Queen City?" I offered, looking up at everyone.

"Say it again," Rosie said.

"Noir Arts of the Queen City," I repeated, trying to judge from their faces if they liked it.

"Dig it," Morgan said as she nodded her head.

"I do, too," Rosie agreed. "Rhiannon, what do you think? Yay? Nay?"

"It's dark. It's sexy. I do like it. Good one, Summer. I guess it is more of a tribe name than Peace, Love, and Fire. So now we just need, like, a tag line to sort of sum up what we do, so that when people see the name they know exactly what it is, and what we are."

"I've been thinking about this for a while," I said. "I've played around with some words and phrases, and anyway, what do you think about this? 'Feats of flame and tribal dance.'" I read the line, each word with deliberation, from my notebook.

"I like it, but it feels weak," Morgan said. "We need to spice it up."

"What about *dangerous* feats of flame?" Rhiannon asked.

I wrote that down as Rosie spoke up.

"And *sultry* tribal dance!" Rosie acted like she was fanning herself. "Woo! It's getting hot in here!"

Morgan added, "Haha! *Sultry!* Now we're talking!"

"Noir Arts of the Queen City: Dangerous Feats of Flame and Sultry Tribal Dance," I said.

I had no idea what I was getting into, and yet nothing held me back. We always had great laughs together at our practices, and I looked forward to it every week. It became my "me time," and I could just focus on my newfound craft for a couple of relaxing hours with friends. Of course, there were also many nights when we would gather and start with a glass of wine (or Bud Light, for Morgan), which led to two glasses, which led to watching videos online of other tribal dance groups, fire dancing gone wrong, and usually at least one clip of Robert Downey Junior. This usually signaled the end of the "meeting" for everyone else, since it meant that Rosie had completely lost focus. And when we were outside, we carefully practiced with our tools, not so much because we were working with fire but more so because of the piles of dog shit from a stray that often found its way to Rosie's rural backyard.

Now all we needed was an audience.

Chapter 11

PATIENCE, RELUCTANCE, AND ANTICIPATION

"I think everyone should learn how to eat fire," Rhiannon announced one evening at Rosie's cabin.

"Um, I wasn't planning on putting fire anywhere near my face, at least, intentionally," I said, although the idea of fire eating did make my pulse beat faster. It sounded sexy and dangerous—somehow more so than spinning the fire poi.

Rosie, who was game for anything without a second thought, said, "Yeah! I've always wanted to eat fire. Back when I worked at the titty bar, there was a girl who did it as part of her act. It was cool as hell. She made a ton in tips, too." I blushed at the reference to Rosie's former profession, and it didn't go unnoticed. "What's the matter? You're turning red! I didn't mean to embarrass you, Summer. You're so modest!"

"It's fine. I just never know what to expect with you, woman," I said, shaking my head.

"I've been wanting to learn how to breathe fire myself," Phoenix said, steering the conversation back to the topic at hand. "I think we need a fire breather in the group, too. So yeah, I'll learn how to eat it."

"You bet you'll learn how to eat it," Rosie told him. This made us all burst into another round of laughter. I caught Adrian's eye when she said that, and the look he gave me sent me into another round of blushing. I hoped that if anyone else noticed, they assumed it was from Rosie's joke.

"The point is that if everyone knows how to eat fire, then it'll be easier to book gigs without having to worry if our only fire eater is available," Rhiannon said in an effort to herd the cats; at least, that is what leading the troupe meetings seemed like on some nights. "If you want to learn to eat fire, you need to read up on the dangers of it. There are risks involved, and I want you all to be aware of them before you commit to this. Even if you don't actively practice and perform it, it'll be good to understand how it's done, so that we can safety for each other in the best way. I'll set up a workshop night for us, where I'll teach you all everything that I've been learning about it."

By then I had become comfortable enough with fire to not be afraid of this new endeavor, and I was simply excited about the idea of it. Fire eaters are badasses, and that spoke to me. I chose to ignore the literature on the dangers of fire eating because I wanted to dive right into my journey into this unknown world. I felt bold, empowered, and consequently, sexy. That night when I got home, I went online to the website that Rhiannon referred us to and ordered a set of torches. Later in the week when they arrived in the mail, I set them aside in the tie-dyed shopping bag that I had begun using to hold my fire poi and waited with part patience, part reluctance, and part anticipation.

"Are you going to Cincinnati Burns this year?" Rhiannon asked Rosie one night at rehearsal as we were practicing with our tools and listening to the radio. I remembered hearing briefly about this festival in between classes one day, and as I slowed the momentum of my poi, my ears perked up. Morgan stopped spinning her poi as well, even reaching into her purse for a cigarette as she listened with curiosity. Phoenix continued to work on a new trick he was learning with his fire staff.

"Yeah, I've been thinking about it," Rosie answered. "Are the tickets on sale yet?"

"They just went on sale today," Adrian said. "We were going to order ours, but we might be able to get a group discount if enough of us go together." He glanced at me as he spoke, and I felt an unexpected stirring.

"I might go, too," I said, feeling a little brazen. "Tell me more about it."

"Well, it's mostly workshops on things like hooping, poi spinning, belly dance . . . ," Rhiannon began.

"Sounds like hell," Morgan said sarcastically.

"Oh yeah, it sucks," Rosie said. "There's a lot of gifting and sharing that happens. We end up just hanging out all day doing the stuff we love with awesome people, then partying all night. It's a hard job, but someone's got to do it."

"How many people are needed for the group discount? If it's five, we can do it." I was already mentally making my plans, and I didn't even have the date yet.

"I think it's actually only four, so yeah, we'll be solid," Rhiannon said. "Let's save our money over the next few weeks, and then we can buy our tickets together. Check your calendars, too, and let me know. It's in June, so we'll need to block off a weekend and not book anything."

"Not going," Phoenix said as he stopped tooling around with his staff. "Even with the discount, there's no way I'm going to be able to swing it. You guys just go, then come back and teach me everything you learn, and I'll hold down the fort here."

"You sure, Phoenix? There has to be a way you can swing it," Rosie said. "None of the rest of us makes very good money, and we're going. I mean, you're already saving money by not buying deodorant."

I couldn't believe she actually said what I was too embarrassed to admit I was thinking.

"I am saving money, and I'm saving myself from toxins. You can poison yourself with deodorant if you want."

"Right, because having fuel-soaked wicks on fire around your head isn't toxic at all. Maybe you just need to prioritize," Rosie answered.

"Maybe you need to butt out," he answered.

"Cool it! Just cool it, you two," Rhiannon said, nearly slamming her hand on the railing. "Everyone here loves this group, what we do, and what we stand for. If you don't, or if you can't keep your opinions to yourself, then leave."

The tension made me nervous, but Phoenix broke it by saying, "I'm staying."

"I'm staying, too," Rosie said. "I'll be here until the end."

Phoenix picked up his staff again and began practicing in the grass. His movements had an edginess that they didn't have moments before, and I could sense that he was still at least a little angry. But the conversation picked back up, and Rhiannon, Rosie, and Adrian went on to tell Morgan and me more about this utopian-sounding weekend.

They said that every summer in the middle of Ohio, Cincinnati Burns rises. I learned that it was a gathering of like-minded individuals who would create kismet in an open field with dance, under the stars, with only the light of dozens of flames illuminating all the lovely faces. It consisted of five hundred or so fire artists who gathered with the intention of sharing their skills and learning from others from sunup until sundown. Fire dancers, tribal belly dancers, and musicians met at a private campground for about four days of classes and workshops that ran the gamut of everything that I could have dreamed of.

Part of my responsibility as a semiprofessional fire dancer, I believed, was to continue my own education, especially since I was beginning to teach poi spinning and tribal belly dance myself as requested by others, so it was an obligation, really, although a lucrative one. It was easy to agree to going.

Chapter 12

THE INTOXICATING ACT OF PERFORMING

Using skills learned from my position at the library, I was able to set up a basic web page with contact information for the tribe. Our group also worked together to create a simple promotional kit that we each began distributing around Cincinnati. At the same time, I had begun actively calling bars and other entertainment venues to try to book the group for any kind of show so that we could get some experience under our coin belts. Some nights, I could hardly sleep at night as fantasies about performing kept me awake. It was such a glamorous notion, and with the formation of Noir, it was becoming a reality.

I was wasting time on Twitter when I got an e-mail from the booking agent for the Cincinnati Sadistic Ladeez, the city's own Roller Derby team. I called the agent back, and we negotiated some details, finally agreeing on a rate, performance length, and date that the tribe would perform for the halftime show at the coliseum. As soon as I hung up the phone, I posted the great news in our online group, reveling in the success of booking our first gig, and such a big one to boot.

Since everyone was either online at work or had a smartphone, we had agreed that it would be wise to set up a private web forum where we could communicate about the tribe and our gigs, once we would start actually booking some. The conversation stayed casual for the most part. It was an effective tool, and as everyone began posting their ideas, it also became a way to get to know each other better and help us bond further.

We were all excited about this first show as a professional fire arts troupe, and we worked furiously to coordinate our costumes, music, and order of appearance. It was agreed that we would wear traditional tribal belly dance costuming, except for Phoenix, who would wear black pants and a fitted black tank top that would nicely show off his muscles.

After three weeks of rehearsing with our fire props and dancing to the songs we had chosen to fill the ten minutes we had for the performance, the night of the event finally arrived. Everyone met up at the Barn, the stadium home of the Cincinnati Sadistic Ladeez. I let my dreadlocks hang down and wore a long, flowing skirt that was black with bright blue trim and had small, embroidered mirrors that caught the light. I also had on a coin bra that I made. It was a simple bra that I had bought from Victoria's Secret and decorated with Middle Eastern coins, cowry shells, and fabric, so that it looked more like a performance piece than lingerie. Rosie and Rhiannon were dressed similarly, in standard tribal belly dance gear that included coin belts and heavy, exotic jewelry. In the backstage area during the first half of the Roller Derby bout, Rosie, Rhiannon, Phoenix, and I nervously rehearsed and prepared our fire tools for the performance. Adrian and Morgan patiently watched and helped out as needed as the bout took place.

Phoenix was stretching his arms and we were off to the side, sort of away from everyone else.

"Phoenix, can I ask you something?" I said to him as I watched him pull his elbows behind his head to stretch his triceps. I noticed that he smelled masculine, in a good way. *Thank goodness it's not offensive tonight,* I thought.

"What?"

"What's your real name?"

"My name is Phoenix," he said as he bent over and picked up his staff, giving it a spin in the air. "It might not be the name that I was born with, but it's who I am."

That's hardcore, I thought. Maybe my birth name was colorful enough that I was satisfied with it. Either way, I no longer wondered what his real name was. He was Phoenix. That was all I needed.

Suddenly, the backstage manager signaled us, and it was time to go. We each lined up in the hallway leading to the game floor and waited for the music. And waited. And waited.

"What the fuck," Rosie said under her breath. "Why isn't the music starting?"

"I don't know," was all that I had to offer. I was nervous but kept my calm as much as possible, breathing deep and trying to focus on this first fire performance that I would give at any second. Word came to Rhiannon from the sound booth that the CD she brought was not working—but Morgan had brought an extra CD just in case. As she ran it to the sound booth, the audience began to get restless. More and more people were getting up to go to the bathroom and buy snacks. Just moments ago it was quiet with anticipation for our act, but soon random conversations began to fill the air in one cloud of sound.

Moments later the CD had been transported up to the sound booth, and Morgan was back at our sides. The first beats filled the air. There were 1,100 people in the audience waiting for a fire show, and little did they know, it was the first appearance of Noir Arts of the Queen City.

The house lights were down, and Rosie, Rhiannon, and I entered the staging area with the candles that we would use to light our fire tools. With cues from the music, we relied on the loose choreography that we had planned and then set our candles on the floor. The songs we used were Americanized versions of Middle Eastern melodies; sitars accompanied with djembes, laid over a beat that was reminiscent of club songs.

We began with a slow walk, holding small sets of palm torches—small wicks cradled within metal cups, with handles to keep our hands from feeling too much of the heat. We swayed our hips in circles as our arms lifted above our heads, moving into a circle as we reached the center of the floor. Once in position, we danced as a single unit, moving our hands in sync with one another so that all six of the flames also moved as one. The effect must have been spectacular, as the crowd, which had been screaming minutes ago during the derby bout, had hushed, perhaps hypnotized by us, or the flames, or very likely, the combination of the two.

I felt so alive.

As the flames died down, Adrian inconspicuously came near the side of the staging area, and one by one, dancing all the while, Rosie and Rhiannon took my palm torches and left the floor. Adrian handed me my newly soaked fire poi and I bowed my head to say thanks. He kneeled down to act as a safety for me as I dipped the poi heads in our candlelight to ignite them. The fire came to life in a burst of light, and I forgot that there were more than a thousand people watching me because all I cared about was dancing with my fire poi and, more specifically, dancing for Adrian. I spun the poi in the air, all around me, and it was perhaps one of my best spins yet. I could feel the energy of the crowd, as well as Adrian watching me. I felt so sexy, so in control. In the quiet moments when I would stop the poi from spinning for a dramatic pause, I could hear their yells. I even thought I heard my name.

"Summer!"

I looked over and saw Adrian pointing at my feet. *Fuck,* I thought. Glimpsing down, my skirt flowing in waves, I saw that my sandal had come untied, and the leather laces were teasing the floor beneath me. *What do I do? What do I do?* What would Rosie do? A professional performer, she would probably make it part of her act. But I wasn't a professional. Or was I? I was getting paid, so yes, I was, technically. *There's not time for this,* I told myself. I planted my feet and continued moving my upper body as though that was part of my choreography, and then the song came to an end. The audience's applause transitioned the sound from our music to their roar.

As I bowed and carefully took my leave, stepping with intention so that I wouldn't trip over my shoelace, Phoenix entered the staging area next with his fire staff. He gently touched one wick to the candle closest to him, then grabbed the fire with his free hand and transferred it to the other wick, so it gave the illusion that he lit it with his fingertips. He then threw the staff into the air horizontally, and as it dropped, two large fireballs rose into the air from either side of the staff, and the crowd screamed with satisfaction. It was obvious that the audience had forgiven the sound crew—and us—for the music delay.

After just ten intoxicating minutes of dancing with fire, we took our bows, blew out the candles, and returned to the backstage area, where we celebrated with smiles and hugs. I felt like I was returning from another world. While we were "on," my adrenaline was pumping with nervousness and excitement, pride and joy. I didn't want to be anywhere else in the world except dancing under the lights with my friends for a responsive audience.

"You girls were incredible," Adrian told us.

"Thanks for letting me know about that damned shoelace," I said, and I stepped forward to give him a hug as Rosie and Rhiannon began putting their things away so we could leave. For a brief moment I wanted to stay right in his arms. He held me close and I could tell that he didn't want to let me go, either. He smelled good, and I was still riding the wave of a high from our set. But I wrote it off. It was such a rush to perform out there for a huge, enthusiastic crowd, and our first performance was officially considered a success. I figured that was probably part of why I was so excited. My face felt flushed from the physical demands of our short but energetic and dangerous show, and maybe partly from trying to hide any attraction that I felt for Adrian. But I had a tribe to attend to.

Our adrenaline calmed down enough for us to leave the backstage area and watch the second half of the bout after we put away our fire gear and fuel. Walking back into the arena, I took in the audience again. So many people. *Did that really just happen?* As I looked around, my eyes landed on Audrey, who was sitting in the front row of the next section down. She saw me and waved me over.

"You guys were amazing!" She said, leaning over the railing to give me a hug. "I'm so proud of you all!"

"Thank you so much," I said. I was so grateful. "Do you usually come to these bouts?"

"No, I'm not really into watching women knock each other down on roller skates, although it actually is pretty entertaining. I wanted to see you guys for your first gig."

"That's so sweet," I said. "I think we're going to watch the rest of the bout since we're done for the night. I'm surprised they haven't started up again yet."

"They did for a minute, I think while you must've been backstage still. But"—she frowned like she didn't want to tell me something—"um, it was delayed because some of the candle wax had dripped onto the skating floor. Every skater who hit that spot would slip."

"Stop it. You're fucking with me," I said, hoping truly that she was.

"No, um, they'd either fall down, or smack into whoever was nearest. That's what they're out there doing right now, trying to clean it up."

I turned around and saw a couple of workers on the floor where, indeed, our candle had been sitting.

"Oh hell," I said. "I guess we're not getting this gig again."

"Just learn from it," Audrey said. "You're going to fuck up. It's inevitable. Don't let it stop you, okay?"

I nodded and told her that I'd see her soon at Dance Mecca, then found my group. I felt terribly guilty about the candle wax, but there was nothing I could do at that point besides accept the compliments that the audience members were showering us with as we made our way to our reserved seats. The attention was glorious. I wasn't used to so many people smiling at me and telling me how amazing I was. I wished I could put the emotions into a bottle that I could open as needed. Even photographers were approaching us, giving us their cards with promises of amazing shots that they had taken during the halftime show.

It was enough to make me feel pretty damn good.

Chapter 13

THE MOST UNNATURAL THING IN THE WORLD

By this time, I had been fire dancing with poi for several months and felt the same awe watching my fellow performers with their own tools as I did when I was dancing myself. I was curious about eating fire. Rhiannon had become a pro at it, performing tricks that many of us didn't think were even possible. She had a way of transferring the flame from her wick to her tongue, to another wick, all the while making it look facile to her spectators. I noticed the precise attention that Rhiannon gave to this act.

"You ready to learn?" She asked me. One of her eyebrows was raised in an arch as she waited for my answer.

"To eat fire?" Even as I said it out loud, I knew that the answer was yes. Of course I wanted to. I wanted to try everything under the sun that would make me feel alive. If there was a way to dance with and manipulate fire, I wanted to know it, practice it, and perfect it, so that it became second nature. The torches were already in my possession, waiting for me to bring their purpose to fruition. "Yes, please!" I replied in a silly, child-like voice that made Rhiannon smile.

"It's on like Donkey Kong."

Once I gave an affirmative to Rhiannon, I knew that eating fire would be part of my destiny. All I had to do next was show up.

I went to Rhiannon's apartment a few days later to take my first lesson. Adrian answered the door when I knocked. "There you are," he said as he opened the door to her apartment. The smell of Thai food greeted me warmly.

"Hey. I didn't know you'd be here, too." He stood in the doorway holding the door open for me, and as I squeezed by to go inside, my shoulder accidentally brushed his chest. I tried to ignore the way my breath caught at this chance touch. "Is Rhiannon around?"

"Yeah, she's outside. I'm cooking dinner for us. You haven't eaten yet, have you?"

"Bummer . . . yeah, I just had a burrito before I left my place. But you guys go ahead and eat. Anyone else coming?" I asked as I put down my purse.

"Somebody somewhere is," he said jokingly.

"Good grief! You kiss your mother with that mouth?" I laughed and shook my head as I waited for his real answer.

"I think the rest of the crew is going to take Rhiannon's little workshop on a different night. They all had stuff going on. You know how it goes."

"Indeed. Well, I could've just come over on the same night as everyone else . . ."

"It's cool. Rhiannon has been stoked that you were coming over. Make yourself at home." He walked back into the kitchen, and I grabbed my fire gear bag, heading out of the apartment to find Rhiannon.

The building had an enclosed courtyard that was decorated with potted plants and ornamental trees, offering privacy from the street and sidewalk. There was a small saltwater pool next to the patio, where I found Rhiannon.

"Hey, girl," I said as I pulled my new fire-eating torches from my bag. She was pouring a small amount of fuel into a can and, still looking at what she was doing, gave a gentle nod with her head to acknowledge me. I watched, aware that the more I talked, the more my nervousness might show. There was a feeling of anticipation in the air, for me at least.

Rhiannon looked up and saw my torches, saying, "Oh no, honey, you don't want to start with those. Here, use these for now," she said, and she gave me a set of torches that had wicks that were as small as the tip of my pinky finger. "These look like baby fire-eating torches." I giggled, but I didn't argue about starting with them. I knew from using fire poi that a bigger wick equaled a bigger flame.

Rhiannon lit one of her torches and then lit one of my "baby" torches. My new, professional set was tucked safely back into my bag, where the sticks would remain for several weeks as I developed a tolerance for the small amount of fire on the borrowed set of torches. "Just touch it to your finger," Rhiannon instructed. I obeyed. *That didn't seem so bad,* I thought. "Get used to it being close to your skin, and then try tapping it in your palm or on your forearm," Rhiannon went on.

This part of the lesson only took a couple of minutes. I expected fear, but rather felt brave and open to this new realm. I experimented with the flame, just nervous enough to remind me that I was alive.

I noticed that Adrian had stepped into the courtyard and was watching us. The space was peaceful as we worked. "Rhiannon, dinner's ready when you are," he said, softly breaking the spell as I observed how the flame reacted to my arm.

"Thanks, babe. I'll be up in a minute," Rhiannon told him as she returned her attention to me. After I was comfortable with the flame on my fingers, hands, and forearms, Rhiannon moved on and taught me how to touch the fire to my tongue. This was more intimidating.

"Bringing a wick that's on fire to your face is the most unnatural thing in the world," I said solemnly as I considered what I was about to do. I had to keep my eyes open, even though I wanted to flinch. I stuck my tongue out as far as possible. Again, this was hard to do when I was bringing a flame to it, however small that baby wick was. I knew that these first attempts were nowhere near the level of art that I had seen Rhiannon perform, and I put my ego aside, ignoring the strange faces I knew I was making. Eventually, after sweating with nerves, shaking my head in disbelief that I was actually doing this, and with my adrenaline rushing, I did it. I put the torch in my mouth, and extinguished the flame and exhaled. I felt like a different person. I was a different person. *Perhaps this is why Phoenix is married to his chosen name,* I thought. I inhaled deeply and kept my head tilted up for a moment, taking in the night sky, not wanting time to move as I came to the realization that I had eaten fire. Then I remembered Rhiannon. I was back in reality.

"Your food must be cold by now. Go eat," I told her. "I'll just relax out here for a while and emotionally recover from all this excitement. I just want to ride this wave while it lasts." I smiled, and I could feel my eyes light up.

"That's a good idea. I am starving. You can hop in the pool if you like, and relax."

"I didn't even think to bring my suit."

"It's clothing optional, and nobody here pays any attention or cares. Go for it! It's the perfect ending to learning the nearly unteachable art of how to eat fire. A good balance, you know, fire and water." With that, I watched Rhiannon leave the courtyard. I looked at the water and then looked at the stars. Orion was faithfully arching his bow brightly in the sky. I had never skinny-dipped before, but I figured I had a little while before Rhiannon and Adrian would return, and at this point in my life, why the hell not? Leaving my clothes within arm's reach by the pool steps, I stepped into the cool water and swam, enjoying the serenity of the water and the sky.

Once the novelty of night swimming had worn off, I swam toward to my pile of clothing and fished for my watch. I had been floating around and swimming for about twenty minutes. Knowing that one of my new friends would eventually pop outside to get me, I got out of the water and dried off before they saw me in the buff. I dressed quickly and modestly, hiding myself as though I was not alone. Which was good, because I wasn't.

"You sure you're not hungry?" It was Adrian.

His voice didn't startle me. I looked at him to see if I could tell what he was thinking or how long he had been there. "Oh! Um, yeah, I'm good," I said as I wrung the water from my dreadlocks, noting how comfortable I felt with his arrival. Any other guy who had walked out at that moment would have made me either embarrassed or suspicious. I realized how relaxed I felt around Adrian.

"Actually, on second thought, yes, food does sound good," I said. "Isn't it funny how swimming can make you so hungry?" I did feel hungry, and the Thai food he was cooking had smelled delicious when I popped in upstairs earlier.

"Yeah, it is. But I'd rather be swimming. Sorry I came down here too late."

I was shocked. *Is he really flirting with me?* I thought. I wanted to throw my clothes back to the ground, grab him by the shirt, and pull him into the water with me. All my reason had vacated. And then I blinked. *He's dating my tribe mate. I can't fuck this up.* So instead of giving in to my fantasy, I just smiled bashfully and picked up my bag.

I followed him up to the apartment, where I had the last remaining bowl of noodles and tofu with vegetables, thanked them both graciously, and went home with my things, including the baby torches.

Chapter 14

ROCK OUT WITH YOUR COCK OUT

After the mostly successful reaction to our first gig at the Roller Derby a month prior, new performance opportunities were beginning to trickle in. We decided that because each of us had various schedules throughout any given weekday or weekend that would conflict with gig dates, we would use a flexible lineup while performing, instead of having to adhere to strict choreographies that would be rendered useless—or not worth a shit, as Morgan expressed—if one person was missing for the evening. We planned out a gig lineup that looked something like this, but could be easily switched around as needed:

Rosie / Rhiannon / me–improvised tribal belly dance
Rosie / Rhiannon / me–fire eating, fire orb
Phoenix–fire staff
Rhiannon / me–fire poi
Rosie–fire fans
Phoenix–fire breathing

We would start with either no fire or "small fire tools," such as an orb, which was a wick that was suspended on a wire that was strung from two small leather loops for handles. It was captivating but not necessarily as impressive as the tools that provided bigger flames. We would then build up, beginning with something like Phoenix breathing fire and ending with something visually spectacular like fire poi.

For the next gig that we planned, Phoenix happened to be unavailable, leaving us with only three performers, all of whom would dance for the finale of our set.

"At the end, you guys can just rock out with your cock out," Morgan announced during practice one night. After the laughter subsided, she took a drink of her beer and explained that all of us would be on stage at the same time with our tools, doing our own things.

"Great idea! We'll call it 'ROCO,'" Phoenix said. "You dance, too, don't you, Morgan? How come you're not performing?"

"I guess I could. Nothing's stopping me . . ." Rhiannon, Rosie, and I looked at one another for approval. Morgan had quickly picked up tribal belly dance and was already on the same level that I was, even though I had been taking classes longer. Making a change like this was the type of thing that we should have discussed on the side and then brought to the entire group. And although I had been thinking about it, the topic had not come up until now. Rosie spoke up first, saying, "About damn time!" And with that, Morgan became one of the performing artists of Noir Arts. We began teaching her everything that we knew about poi spinning and fire arts.

On the night of Morgan's first lesson, Phoenix told her, "Just remember, safety third!"

Morgan's eyes got big for a moment; then she smiled and wrinkled her nose. "Oh, you."

"What prop do you want to learn?" Rhiannon ignored Phoenix and was looking at the various tools we had laid before us on the lawn, most of them cooling from having just been lit. "We have fire fans, palm torches, fire poi—but you won't want to start with those since you haven't spun poi before now—fire eating torches . . ."

"What's the easiest? Like, the quickest to learn?" she asked.

Rosie let out a laugh that was almost a snort. "Honey, none of them are easy. It's fire. They're all hot. They all burn. You have to decide which one calls to you."

"Well, the palm torches look easy. I mean, they're small. What's the worst they could do?"

"They can burn the palms of your hands," Rhiannon said with the impatience of a parent who cares about his child making a stupid decision. "Like Rosie said, this is the real deal. Are you sure you're ready for this? Because the worst they could do is catch your costuming or hair on fire, while you have an audience. If you're lucky, they just get too hot while you're holding them. That's part of the job."

"Fine," Morgan said stubbornly. She turned away from Rhiannon and faced me, quickly rolling her eyes. "Summer, what do you think?"

I looked at the fire props before me, considering. The poi and staff definitely took more prep-time before lighting them up; some people spent months practicing before adding flame to the props. The fire fans provided tons of flame—way too much for someone new to fire dancing. It seemed as though palm torches were the way to go. "From what we have here, I'd say that if you want to do fire, starting now, your choices are likely going to be either the palm torches, or learning how to eat fire."

"I'm not putting those things near my face," she said indignantly. "I'd burn my eyebrows off."

"That's the risk we take every time we light up," I said.

"No one's going to force you to use fire when we perform," Rosie added. "You have enough other skills to bring to the group."

"Hold the phone," said Rhiannon. "That's not fair. Why should we risk everything, and let one person not put in the same effort? I busted my balls to learn how to use my props."

"Let's think about this for a minute," Rosie said. "Morgan brings it just as much as any of us, between her music mixing and her safetying for us.

And she can belly dance. We can't force somebody to eat fire, for fuck's sake."

"I can learn the palm torches. I can learn the fire orb. And like you said, I can mix our music, belly dance, and safety. Take it or leave it."

Is this really happening? I thought. "I'll take it," I said. "What is happening here? Morgan can perform with us, and then we'll have one more person to add to the finale whenever we ROCO. So let's just do that. ROCO."

Rosie and Rhiannon seemed agreeable, and I thought to myself how funny it is how we sometimes let our emotions flare up. But maybe that's one of the reasons I loved them so much.

As Morgan integrated with us as a performer, we used the ROCO ending quite a bit over time. For us it was ideal, and it was nice for the audience because they could not possibly get bored—there was so much to take in. The eye could bounce around from dancer to dancer, flame to flame.

But not all the shows we began booking were able to feature fire. Often, as our calendar filled with gigs, we would find ourselves dancing at coffee shops or restaurants, for free food, beer, and tips. If we were lucky, we would get a split from the door when there was a cover charge. I was fine with all of this. I had come to love my tribal sisters, not to mention Phoenix and Adrian, and I simply enjoyed dancing and performing with them every chance I could get. By fire dancing in particular, we had developed a trust in each other. At any given time, we were responsible for the safety of one another, and we respected the unique qualities of each dancer's flavor. Rosie became known for her sensual style and had no problem accepting side gigs in burlesque shows, where she would do a solo, performing alone on stage instead of with a group, to a sexy song. She didn't even have to remove all her clothes because her stage movements alone were enough to make jaws drop to the floor. In her acts, she threw her hair back in time with the music or climbed a pole with the stamina of an athlete, all the time connecting with the audience by wink-ing at them, her mouth slightly open as she demanded their attention.

Rhiannon had a very different stage presence. Hers was one of femi-nine, maternal strength. She often danced with a large sword called a scimitar, balancing it on her head or even her hip as she danced. Morgan was bold in her movements, often leading the improvised dancing with a confidence that I admired and would soon develop from experience. I danced with just the slightest hint of flirtation. Those watching us did so with a respect for the art form and an appreciation of our skill of the dance. Together, the four of us created quite the spectacle for any given group of people looking for entertainment, diversion, or just something different.

Chapter 15

CINCINNATI BURNS

I packed up my hatchback with my fire gear, a few tribal pieces—a skirt and a belt were must-haves for festivals, I was told, where spontaneous dancing was as guaranteed as drum circles at 2:00 in the morning—camping gear, and my enthusiasm. After meeting everyone at Rosie's, we all squeezed into my car with questionable directions, a huge bag of Twizzlers, and an MP3 player. During the car ride, we talked about dance, music, our jobs, and our families.

It was only a couple of hours, but in that time I felt like we became even closer as a group. I couldn't help thinking about how much I loved each of them. I cherished them. Plus, I was overwhelmed with excitement for the variety of classes that I planned on taking: makeup for stage performances, zills/finger cymbals, yoga for dancers, African dance, partner acrobatics, fire arts, hoop dancing, poi spinning, shimmies, and business for performing artists, covering topics like booking gigs and having specialty insurance.

Eventually we pulled into the parking area of the campground. The first thing we saw was a camper with a homemade banner. It was a white bed sheet, painted with the words WELCOME HOME. It made me feel good, like I had indeed just come home. The campground was sprawling with tents and cars, blankets on the grass, and strangers who looked like me and my friends walking along the gravel paths, greeting one another. As we pulled up to the gate to present our tickets, I noticed a few candle-lit red paper lanterns rising above the tree line. By the time we parked and got out of the car, more than one hundred lanterns had begun to drift through the sky, and we heard hoots and hollers from the field beyond the tree line, in the area I would come to know as the "Main Play." We all smiled at each other, knowing that it was going to be an exceptional weekend.

The grounds had primitive cabins with about a dozen bunk beds each. The cabins lined a large lake and were nestled within acres of wooded land. Dirt paths led us from one place to another, and there were several barnlike buildings where most of the workshops were held. A large club-house included a cafeteria, where meals were served during the day and shows were held at night. Outside of the clubhouse was a vending area where everyone shopped and bartered for a variety of fire arts and belly dance accessories, books, music, and jewelry.

Rhiannon and Adrian moved a couple of bunk beds together in the small cabin we were all going to share. Morgan bunked beneath me, and Rosie took the newly-double bunk above the couple, joking that they had better not keep her awake too late into the night. I smiled to show a good sense of humor when Morgan added, "Brown chicken, brown cow!" but I cringed at the idea that we all might share such an intimate space. Of course, then I felt guilty; *I have no right to be jealous,* I reminded myself.

After we had gotten settled and evening approached, each of us began to wander in different directions, curious to see the layout of the festival and if we had any other friends, including Hypnosis, who had stumbled into the campground.

Tents and cabins lined the edge of the tree line, and at each camp I found strangers who would no longer be strangers by the time the weekend was over. People played guitar, hula-hooped, juggled, spun glow poi, talked, hugged, danced, and grinned from ear to ear. It really was home; everyone here was either a fire artist or performer of some kind already, or was aspiring to become one. Some would begin their transition from glow or practice tools to fire props during the four days of the event. I could sense the excitement from the fresh new faces of those who were there to learn, as well as anticipation from the pros, who were happy to be teaching. I was somewhere in the middle, and while part of me wanted to check out everyone else to see where I fell in the hierarchy of talent, I consciously chose not to, for I knew that to try to compare myself to others would be my creative death. This environment in particular is where the best came from all over the world to share their knowledge, and where there was no reason for competition. Everyone was on the same level because everyone wanted to learn from one another, be it to further their current skill set, or to pick up an entirely new toy or prop and start from square one. Although fire arts in particular were not new to me, I felt a curious excitement at what the weekend could bring.

The day was losing its last light as I was eyeing the vendor booths, which had banners hanging over the closed sections of their tents. They were to open the following morning, since everyone was getting settled in on this first night. As I wondered about all the goodies, I felt a gentle hand on the curve of my waist.

"Hey, you!" It was Adrian.

"Hey. What's up?" I responded as his hand dropped away. I quickly noticed that he was alone, and for a split second considered whether he would have touched my waist if Rhiannon had been with him. Not that I minded the minor show of friendly affection.

"Just checked out the Main Play. It's sweet! They have a DJ set up in the middle on a stage, and the fire dancing area is marked off. It's a huge space. Lots of folks just hanging out for now. Want a hit?"

"Duh," I said sarcastically as I took the pipe from his hands and inhaled a little weed. "Where's Rhiannon?"

"She's back at our camp hanging out with Rosie by now, probably. How about we go up to the Main Play and finish this bowl?"

"Sounds good, but"—I hesitated—"we should get back to camp. Thanks for the hit," I said as I started to turn away.

"Aw, come on," he said. "You know you want to."

My chest swelled. "You don't know what I want," I said, returning his flirtatious tone.

"I know what *I* want."

I wanted to say, *And what* do *you want?* I felt the power that I had over him, that he was giving to me, and I wanted to see how far he would go. But at this point, I could feel that passersby may notice us and the way we were looking at each other, wanting each other, but withholding from moving in. "You want to get in trouble," I said, thinking of Rhiannon and wondering where she may be.

"I don't like trouble, but trouble sure likes me," he said with a laugh.

I smiled out of the corner of my mouth and, ready to rest up for the following day, I headed to the cabin, with him next to me.

"I just think it's the smart thing to do," Rosie was saying to Rhiannon as we approached our festival home base. The campfire was burning, giving their faces a soft glow. "I'm burned out from working at the party store. The pay is shit; the hours are shit; the customers are shit. There's no future there, and I want something to look forward to. None of us are making a living from dancing, and we won't be able to do this forever anyway."

"Is something wrong?" I sensed that all was not well, although I was unsure of what Rosie was getting at.

"Aww, no, nothing's wrong. I was just telling Rhiannon—"

"That basically she's going to quit the group," Rhiannon finished for her.

"What's she talking about?" I looked from Rhiannon back to Rosie as Adrian poked at the fire. I felt like I swallowed a large rock that landed in the bottom of my stomach.

"I think I'm going to go back to school. Get a degree. Get a career. A 401k. Benefits. It's not a bad thing, and it doesn't mean that I'm going to quit the group, so don't even think of that," Rosie answered.

"Okay, well, good for you," I said. I wanted to be supportive of my dear friend but could not deal with the idea of Rosie leaving the tribe. My mind quickly did the math. We were like a family, and performing together was what solidified that and kept us together. If we didn't have weekly rehearsals and scheduled gigs, then we would have no firm reason to see each other once—or three times—a week. I needed them, including Rosie.

"Thanks, babe," Rosie responded with a smile that hinted at sadness. "It'll be fine. I don't want anyone to worry, especially this weekend. Let's just have a good time and ROCO."

We smiled; that was the only kind of finale any of us wanted to think about right now.

"Shit! Look what time it is," Rosie said, checking her phone. "The showcase is about to start. Let's go and try to grab some seats together, if there's still room."

"I'll squeeze some people around and make room if I need to," Morgan said as she lit a cigarette. "But yeah, let's head over. I don't want to miss anything."

The performance showcase was held inside an intimate little barn that served as a theater. Morgan did indeed somehow manage to politely squeeze and "excuse us" enough to score some room on a bench near the stage. The opening act was a comedy duet that made us all laugh; at one point Rosie snort-laughed, and by the end of the act my sides hurt. Next up was a woman who went by the name Nailface Nina.

Nina had high cheekbones and deep-set eyes. She was not conventionally pretty, but she was beautiful in a way that some of the strangest-looking supermodels are. She had a long face with pale skin. Dark hair framed her cheeks. Her eyes would not let me look away. At the beginning of her act, she walked out to the middle of the floor that served as the stage and proceeded to dramatically drive a steel nail through her nose, right into her face. I was in awe, sweating with nervousness for her.

There is a certain beauty that is found only in people who are undeniably unique and, often, is recognized only by others who are different themselves. Because of my own act of—it's so hard to say—self-mutilation, I could identify with Nina in a way. But I admired that she was using it as an act of entertainment, of shock and awe. Looking back, perhaps I was seeking shock and awe, too.

"Next, I'll need a volunteer," Nina announced. Before my brain knew what my hand was doing, my arm shot up like a bullet. Nina laughed and said she liked the fact that I had no idea what I was volunteering for. Others chuckled with us as well, and I blushed with excitement that she chose me. Rosie, sitting next to me, smiled from ear to ear, and Rhiannon waved her hands in a *get up there* gesture. I walked nervously to the spotlight, just a couple of feet from this incredible being. Like any practiced performer, Nina asked for my name and thanked me for volunteering, all the while with a nail stuck in her face.

"Your job is to remove the nail," she announced.

I nodded my head. That seemed easy enough. I'd just use my hands to carefully . . .

"Without using your hands." Could I turn any redder? Could I possibly sweat any more? The audience went nuts with nervous laughter, and I imagine they hated the idea of watching but loved it all the same. Every one of us was a freak in our own right—for having our own physical abnormalities, for practicing unnatural activities, or just for loving to take it all in. I loved being among my own in this strange collective. As a fire dancer, I loved "letting my freak flag fly," as they say. I took a step toward Nina with my hands obediently behind my back, leaned forward, pulled my lips back, and gently bit down on the little bit of nail that was still available to grab. I pulled my head back, daintily took the nail out of my mouth with my hands, and gave it back to the star. Nailface Nina had shocked the audience, and me, but she had also entertained us, made us cringe, and made us laugh. My life seemed changed, and I realized that I was most comfortable when I was out of my comfort zone.

After the applause and a bow with Nina, I returned to my seat, and she went on to perform the human pincushion, in which she embedded needles in her cheeks. It was thrilling, too, but, for some reason, the nail trick just blew me away more than anything. The show continued with top-notch entertainment: burlesque strip-teases, knife throwing, belly dancing solos, fire arts, and comedy routines. For the rest of the night after the performances were over, I talked my friends' ears off about Nina and her act. Not that they seemed to mind, but I could tell that they weren't quite sure what my fascination was. One thing that we had in common was that we were all passionate, and so even when we were enthusiastic about different things, we still shared the excitement itself.

Back at our cabin for the night, I noticed that the campground had begun to settle and the sounds of passersby, guitar playing, and drumming slowly fell quiet. Everyone was putting the day to rest and mentally gearing up for the following morning.

Once in my bunk, I had a hard time falling asleep. At least my earplugs blocked out any remaining random noises, but that inevitably left me with only my thoughts about Adrian, after my mind wound down from Nina's human blockhead act. I let myself go into a fantasy of such unrealistic detail that I eventually forced myself to stop thinking about him. It was fun, though, to see little scenes play out in my mind's eye, scenes where he was unbound. I replayed the times that he had given me piercings, and let my mind see what would have happened under different circumstances. Maybe when he was giving me the navel piercing, his hand would have grazed the top of my skirt . . . I shivered just imagining. Then I shook my head to really clear my thoughts. *This is absurd,* I thought. But at least it was harmless.

I turned to my side, trying to get comfortable enough to sleep while not disrupting Morgan, who was already asleep beneath me. Rosie was a few feet away on her top bunk, breathing in a soft, rhythmical way that told me she had already drifted off as well. I knew instinctively that once she went back to school, we would play the "we promise to always be friends" game. It was the game of denial, where we would vow to still hang out and stay in touch, wanting to, meaning to. Our lives, however, were destined to change since we were only in our twenties, and I was sure that our best intentions of staying close were doomed to eventually fail. I finally fell asleep, missing her already.

The bunk bed was relatively comfortable, and the room had a faint cedar smell that went nicely with the drifting smoke of still-smoldering camp-fires outside. I had slept well, surely with help from the earplugs. I woke and stayed in the bed for a while, listening to the birds and sensing the quiet breathing of my friends. I stretched my arms over my head as far as I could. I was so happy to be waking up in this space, just a blink of an eye away from the first class of the day. These thoughts stayed in my mind until I was no longer able to ignore my bladder, and I finally had start moving. I slipped out of my warm sleeping bag and climbed down the bunk as nondisruptively as I could, being careful not to wake Morgan. I remembered from our college days that she wasn't what one would call a morning person.

The cabin's bathroom was cold, including the water that I used to wash my hands. I splashed some on my face, brushed my teeth and my hair, and opened the door to find Morgan.

"Girl," she slurred.

"I tried to be quiet," I apologetically whispered, not wanting to stir the whole cabin.

"I'm up now. Let me get in there and get my business done," she said quietly, humorously emphasizing *business.*

I was relieved to see she was in a decent mood. "Want me to wait for you outside? We can try to find some coffee together."

"Sure," she said with her eyes still half-closed.

The sun was up, although still low enough to be shining its rays through the trees. I sat on the small porch in front of our cabin to eat a banana and go through a small tote bag I packed for my days. It held a notebook and pen, a bottle of water, some energy bars, and my poi set. These things became part of my survival gear for the weekend.

Once Morgan joined me outside, we wandered around the camps, and as we walked, a woman with a loose braid was calling out that a tribal belly dance workshop was starting soon. She was wearing a tribal outfit and had a round stomach and a mellow vibe. Even though it was in the morning, I was sure that she was high. Morgan and I looked at each other and shrugged, then followed the woman to a small open space next to a large oak tree. A slight wind blew the leaves just enough to force resting dewdrops down to the ground in a miniature rain shower. Watching the work of gravity on the drops, I adjusted my focus and saw Audrey walking toward us from the other side of the tree. She walked through the "rain," smiling at no one, just strolling along. I felt lucky to have her as a friend and thought that the scene could be a painting that I was viewing, because everything about it was that lovely. And, about to embark on taking an impromptu class in the middle of a campground in the wet grass, I loved everything about that moment.

When Audrey got closer, I nodded my head toward the teacher and, skipping any natural hellos, said, "She's teaching a class now."

"Heck, yeah. Morning belly dance. Let's do it," she said.

There were perhaps twenty festival-goers who had gathered next to the tree with the teacher, including at least one guy, and one woman who was topless. I found this to be disconcerting at first, and without a specific reason, I felt a little backward for even noting it. I needed to get over the fact that I was taking a belly dance class next to a nearly naked person. Was I comfortable? No. Did I mind? Not really. I thought, *Morgan and Audrey don't seem to think anything of it, either, and neither does the guy in the class, so why should I?* I did wonder, though, how I would feel if Adrian were here. I knew that even though I had no right, I would probably feel a twinge of jealousy if I noticed him noticing the other dancer. But Adrian was with Rhiannon, and I knew I shouldn't even be thinking like this, so I succumbed to enjoying the festival on my own and with Audrey and Morgan.

After the class, which offered just enough movement to loosen our muscles a bit, everyone, including Morgan, quietly and slowly scattered around the campground again. I picked up my shoes from the grass and had them in one hand as I stood up to find Audrey next to me.

"I really like the way you dance," she said, tilting her head to one side.

I blushed. This was my teacher; she set the bar. "Thank you," I said quietly.

"Maybe we can dance together more. I think we'd be good together." She gave me her subtle smile and then said, "I'm going to walk around a bit and see what I can get into. See you later."

I lifted my hand in a wave and then realized I was waving my shoes at her. But she had already turned to drift around the festival, leaving me free to do the same.

"You going to drink tonight? I brought some spirits for later," Rhiannon said. We had run into each other in between workshops that afternoon and had stepped just into the trees, off the main path. We were sharing a small bowl of weed that she offered me.

"I kind of doubt it. I so don't want to be here with a hangover," I said, knowing that it wouldn't take much alcohol to ruin my next morning.

"You're such a lightweight, Summer."

"I know. I'm a cheap date." I laughed.

"I guess I am, too, when it comes down to it. But Adrian doesn't seem to mind."

I said nothing this time. That's the thing about being a little high—you can sober up if you need to. And I felt the need to.

"I love him," she continued. "But sometimes I wonder how much, or if, he loves me."

"If?" I asked.

"Well, not *if*, I guess. I mean, I know he does. Somehow. Sorry if I'm getting all sentimental. We have some issues, I guess you'd say. It's hard to be one hundred percent at peace in a relationship when you're with someone who doesn't believe that you can belong to anyone. That everyone is free. Ya know?"

"I guess I don't know," I admitted. "I've never been in a serious relationship with anyone."

I handed the bowl back to her and our hands touched. We stood looking at each other. I wished that I could read her better.

"You'll find love, Summer. I love you, dear. Everyone does. You're a good friend."

"Thanks, Rhiannon," I said with hidden guilt. I loved her, too, but I still wanted to—let's face it—do naughty things to her boyfriend.

With Rhiannon and Adrian still on my mind, Rosie and I went to the Cincinnati Burns networking lunch together. There, we witnessed a professional sideshow that came in from California for the weekend. While we ate scrambled eggs and drank orange juice, the sideshow act performed glass walking, sword swallowing, and more. The event was great, but it was even better when I saw that Nina was there in the audience.

"You should go over there and tell her how much you loved her act," Rosie said to me.

"Do you think so? She'll think I'm weird," I replied.

"You *are* weird," she said with a wink. "No, really. Think about how much it means to you when someone tells you the same thing." Indeed, there were few Noir Arts shows where we didn't have fans approaching us after our sets. Women would ask if we taught dance classes anywhere or someone would ask for a business card so they could book us.

I knew she was right. I walked over and said hello, and Nina remembered me as her volunteer from the night before. "I can't even express how much I loved your act," I told her. "I've never seen or heard of anything like it, and it just blew me away."

"Aw, thanks," she said humbly. We talked for a couple of minutes about where we were from and other pleasantries. She surprised me when, just before she walked back to her table, she said, "You know, if you're interested in learning human blockhead, I'll be happy to help walk you through it. You can call me, or we can talk online. Just let me know." She paused as I nodded my head and then added, "I think it's important to share this knowledge with others, or it could become a dying art, even though some performers don't want others to know how it's done." While, as a fire dancer, I had always been happy to share my knowledge, I had always done so when getting paid to teach a workshop or class. I spent quite a bit of my own money learning these arts, and I saw teaching as a way to put the money back in my pocket or reinvest it in more lessons, study, and research. I was honored that Nina would so willingly offer to share with me this skill, and without compensation.

"Thank you so much," I told her graciously just before she walked away. I honestly had not been thinking about learning the trick myself, but Nina had planted yet another seed.

After our lunch I made my way to a yoga class that took place in the middle of a field. It was just as delightful as I could've expected, and, feeling limber, I went to the next workshop I was interested in: "Hooping for Burlesque." The instructor, a hooper simply named Halo, began the class with some advice as about fifteen students began to stretch and practice basic moves with our hoops. "Leave your shoes and your inhibitions at the door. This class isn't just about how to hoop. It's about how to tap into your sensuality and express it through your hooping. Don't worry about what you look like. Don't worry about who else is in the class or where your level is compared to her. Don't worry about who might see you as they walk by. Don't worry about what you're doing later today. Keep hooping. Don't worry about your hair, or your outfit, or your car. You are not the things you own. They do not make you. You are not your job. You are a dancer. You are a mover, an artist, an express-yourself-any-way-you-can unique person. Keep hooping."

And we did. The first few minutes, the lecture, if you will, opened my eyes to a new way of seeing others, and even myself somehow. Even though I felt free before, after Halo's mantra, I felt even more so. Although I had always played around with a hoop here and there at the studio and at practices, I felt like I was connecting with it for the first time. I was light, and my spirit was lifted. Like when I first started my dreadlocks, I felt again that my insides matched my outsides.

Those first ten minutes, although brief, were powerful enough to allow the students, including me, to feel attractive in a new way. This alone is an absolute necessity for any performer who takes the stage, even if she fakes it during her set. I discovered that when I felt beautiful, I looked the part as well. It was a lesson that this class reinforced, and that I could sense in the ways men treated me. When I was in my stage character—a confident, bold fire eater whose job was to captivate, thrill, and push people out of their comfort zones—men would flirt with me relentlessly. But when I was in my day-to-day street clothes, without makeup or excessive jewelry, I was often overlooked, treated as part of the background. And I was okay with that. The attention I received while "on" was enough to carry over into my mainstream life, where people looked at me and saw nothing special. My dancing had become a secret that I withheld from others until I felt they were somehow worthy of a piece of my heart; that's how much I loved dancing with fire.

After warming up with the hoops and setting the atmosphere, Halo began to teach us her techniques for burlesque dancing for hoopers. I had fun with the remainder of the class, which focused on specific hoop tricks and dance movements that were sexier than the hooping style that most of the students or I had already practiced. One lesson was on how to recover gracefully and seductively when we dropped a hoop, which I had seen happen to every hooper at some point, by bending the knees to pick it up but then keeping the hands on the hoop, on the ground, while straightening the legs first, then raising with a flat back. The result was that it looked like I meant to drop it, just so that I could show my long legs, instead of the reality that gravity worked its force against the hoop.

Class ended with hugs and applause for Halo's amazing teaching, and we slowly scattered to our next workshops. Leaving, I passed a small hill and saw a yellow motorcycle parked next to a tent. A string was attached between two trees, serving as a sort of entrance to the space, and on the string was a sign that announced, THE HOOKAH IS OUT. I was intrigued.

"Come on up," said a friendly, masculine voice. I walked the ten or so steps up the hill, bending slightly to go under the sign, and found a few people sitting on the ground sharing a hookah. I saw Audrey through the smoke and sat down on the ground next to her.

"Are you having a good time?" I asked.

"Couldn't be better. How about you? What do you think so far?"

I paused, looked around, and said, "I think I can't wait to light up my fire poi tonight." I was surrounded by strangers that I knew were friends. The music, the smoke, the dancing—it was yet another surreal experience that I knew I would have missed out on if my life path had not crossed with Rhiannon's at Permanent Productions. It also led me to Audrey, this kind, reserved dancer. I felt lucky.

Throughout the festival I would continue to randomly pass Rosie, Morgan, Rhiannon, and Adrian. The girls had planned their own schedules that included a variety of classes in dancing with fire fans, palm torches, and poi.

It was around seven o'clock that evening when I stopped at a food booth as I made my way back to the cabin, where I found Adrian starting a campfire for the night. "I just got a quesadilla, and it's stuffed. I don't think I can eat it all. You want some?" I asked him.

"Nah, thanks. I actually just ate." The campground was alive with laughter and music in the background, but we sat in silence for a moment with the crackling fire. "Did you see that they have fire hoops for sale?" he asked me.

"Ah, no! I've been busy with classes all day, and trying to take notes in between so that I don't forget anything." I looked around us, lost in my own headspace. "I can't imagine being anywhere else but here, in this space, in these moments. Surrounded by other dancers and jugglers and hoopers, and having fire connect us all. It's like family, and yet I've never met these people. We have to come back next year." I was still euphoric from Halo's class earlier in the weekend.

"You should get one of the fire hoops, ya know. I saw you in that class earlier, and you were amazing," he told me without breaking eye contact. "I'd love to watch you do the same thing with fire."

My face flushed and I felt flattered by the way he looked at me. I smiled but said nothing, and was only slightly embarrassed that he had witnessed the burlesque hooping. I had been dreaming about fire hooping, but it seemed so much more dangerous than spinning fire poi, which were never terribly close to my body unless I intentionally put them there. For example, I like to do this playful and unexpected move that's called a "butt bounce." I spread my feet apart and swing the fire poi under my legs, and let them hit my butt, so that they bounce back and swing forward again. With a fire hoop, I feared the unpredictable nature of where the wicks would be on the hoop as it wrapped around my waist, or even around my neck. But something about the way that Adrian was looking at me made me want to dance with a fire hoop, and I knew that it would happen, perhaps even that night.

Part of my consciousness told me that this conversation was somehow wrong, that it might not have happened if Rhiannon was with us. There was an invisible exchange happening between Adrian and I, not unlike when he gave me my piercings and we connected. I could hear a voice in the back of my mind wishing that he was unattached, but I refused to even acknowledge it. I recognized it as a wedge that could be driven between Rhiannon and me, as well as between our tribe. No amount of flirting or even a crush was worth that. Although I had to admit, I appreciated the masculine attention from someone who knew me, as opposed to a random audience member.

But I needed little prodding about getting the fire hoop, and tried to be casual when I said, "We could use a fire hoop in Noir, couldn't we?

The vendors probably close soon, and the Main Play will be pulsing before too long for the open jam. Tell you what. I'll be back. See you in a bit." I grabbed my wallet and walked away, leaving him by the campfire until our paths would cross again that night.

I saw Morgan walking toward the cabin as I left. "Hey, you got a light real quick? Where are you off to? You look like you're up to something," she teasingly said as we neared each other on the path.

"Maybe it's a surprise," I said with a raised eyebrow, pulling out a lighter and holding it up to the cigarette in her mouth.

"I can't even imagine," she said.

I simply winked as a reply and waved casually, heading to the vendors.

Everyone gathered at the barn-turned-theater to watch more professional soloists and groups from around the country perform on this, the second night of Cincinnati Burns. I was so inspired by them that I felt like creative energy was pouring out of my own body, rising to the stars above. I wanted to hug everyone. I was filled with love for what the dancers had created and shared, and what I was now inspired to create and share myself. Plus, I was a world away from the realities of my day-to-day life.

While most of the audience had stayed at the barn after the performance, I retreated to a cabin where the musicians of Hypnosis were jamming together. I had only seen them sporadically throughout the festival and wanted to spend some time listening to their music. The cabin was lit with just enough candles to allow everyone to see each other, and it held about twenty people, who came and went as they mingled between there and the barn. It reminded me of Dance Mecca, in that pillows lined the walls along the floor, where people sat comfortably listening, watching, being. I noticed that while most of my own tribe mates were elsewhere, Adrian was inside the cabin, sitting with some new friends that he had made.

The music began falling into an improvised song. Being a weekend event for dancers, it was no surprise that the empty space in the middle of the cabin shortly contained the moving body of one of the girls who had been sitting on a pillow. She danced, the musicians played, and it was picture-perfect.

The music never stopped, and dancers quietly took turns on the floor, creating what seemed to be a single dance. Throughout the evening, the music slowly transformed from one melody and tempo to another. As it did, the single dancer sat down and another one would take her place. This went on for about an hour, until the space was free, and I felt comfortable enough to join in. I shyly stood and took the floor. I didn't belly dance, didn't try to re-create any of the combinations that I had learned that day, attempt a new shimmy, or show off any of the signature moves that I always found myself doing. I just moved my head, arms, legs, fingers, feet, eyes . . . to the music. Every melody that the musicians gave me, I returned with a movement that I felt complemented it. I—now, more than ever—was in my element. I knew that the people within that small space were in the same headspace as I was, filled with joie de vivre.

When the dance felt complete, I carefully stepped between the people sitting next to the door to go out for a moment and breathe. Just before I made it to the exit, another girl stopped me. I recognized her as the teacher from the "Advanced Techniques for the Stage" workshop earlier in the weekend. Before I had a chance to tell her how much I had enjoyed her class, she pointed to me. "That," she paused, "was the most incredible thing that I've seen tonight." And then she walked away. I was left feeling humble and filled with gratitude. I had seen so much during the actual show earlier in the weekend, and I was happy to have contributed to an evening of improvisational and organic movement, whether it was for the two hundred people at the main stage, or the twenty in the cabin.

I had brought my zills, which are also known as finger cymbals, and, resting from the dance but not ready to be still, was eager to chime in to the song. I had taken a zill workshop that day for the first time. While the musicians tuned their instruments and fooled around with different melodies, I noticed a slim young man who was watching me place the zills onto my middle fingers and thumbs, as I was shown to do. He had a goatee and long red hair that was pulled back into a loose ponytail. He was wearing cargo shorts, sandals, and a Sublime T-shirt. A multicolored, beaded necklace hung from his neck. He played a very simple rhythm on his drum and then nodded to me, indicating that I should repeat it with my zills. We began playing a flirty game of call and response, where he continued to play a simple but changing rhythm on his drum, and I repeated the rhythm with my zills. To do this, we had to pay close attention to each other; I had to block out everything else around me so that I could concentrate on his beats. I had never felt particularly percussive but enjoyed our game of nonverbal communication. After several minutes of him leading, I began to call with my own rhythm, and he responded to me. Everyone else in the cabin seemed to disappear—I was that focused. When he and I unpredictably created the same rhythm at the same moment, I completely stopped and fell backward to the floor in a fake faint of ecstasy at the perfect timing and unexpected precision.

"She's having a zillgasm!" Adrian was apparently enjoying our call-and-response game himself. I blushed because I realized that it was obvious how much fun I was having. Between the music, the dance, the lake, and the stars, I was filled with bliss.

With the serendipitous magic broken, our laughter filled the space in the cabin. It was time to switch gears.

"You just have to keep practicing. Find a rhythm and do it over and over, ten thousand times," the drummer said softly to me. I noticed how green his eyes were. "Like polishing a stone."

My lips parted with a subtle gasp as I thought of the smooth rose quartz that Rhiannon had given me. I reached into my pocket, pulled it out, and held my hand to him with my palm down, hiding the token. I felt a Mona Lisa smile form as he accepted my "polished stone" without speaking. His eyes lit up.

I put my zills away and tried to slow my heartbeat to a normal level as my awareness of the music and people returned.

I was nearly delirious from the festival. Wanting to go to bed at a decent time to sort of mentally and physically recover from everything I had been experiencing, I was on my way back to the cabin when I saw Audrey standing by the lake.

"Hey, you," I called to her. She turned and waved as I made my way over.

"I was just looking at the paddleboats over there. They look lonely."

I gazed across the water and saw that, indeed, they were calling to us. Six boats that had faded and chipped paint lined the dock on the other side of the lake under a spotlight.

"Let's do something about that, shall we?" I asked. She smiled and nodded, and we made our way across a footbridge and over to the small dock, making small talk about our day. When we reached the boats, we put on lifejackets that hinted of mildew and climbed into an orange paddleboat that had a small puddle of water in the bottom of it. It was the first time that we had a chance to be alone, so I took the opportunity to pick her brain.

"So, what's it like to be in Hypnosis?" I asked as we began pushing the foot pedals.

"It's good. It's awesome. It can be hard. What about Noir?"

"Same," I said as I tilted my head. I didn't want to say anything negative, and I could tell she felt the same way.

"We're being pretty diplomatic, aren't we?" she asked.

"I think we have to be," I said, "since we're in the same boat."

Audrey laughed with me. "We have umpteen dancers and musicians," she said, "and we're all incredibly creative and passionate. Sometimes it's a little hard to keep everyone focused, and sometimes we drive each other a little crazy, but we're family. It's never such an ordeal that I would consider leaving or anything like that."

"Right, right," I replied. "Our tribe is relatively new compared to yours, but it's similar. I try to keep everyone happy as much as possible. Sometimes there's a tiff over something minor, like what color our costuming will be for a gig, or what song to use for a fire-eating number, but it's never been anything that we couldn't work out. There's equal say in pretty much everything."

"Don't try too hard, Summer. You might be able to keep everyone happy for a minute, but don't expect it to last forever. I tried that myself, and I can tell you it's not worth the strife."

"But everybody seems happy in your group."

"We put on our show. I mean, it's not bad or anything like that, but when you're working with a group like you and I have, you just have to expect drama. Everyone's creative. Everyone's emotionally invested. Tensions can run high. I just want you to be prepared, in case shit ever hits the fan. Which I hope doesn't happen," she added.

"Can I ask what's the worst thing that's ever happened? I mean, you sound like you have experience."

"You can ask," she said, turning to look at me for a moment, then looking toward the beach.

"You can trust me," I told her.

"I know," she said. "For the most part, everything's just grand. Really, like unbelievably smooth. We love each other, like brothers and sisters, and some like lovers. But trust is a huge part of being in a tribe like this. It's a given." I could tell she was having a hard time going on. "One night, we had a gig where we were dancing as part of a Labor Day festival on the river. It was one of those gigs where tips were expected to be the biggest draw for us. The guaranteed pay was minimal by the time we split it up between all of us. We had two sets that were only, like, fifteen minutes each; just enough time, you know, to gather a big crowd, entertain them, and then pass the hat.

"One of our musicians at the time, Gerald, had put down his instrument, taken off his hat, and gone out into the crowd with the dancers to accept tips. The rest of the band continued playing a song to keep the crowd there long enough to get paid, and then the song ended. Gerald said he'd count everything, so we gave him the money we collected, which seemed like a ton in singles, some tens, even a couple of twenties. Then we started packing up the gear and changing into our street clothes. I mean, you know how uncomfortable our outfits can be."

I nodded in agreement with her. I've gotten scratched from the coins on my belt and bra, and *cozy* is not a word I would use to describe belly dance garments. They're more like *tolerable*.

"I'll be damned if I didn't walk around the corner backstage and see Gerald take a wad of the cash and shove it into his pocket. He knew I caught him, but he denied it. We ended up in a yelling match, and the stage manager had to break it up, telling us that we were interrupting the next act. I was embarrassed by that, and pissed at Gerald. We had a big meeting about it with everyone in the tribe, and it was agreed that it would be best if he left. I haven't seen him since, and we don't mention his name."

"But everyone knew you were telling the truth . . . you wouldn't have a reason to lie about something like that."

"Exactly. He was a great part of the tribe—until he fucked it up. But it caused a rift for a while, because the guys wanted to take his side, and the girls took my side. Thank God the dust has settled. I don't want you to get burned like that, that's all. I've been there, being in a tight group, 'just for fun.' Heck, I am there. It's wonderful, until it's not."

We paddled on in silence for a few moments, creating small waves behind us across the lake.

Audrey turned to me. "Want to play truth or dare?"

"Okay," I said as my eyes flashed with excitement. "Hmm. I'll go first. Truth: Are there any *issues* in your tribe?" I said it sarcastically, half joking but half serious. I felt pretty lucky that those of us in Noir got along so well. I wondered if it was common in other belly dance groups and I still wanted to know more about Hypnosis.

"What's the dare?"

"I guess I should've been prepared for that. Um, I dare you to . . . scream out loud, 'I love myself!' But you have to yell it loud enough that someone on the shore can hear you."

She laughed and, to my surprise, took a deep breath and hollered, "I love myself!"

We giggled quietly as we waited for a response from the shore. When we heard a male voice carry to us from the small beach, over the water, saying, "Good for you!" we both burst into laughter. But it left me wondering why she didn't answer my question, and I felt guilty for asking.

It was like she read my mind when she said, "And to answer your question, I wouldn't say that there are any *issues*, per se. It's a family, and we have ups and downs. We pretty much always come together for the art, though. It's the thread, the single thing that's important enough for us to put everything else aside. Relax, Summer. I'm sure Noir Arts is going to do just fine.

"Okay, now it's my turn," she continued. "The dare is to . . . " and she started giggling before she could finish.

"Oh God."

"Suck your own toe."

"That's fucked up, Audrey."

"You have to do it."

"Maybe not. What's the truth?"

She lost her smile and looked at me with a level of concern that reminded me how serious this game can sometimes get. "I feel like I already know you. Like, really know you. But I want to know you . . . on a deeper level. You seem so happy all the time, but you must be human. So my question is, what's your lowest low?"

I stopped paddling, considering if I wanted to confide in her, if I trusted her enough to share my darkest secret. I was so embarrassed by the suicide attempt. No one else knew, except my family, whom I knew loved me unconditionally. But I wanted to give Audrey what she wanted. I wanted us to be closer, and there's an undeniable magic that takes place when the sun is absent. It made me feel safe, comfortable, as we floated along.

As relaxed as I felt, however, part of me wanted to keep our conversation from getting macabre from my embarrassing past, so I said, "You must really want to see me—oh my God, I can't even say it—suck my toe." Even as I said it, I knew I was going to share with her my suicide attempt.

"Your choice." She shrugged.

"Okay." *Like a bandage,* I thought. "My lowest low was when I took a razor and tried to slit my wrists." After I said it, I waited for her reaction before going on. When she remained silent, I continued matter-of-factly. "I put up with a lot of bullshit from other kids when I was in high school. They called me names in the hallways, on the bus, even on the street when I would walk home after school. I felt worthless. I felt grotesque. I hated what I looked like, mostly because they drilled it in daily that I looked so ugly. I had acne on my face, my back, my fucking shoulders even. They called me *craterface.* They made fun of the spider veins in my legs when I actually thought I could get away with wearing a skirt one day. I didn't have boyfriends." An owl hooted in the distance, and I paused for a moment.

"I just couldn't take it anymore one day. I guess there are a lot of ways that you can do it, but I wasn't thinking about anything other than the pain I was in. I took a razor from the bathroom."

"Was there a lot of blood?" Audrey asked somberly.

"Enough to freak out my parents. My dad came into my room shortly after I started, and he saw what I did. I didn't even try to hide it from him. Honestly, I was glad he found me. It wasn't that I wanted to die. I really just wanted the bullying to stop.

"So that's it," I said with a sigh. "That's my lowest low." When I began paddling the boat again, she did the same.

"Since then, you haven't . . ."

"No, no way. Once I got out of high school, I was fine. It was so toxic. Hard to believe anyone survives it."

"I love myself!" Someone from the shore shouted out, and we laughed. Ready to move on to a different topic, I was relieved to have something break the heavy weight of my confession.

"Ironic, isn't it?" I said.

"Yeah, it is," she answered. "I'm glad you're okay now, Summer."

"Thanks. Me, too. If things had gone differently, I wouldn't have ever found tribal belly dance, fire arts, or cool people like you." Then suddenly, I had an idea. "You know what would be cool?" I asked, nervous and excited.

"So many things. But tell me what you're thinking," she replied.

"If Hypnosis and Noir combined forces," I said, not thinking about the logistics, the pros, or the cons.

Audrey slowly nodded her head, her gears turning with the idea. "That could be interesting," she said slowly, once again displaying her diplomacy as she bit her lip.

"I mean, it's something to think about, anyway," I added. "We'd have to convince everyone in both groups."

"And then we'd be splitting the small pay that we get from having that many more people, and trying to arrange practices and book gigs around that many more schedules . . ."

"Hmm. Yup. Well, it was fun to think about for a minute," I said, coming back to reality.

"That doesn't mean that we can't dance together sometimes. We're all still part of the same community, after all."

I nodded in agreement as we began to paddle our way back to the dock. I looked at her and said, "I think we should."

The third day had come and gone, and when the sun fell beyond the cloudy horizon, I got out my fire gear. There was a drummer playing a beat nearby. I was driven by music, and although I didn't mind dancing with my fire poi to silence, a rhythm always moved me more. It somehow guided me to move more intuitively. The melody or beat carried my body for me. Before I dipped my fuel-soaked wicks into the bonfire that dozens of people were gathered around, I followed the sound of the drum.

I made eye contact with the drummer, who nodded and smiled at me. I recognized him immediately as my "zillgasm" partner and felt warm with his familiar presence. I lit the poi and found an open area nearby where I could both hear the drum and share my art. The drummer was only wearing patchwork shorts and the same beaded necklace from the last time I had seen him. Either from the heat of the bonfire or the physical beating of the drum, his hair was sticking to his shoulders with sweat. I am not going to lie—it was sexy, and I shyly took it all in. He watched me as I fire danced, and I kind of liked that. It made me feel sexy. Others sat around the circle, some playing their own drums, some casually watching me spin. Slowly the fire on the poi became smaller and smaller, until the only sound was the music once again, and my heavy breathing. As the fire on my poi eventually died down to two disappearing blue flames, I handed them to a nearby fire safety, who extinguished the remaining fire and gave the poi back to me, slightly smoking and still hot.

"Kyle," the drummer said as he stood up to give me a friendly, nice-to-meet-you hug.

"Summer."

He nodded and kept my eye contact, and I felt as though he was reading me, in a good way. We were connected before we had a chance to connect. I learned over time that this was a natural result of dancing with fire while someone played music. The music was my fire. I needed it, and it gave me life. Kyle was one of many people who provided me with the music, which made me thrive. I think he recognized that when we met. Our mutual gazes said everything that would need to be said.

Later in the evening, I stopped by Audrey's cabin to see if she was around and say hello. I found her sitting next to a small campfire that she had built.

"I just met someone interesting," I said to her as she looked up at me with a smile.

"Oh yeah?" She asked. "Tell me about him. Or her. Whatever, just keep me company. The rest of my group is still out playing. I just needed a little downtime."

I sat down on the ground across from her and told her about Kyle, the zillgasm, and the drumming. I added, "This place is magical, you know? I feel so different."

"It has that effect on people. I think it's because so many of us here share the same interests. We're all open-minded, free spirits who just want to express it. I'm glad you met Kyle. I've known him for a while through the belly dance community. He plays the drum in a two-man band, mostly at coffee shops. Really cool guy."

"He seemed cool. We didn't talk much at all, but I felt so comfortable with him, like we've been friends for a long time."

"I know what you mean. He's super into yoga and also runs an organic farm for a living. He plays music on the side, teaching and stuff. But he's a hell of a drummer, and his partner, Edward, is amazing, too. He plays the flute and the guitar. Not at the same time, of course."

"His 'partner?'" I asked, surprised.

"His *musical* partner."

"Of course," I smiled. "I'd like to hear them play sometime. I wonder, do you think they'd perform with Noir? It would be cool if we had some musicians to work with, instead of using recorded music all the time."

"I'm sure all you'd have to do is ask. What could it hurt?"

"Okay. I'll e-mail our group later and see what they think. I've been working on booking us at a new restaurant, and this would be perfect. Is Edward any good? Like, are they good enough to play music while we dance?"

"Yeah, they've been playing music together for a couple of years now, so they'd probably be the perfect fit."

I nodded my head and gazed into the campfire, my gears turning with this new possibility. "I felt like we bonded tonight, even though we didn't really talk."

"That's the best way to get to know a person, I think," Audrey said, looking into the fire. "Words can just get in the way, but you can get to know a person as much as you need to between dance and music. They transcend conversations."

"Are you guys ready to light some shit on *FIRE?*" The DJ had stepped up onto his stage, put on a headset, and begun mixing underground house music for the hundreds of fire dancers who had gathered at the Main Play. Night had fallen, and the stars were beginning to show themselves, sprinkling their magic onto the field. Onlookers had formed a circle around the fire floor, which was the marked-off space that fire performers were allowed to use. Once our tools were lit, we had to stay within the fire floor, for safety. A line of twenty or so dancers was off to the side, where they waited patiently to dip their tools at the fuel dump, spin off the excess, and then enter the designated space.

All the love and positive energy from my teachers, fellow students, and many audience members was rising into the air. I felt surrounded by friends, and so I was comfortable despite the fact that Rosie, Morgan, Rhiannon, and Adrian were nowhere to be found. I slowly walked around, watching everyone else and smiling, joyful to be a part of this experience. In addition to my notebook, water, and poi, I had a new accessory resting on my shoulder: a fire hoop.

It was white, and the wicks were clean and soft compared to the black and sooty wicks of my torches and poi. I knew when I had approached the vendor who was selling fire hoops that I was going to buy one, but I still hesitated as I browsed the small selection. The hoops were similar, except some had seven wicks and some had as few as three wicks. The sizes also varied slightly, so I was glad when the seller allowed me to play around with them to see which "fit" me best. I asked a few questions, not so much because I had questions but more so because I was stalling. I was about to hand over $140 and confront my fear of the unknown: fire hoop dancing. I even browsed some of the other props that the vendor was selling but never took my eye off this one hoop that seemed to be calling to me. I wanted to make sure that no one else was going to buy it and walk off before I committed to it. It had five wicks and was a larger size. It felt good when I hooped with it, although I unconsciously held my breath every time I saw a wick go near my waist, which was basically with each rotation of the hoop. I needed to relax.

Once at the Main Play, I wanted to get to know this hoop, this new friend, better before I introduced it to flames, and so I found a free spot of grass, set down my things, and looked it over, spinning it around my hand to get a feel for it.

Surrounded by the pumping music, the dark-blue sky, and other fire dancers, I lifted the hoop above my head, brought it down to my waist, and gave it a gentle push. It felt natural, not very different from other hoops I had played with. As I paused for a moment to consider the hoop, again, just feeling like I was getting to know it and trying to get over the apprehension I felt about lighting it on fire and dancing with it, Adrian walked up.

"Have you seen anybody else?" he asked.

"No, I've been keeping my eyes open for them. I'd like to wait to light this up until they're here because I know they won't want to miss it."

"Right on," he replied as he, too, surveyed the scene. By then, the folks who had been waiting in line to dip their tools in fuel had entered the fire floor and were all dancing with their props. Poi spinners, staff spinners, fire eaters on stilts, and hula-hoopers were spread out, moving to the hypnotic music for their own love of fire dancing and to the amazement of the onlookers at the circle's edge. As the fire on each tool went out, the dancers left the floor and new ones took their places. It was an endless stream of fire, and the river of individual flames never died. An hour or so went by as Adrian and I hung out at the Main Play. Every once in a while we would take a turn to walk around the field and look for Rosie, Morgan, and Rhiannon, but they, too, were surely somewhere safe, having a fantastic time.

"You should just light it up," Adrian told me. "I'm dying to see what you can do with it."

"I don't know . . . the line's so long over there, and I'd hate for the girls to miss my first burn with it."

"How about if I wait in line with you? Then it won't go so slow. If you think about it, you owe it to all the other dancers, ya know? Every person here is contributing to this night. I'm here to support my friends and have a good time, but you have a talent, and you should share that. Don't hold back; don't keep it to yourself."

I looked at him and knew that he was right. This was a philosophy that had driven me so far, and I knew that I had something special to share with an audience, with my friends, with the world. I wanted to be able to look back at this weekend with no regrets. The following day we would all return home, to our jobs, our dishes, our bills. It was time to do what I loved, and there was no better place to do it.

"You're totally right. I can always light it up again when we find them, too. We have all night, after all." With a deep breath, I gathered my things and we walked to the fuel line. Once we were there, it seemed to take forever, despite the small talk we shared together and with the people in line with us. But finally it was my turn. The table with paint cans of fuel was in front of me. As I dipped each wick in the fuel, I counted them to make sure I definitely dipped each wick exactly once. I felt the actual countdown to lighting it on fire. As I dipped the last wick, I said to Adrian, "This is actually happening now."

"Virgin burn!" Adrian exclaimed, and the others nearby clapped and hollered the same. They cheered me on as I spun off the excess fuel from the hoop and then walked back toward the fire floor, ready to dance.

"Do you have any advice for using this?" I naively asked a nearby girl who was holding her own fire hoop. "I've been fire dancing for a while, but I've never used a fire hoop."

"Yeah. Have fun!" The girl smiled. And that was all the formal instruction I received.

Once I was beyond the gathered onlookers around the edge of the circle, I saw Halo with her fire hoop nearby. Between the music and the fire, body language was much more effective than trying to speak, so I cautiously got closer to her and made eye contact, showing Halo the unlit hoop and raising an eyebrow as if to say, "Can I get a light?" Halo smiled after she recognized me from her workshop and then she noticed the virgin wicks. A sentimental look came to her face, and I could sense that she remembered the first time she lit her own fire hoop. Halo nodded her head and touched one of her well-used, lighted wicks to each of my new fuel-soaked wicks as I slightly turned the hoop, one, two, three, four, five times.

Halo mouthed the words "have fun" and then walked a safe distance away so that both of us could dance among the rest of the fire spinners.

Adrian was the catalyst for this experience, and I hoped that I would live up to his expectations, as well as my own. The flames were warm and so I continued to move the hoop around in the air just to try to control the fire. When I paused to look for Adrian in the crowd, I saw that the flames took on a life of their own, flicking at my wrist. I had to trust that he was around, and so I turned my attention fully on the fire hoop. I was surrounded by others, but I was alone.

Undaunted, I finally lowered the hoop around my waist. Since I was used to working with fire creatively, I was comfortable with the flames, but I still felt like I had just met a new person who was destined to become an intimate friend. I wanted to get to know the hoop to better understand my relationship to it, especially how to anticipate the flames as they found their way in unending circles that flicked at my hair and shoulders. I became unaware of anything else going on around me and simply felt as if I were a butterfly among fireflies, under the stars. The hoop felt right, and I allowed the mantras from Halo's class to guide me to not worry, not worry, not worry. Let go. Dance. Live. Love. By the time I caught my breath from the sensation of working with this mysterious hoop, the flames had died down and all that was left were five small blue ghosts that the wind gently blew out: one, two, three, four, five.

I held the hoop in one hand as I walked back toward the edge of the circle, looking for Adrian again.

"That was really sexy." I heard a voice over my shoulder. I turned to see who it came from. It was him.

"Oh, thanks. It felt good," I told him, still sort of buzzing from the experience. I looked into his eyes, and the magic of the festival seemed to have cast a spell on me. Had his eyes always been so blue? He took a step closer to me and put his hand on my waist, pulling me toward him. My lips, ready to kiss him, involuntarily parted, and then I heard Rosie's, Morgan's, and Rhiannon's voices. Disappointed by the interruption, I pulled away from him and then mentally chastised myself. *That was close,* I thought. The possibility of tasting his lips was driving me mad, and yet I knew it was wrong to want him. I had to snap out of it and be present.

"You got a fire hoop! Oh my God, Summer, you were beautiful. That was amazing!" They chorused. It took me a second to realize they were talking about the fire hooping.

"You got to see it? I'm so glad. I waited forever, looking for you guys, but I finally just had to go and light up. I'm so happy you were here for it," I told them sincerely, blushing at their praises.

"Hellz yeah, girl. I'm glad, too." Morgan smiled. All of them hugged me tight, although Rhiannon had a brief look in her eye that told me she may have seen more than just my hooping. When we separated, I looked up to the sky again. It was incredibly dark, and the stars filled it from horizon to horizon. The five of us found an open spot of grass along the edge of the fire floor and sat on a blanket so that we could take in the beauty of all the other fire dancers. Without shirts, in outrageous costumes, and some completely naked, the fire artists shared their own flavor and danced for their friends and for themselves. There was so much love in one field. With no one feeling competitive, everyone there was able to be free.

"I think there's just one thing that can make this even better," said Rosie as she pulled a joint out of her pocket. "Someone gave this to me earlier after he saw me take a burlesque class. He just handed it to me, and said, 'Damn.'" We had a good laugh at this, and our group passed the gift around until the last breath of warm smoke was exhaled. Then we sat quietly and listened to the DJ's music and watched the flames dance endlessly, until the sky began to subtly change from black to a blue-and-orange shade of dawn that I rarely experienced.

I looked up into the fading stars and gave thanks for the life path that had brought me to this place, this moment. It was the perfect way to end the weekend. My body and mind were tired, full, satisfied, and spent. I slept well. I breathed in my surroundings, knowing that before long we would be back at home and working on the next gig.

Chapter 16

CHEZ ES SAADA AND
THE WARDROBE MALFUNCTION

Free food, free drinks, plus tips. Every other Saturday night at Chez Es Saada, on the east side, and—drumroll, please—I have two musicians to play music for us. Kyle—you may have met him at Cincinnati Burns—plays hand drums, and Edward plays a variety of flutes and wind instruments, plus the guitar. Kyle seems to be cool as hell, and they both come with a good recommendation from Audrey.

I posted this in our online group as soon as I was back home and on the grid again. I got quick responses:

Rosie: Awesome! In.
Morgan: On it like Blue Bonnet.
Rhiannon: I'm down with this.
Phoenix: Wish I could, but they won't let me blow fire inside.

While I knew that Phoenix would not be able to perform with us for this gig, chances were good that if things worked out well with Kyle and Edward, they would be playing music for our fire gigs in addition to the belly dancing ones.

So, for free food, drinks, and tips, we began dancing every other Saturday night at a new little Moroccan restaurant called Chez Es Saada, which was owned by an endearing older couple who made sure that we ate well. They matched each other physically, like they had spent so much time living and working together that they began to take on each other's characteristics. They were both short and slightly round, and had very short, dark hair. The woman even had a few sprouts of hair on her chin that I so badly wanted to just pluck off her face. On a good night in their restaurant, we would make about a hundred dollars after shimmying around the diners. But the food—the food is what we honestly performed for. It was the first time that I had had couscous, or tasted saffron. The flavors were as mysterious to me as I hoped to be to those who watched me perform tribal belly dance. The sheer fun of the evenings was the other reason that we worked at Chez Es Saada so enthusiastically. The pay was a bonus.

Kyle seemed to call the musical shots between himself and Edward, who was obsessed with string and wind instruments and would sometimes even play two flutes at the same time. He would trance out during their sets and stare off into space, at us, and at the audience. It was his utopia. Their music was Middle Eastern in nature but fused with sounds from Egypt, India, and even Ireland. It was also improvised, so neither they nor we would know what type of song would be played next, or how long any particular song would last. We began calling it tribal belly dance roulette, and we would each dance to the song based on which of us was inspired, or tired, at the moment.

While Kyle and Edward became staples at this gig and would play music every time we were scheduled, Rosie, Morgan, Rhiannon, and I would take turns performing, for several reasons. It was a small space, so there was not room for all four of us at the same time, and if only a couple of dancers were there, then each performer would at least make a few dollars, as opposed to making even less by the time the pay was split six ways instead of four, for example. This also allowed us to have flexible weekends, so that no one was married to the schedule.

The tribe would perform from seven to nine p.m., always hoping for a crowded house. Sometimes few diners would show up. On these nights, we optimistically looked at the gigs as practice time, which I felt I desperately needed since I was now dancing for more than my own enjoyment. Chez Es Saada was my first regularly paying dance gig. The music could be a challenge to dance to because it had little structure. I joked with the girls that if we could successfully perform to this, then we could perform to anything. And we did.

When I was scheduled for the evening, the other dancer would often meet at my apartment. We would put on our makeup, including heavy black eyeliner, Indian bindis on our foreheads or around our eyes, and tribal markings made with liquid eyeliner. Our costuming typically included heavy jewelry from the Middle East, ankle bells, and veils: the whole kit and caboodle. Of course, after two hours of performing (with only one break, halfway through), we would end up with streaked makeup, black-bottomed feet from the carpet that was rarely cleaned, a full belly, and a small handful of money.

The rotations were going well, and it was just a couple of weeks after I had made a pair of "harem" pants out of an Indian sari that it was my turn to dance with Rosie. The baggy pants served as a flash of color on my legs as I spun in my twenty-five-yard skirt that lifted around my ankles when I wore it, rippling in waves of texture. They felt a little too baggy around the ankles in particular, but I thought they looked great.

"Well, they're supposed to be really big," Rosie told me when she saw them. "That's why your ankle bells will go on the outside of them. The bells will help hold the material in place."

Okay, I thought. *She knows more about costuming than I do.*

The pants were fiery shades of pink and red that faded into an ash gray from the knees up, then faded back into the pinks and reds. I had chosen the pattern because of my fire dancing. Not that I could light up while wearing these . . . the fabric was highly flammable. But they were perfect for tribal belly dancing at Chez Es Saada. On this particular night, I chose to let the pants shine on their own and simply layered some belts and large fabric tassels over them, instead of wearing them underneath a large, long skirt as they were intended.

Once we were "on" at the restaurant, Kyle was drumming away on the doumbek and Edward was heavy into a flute melody during a spirited song titled "Ishtar." I took a step, lifted my foot too high, and then set it down too close to my other foot. The second sound I heard was Edward's flute making a quick ascending note that reminded me of an elephant blowing its trunk. The first sound I heard was the ripping of fabric.

Immediately, my face turned red, and I sat down next to Rosie at the booth that was reserved for the dancers. Not the most professional thing to do, but we had no backstage, and to get to the bathroom, I would have had to walk (or dance) my way past several tables with a gaping hole in my pants. "It's not that kind of show, Summer!" Rosie whispered to me when I sat down, my face as red as the pants.

"You mean we weren't supposed to literally ROCO?" I tried to make light of it as I drank from a glass of water at our table. Light tears came to my eyes, an unstoppable physical reaction of embarrassment. I knew that it was funny to everyone else, so I figured I might as well enjoy the fiasco as much as I could by seeing it through their eyes.

"Not for this place, at least," she said as I used a napkin to dab at my eyes. "You're also going to smear your mascara. Here, let me help you."

"Thanks for the tip, Rosie," I said, "but I don't think anyone's going to be looking at my face, at least until this hole is fixed."

Rosie sat at the table with me through the next song, helping me to hide the rip so that I could at least leave with dignity.

"What would I do without you?" I asked her as she pulled some pins from her purse. "I'm a hot mess."

"Oh, honey, you're hot all right, but you're not a mess. At least your panties are pink and red. It could've been worse—you could be wearing a thong, like me, and have shown your whole ass."

"Rosie!" I whispered. I was already embarrassed enough.

"What? You'll be fine. Everybody's probably forgotten about it by now."

She was right. The diners were having their own conversations, Kyle and Edward were tuned in to their music, which was wrapping up, and the waitstaff was busy serving water and taking dishes. I was reassured by the normalcy of the room.

"That was awesome." Edward had come to our table. "You just kept right on going and handled it like a pro."

"I sure don't feel like a pro," I said. "I don't know what I was thinking, first of all. I should've just bought the damn pants instead of trying to make them myself. But what's worse is that I didn't even have a place to go to. I've had to sit here in front of everyone and wait for the moment to pass instead of getting the hell out of dodge."

Kyle joined us as Edward continued. "At least you were camouflaged," Edward said. "I'm probably one of the only people who really noticed, *camo girl*."

I must have fluttered my eyes, which is the most subtle and yet effective way I have of showing annoyance. Rosie and Kyle picked up on it.

"Maybe we should just let it go and move on, Edward," Kyle said lightheartedly.

"Ah, she doesn't mind it; do you, *camo girl*?" Edward asked me.

"Actually, you know, you can just call me Summer."

"All right, *camo girl*."

Kyle lost his smile. "Dude, cool it."

"Okay, okay, I get it," Edward said. "Summer, I crossed the line. Forgive me for making a joke?" He held out his arms for a hug.

"Forgiven," I said, wanting to just keep the peace.

Kyle picked up his glass of water from the table and took a drink. "Well, ladies, we have about five minutes before the next set starts. Any requests? Suggestions? Complaints? Suggestions come to me, complaints go to Edward."

"I have a suggestion," I said, leaning toward Kyle and looking at my three friends.

"Ma'am?" he said.

"Let's never stop doing this." I sat back in the booth. "I love you guys; I love dancing and being with you, Rosie. This is the best way we could possibly spend a Saturday night, ripped pants or no."

"I'll drink to that," Kyle said, lifting his glass.

Edward, Rosie, and I followed suit, raising our glasses and toasting each other.

"To dance!" I said.

And they replied in unison: "To dance!"

Chapter 17

SIDETRACKED

The Gypsy Hut was a maze of rooms with wooden floors and black walls that were touched here and there with artistic graffiti. It was a two-story brick building and had a fenced-in patio with picnic tables and potted trees. The place was known for their custom hot dogs, of all things, and they had hired Noir Arts for a New Year's Eve party.

We were hanging out at the bar prior to our set. After she'd seen Rosie sipping a Cosmopolitan, Morgan asked the bartender for a Bud Light.

"Where's the rest of the gang?" Morgan asked.

"Rhiannon and Adrian are floating around, and I saw Phoenix outside setting up his fire-breathing space," I said.

"Good," she said. "What are you drinking? It's on me."

"Actually, just water is fine for now. I'll let you take care of me later, though," I said with a wink.

"It doesn't hurt to have just one, ya know," Rosie said. "When I worked at The Office, I had to build up my tolerance because the guys would constantly want to buy me drinks. And I'd let 'em, too, because then the bartenders would share their tips with me."

"You must've done pretty well there, Rosie," Morgan said as she pulled out her pack of cigarettes. "One of you guys have a light?"

I reached into my purse for a lighter and indicated that I would light her cigarette for her.

"Thanks," she said. "It's impossible to have a drink without a smoke."

"I learned how to do that, too," Rosie said. She looked at her nails and continued, "But I'm glad I don't have to do any of that anymore. It was good while it lasted, but that kind of gig can wear a girl out. It can wear down your soul."

"I've actually been really curious about it," Morgan said. "I'm still paying off my college loans, and I don't think I'll ever get out of debt."

"Oh, Morgan, don't do it," Rosie told her, putting her hand on Morgan's knee. "They'll eat you alive. It's good money, but it's not for everyone."

"You can't be serious, Morgan," I chimed in. "I can't picture you working at a strip club. Unless you were a bartender, or a bouncer maybe."

"What's that supposed to mean?" Morgan said. Both she and Rosie were looking at me like I had offended them both.

"It's supposed to mean that I know how emotionally hard it would be for you. You're an outright feminist. When we met in college, you didn't shave your legs, you refused to wear a bra, and it was you who introduced me to Gloria Steinem. How can you go from that to tribal belly dancing, which is totally empowering, to taking your clothes off for drunk perverts?"

Morgan sighed and took a draw of her cigarette. "Yeah, I guess you're right. It was just a thought."

"It's not that bad, but I guess it sort of is," Rosie said. "What was college like? It's something I've dreamed of ever since I got my GED."

"In a word, it's fun," I said. "We partied so much. Every day we'd spend time hanging out between classes, studying together, talking about big ideas and life in general, and then nights and weekends were time for play."

"It was pretty awesome," Morgan said. "Despite being a money suck. That said, it might've helped if I'd majored in something other than philosophy."

"Stop philosophizing—we've got a show to do!" Rhiannon had popped over our shoulders. "Follow me and we'll get started."

Our set on stage went so-so. Perhaps because a couple of us had had a drink, perhaps because we were too much in our own headspace to be "on." We continued to smile throughout the performance, even when I messed up a cue because I was distracted. Adrian was sitting front and center, practically drooling. I lifted my chest a little higher, feeling like an exotic bird playfully doing a mating dance. I even giggled to myself a little but came back to the moment after spinning around and seeing Rhiannon. We were still performing, after all.

Once our songs were over and we took our bows, we began mingling with the crowd, accepting compliments, and answering questions from our fans. I had fun flirting with Adrian from a distance; we sometimes played a game where we would make eye contact from across the room, or brush past each other without showing outward acknowledgment. This secret code had me on edge.

"Don't do it." I simultaneously felt someone's hand on my arm and heard the voice in my ear. It was Rosie. "It's already a mess, and you don't want to be a part of it."

"I don't know what you're talking about," I said, trying to guess if she could sense my crush, and my waning ability to keep it at check.

"Adrian. I can see it. I've known him for a long time, and I've known Rhiannon for longer. You might think it's all fun and games, but trust me, sister, just stay away from him. Don't let him suck you in."

I was busted. But she didn't act like I was completely in the wrong, so I didn't dispute her. "I've had a crush on him since we met. Since before I met and knew Rhiannon. I haven't done anything."

"I just wanted you to have fair warning, sugar," she said. "Besides, imagine the clusterfuck it would create if our whole tribe started fooling around."

Trying to end on a sarcastic and funny note, I opened my eyes wider and said, "That would be awesome."

"Get out of here," she said, gently pushing my arm. "The things that you say sometimes."

"I will get out of here, to get changed at least," I said. "This coin bra is scratching the heck out of me."

"I'll walk with you to the green room. I want to check on my purse because sometimes people get in there that shouldn't be in there."

"I know," I said. "It'd be nice if they'd give us a lock or something."

We walked upstairs where the changing area was. I opened the door and flipped the light on.

"Oh!"

"Who is it?"

"It's Summer. Sorry!" Before I could look away, I saw Phoenix and a girl I didn't recognize sitting on the couch, blinking from the sudden light, and pulling at their clothes.

It was my turn to say, "Oh!" I turned and walked out, passing Rosie. "Uh, you may not want to go in there just yet," I told her.

"Yeah? Somebody having a little extra fun?"

Then Phoenix and the girl came walking through the door, hand in hand.

"How'd you like our set, Phoenix?" Rosie asked him.

"Damn, I missed it tonight," he said. "Hey, I'll catch up with you later, babe," he said to the girl, who squeezed his hand, grinned at him, and walked toward the steps to go back downstairs. "Sorry. I guess I got sidetracked."

"Well, it would be nice if you'd stay out and support your tribe, instead of fucking around with the patrons," Rosie said to him. Her words were blunt, but she said it in a joking way.

Phoenix held both of his hands palms up and looked from one to the other. "Watch belly dancers that I see every weekend, or actually meet someone new while we're out. We weren't fucking, by the way."

"Right, you would need less time than one song," she said, poking him in the ribs.

"If you don't like 'watching us every weekend,' then are we doing something wrong?" I asked, offended by his remark. "I know you might get used to it, but if you do, then that means anyone in our audience could."

"Ah, no, it's not like that," Phoenix said, crossing his arms over his chest. "You guys are great, really. But I, like, live this stuff. Don't think anything about it, okay?"

"That's fine, then," I answered. "We've been back here long enough, though. I'll meet you all outside for your fire-breathing set in just a minute, after I change."

"Don't change too much," Rosie said jokingly as she pulled some lip gloss from her purse. She put on a dab of it expertly without a mirror, dropped it back into her purse, and left with Phoenix for the fire set.

Chapter 18

OOMPA-LOOMPAS, HOES, AND ASSHOLES

Winter rolled along with regular practices and some smaller gigs, and in March Noir Arts was booked to perform in Columbus, Ohio, for an after-party during a famous bodybuilder's fitness expo. The party was basically a bar full of testosterone-filled weightlifters accompanied by loud music and strobe lights. Rhiannon had booked this gig through her friend Brad Fields, who built massive, artistic structures out of PVC pipes. Noir Arts was hired mainly to perform with fire on the front lawn of BoMA, the Bar of Modern Art. It was several hours away, we had someone designing costumes for us, and it paid well. We were beyond excited. The fact that we had a costume designer alone perhaps inflated our egos, but that was part of the reward for putting so much hard work into a project.

We arrived at BoMA early to try on the costumes, which we were to wear not for fire dancing, we discovered, but for afterward. The offer was something like, "Do you want to make some extra money? Wear this and pass out candy during the party." *Well, okay,* we agreed in good humor. The costuming was inspired by the oompa-loompas in *Willy Wonka and the Chocolate Factory.* Mine in particular consisted of orange suspenders that held up a pair of green booty shorts with white polka-dots, plus a bright green top that was not as revealing as a *brassiere*, but sexier than a sports-bra. I was in.

Brad was constructing the PVC sculpture, which filled the theater in BoMA and was maybe two stories high altogether. He needed help, and we performers had muscle, so everyone involved worked together to do as he instructed. As I lifted my section of PVC, I struck up a conversation with the guy next to me. He was about my height, covered in tattoos and piercings, and had a mohawk.

"So, are you performing?" I asked him in an effort to make small talk, since we were sort of teamed up.

"I'm one of the suspension guys," he told me. I had heard about groups of people who basically surgically insert metal hooks through their skin, usually in their backs, and "suspend" themselves from things like trees. That was all I knew about it, and it was all I wanted to know—even though I was drawn to Nailface Nina's human blockhead act, suspension freaked me out for some reason. Maybe it was the difference between one being an entertaining performance, and the other being a practice that people just *did*. It felt surreal to be standing next to—and about to perform with—someone who practiced suspension.

"What do you do?" he then asked me.

"I'm one of the fire dancers," I replied.

"Man, I don't fuck with fire," he told me. *Hmph.* I felt like I had won in the freak show.

When we finished setting up, everyone went back to getting ready, and I set out on my own.

"Brrrr. It's still winter outside," Morgan said as she walked up to me, rubbing her arms to warm up. "I just went out for a smoke. It's way too windy for us to do fire."

"I was afraid of that," I said.

"I already talked to Brad. He said that it's fine, and that we can just dress up in the oompa-loompa costumes and pass out the candy."

"Good. At least we can get paid for something," I said. "Let's head up to the dressing area and see what we've got."

These were not the oompa-loompa outfits from the movies. These costumes exposed our midsections, the part of the body that most women in the general American population would never want to bare in public, much less at a bar filled with fitness enthusiasts. My cohorts and I, however, came from a healthy background of tribal belly dance, in which we celebrated the fact that our bellies were as "soft as a pillow and round as the moon." By the time we got dressed, the party had begun, so we grabbed the bags of candy and went out boldly among the drinkers.

I could feel the bass of the music pumping through my chest because it was so loud, and the lights played tricks with my eyes as they flashed in time with the songs. Guys were lined up around the bar, visibly checking out the women who were standing around with drinks in their hands. I do not know what the fitness expo itself was like, but I am sure that the patrons at BoMA that evening were thrilled to mingle with their kind. It was not unlike when I would go to a hippie festival, for example, and be around other hippies that I automatically felt in union with. Well, yes, actually it was unlike that, but I was trying not to judge.

Brad approached Morgan, Rosie, Rhiannon, and I once we were on the floor. He had to practically yell so we could hear him, and we all leaned in to hear. "Girls, two things: The club owner wants to see people dancing inside of the dome, so I need you go grab people and get them out there. Also, climb up the dome as high as you feel comfortable and dance around on the piping. It'll look great."

"But the suspension people are on it. I don't want to mess up their, whatever you call it," Rosie said as loud as she could.

"Don't worry," Brad said. "The PVC can hold you with no problem. Just climb up, dance around, swing around. You'll be fine. If you look like you're having fun, then the patrons will have fun, and we'll have fun and make a little money. Do a great job, and they'll have us back next year."

Rosie was the first to grab onto the PVC and hoist herself up. I walked to the other side of the dome and followed suit, and I watched as Morgan and Rhiannon began to work the crowd. We were all having a blast, and we were completely *on.*

After a few songs, Morgan and Rhiannon came back and started to climb the dome, so I got Rosie's attention and we came down to the floor to switch it up. The whole time we were up on the dome, only a handful of people had made their way to the center, and their stay was brief. I hoped that we would have more success in getting people inside. Rosie disappeared into the crowd, and feeling confident, I continued in my character, dancing like I was having the best time of my life. It was not a far stretch.

I tried to set an example and inspire other people to loosen up, perhaps letting go of some of their inhibitions and relaxing enough to not worry what other people thought about their hair, clothing, or biceps. I loved it, and I had a strategy in mind. I planned to dance up to the patrons who were at least near the dome, thinking they might be more likely to take a few steps inside. I made my way to a muscular man who was talking to two cute women—one had long hair that was pulled back tightly into a clean braid, and the other had a short bob—and I tried to get them all to dance with me.

The music was so loud that trying to speak was pointless. Only gestures would work to try to convince them to take the party inside the dome, to the middle of the floor. I was doing my job, I felt. But did I mention that the girls were cute?

The man looked at me with a hint of disdain, leaned toward me so I could hear him, and said, "Back off, ho." He might as well have slapped me in the face.

Fortunately, the two women who were standing next to him were not as mindless as I would have assumed. They looked at me with sympathetic expressions, looked at each other with affirmation, and then tossed their vodka martinis into his chiseled face. He looked pissed as he wiped the drinks from his face and made a 180-degree turn to leave the dance floor. The two girls set their glasses down and moved to a different part of the bar and I, in shock, made my way toward the dome.

I held my response at bay. I was still working. My body continued as if nothing had happened, and I climbed the dome, feeling a safe distance from the hostility below. But my mind was stuck in that moment. It had a familiar sting, a phantom pang from my teen days. I suddenly recalled the time I was sitting at a bus stop when a car of boys drove by. I looked up as one of them yelled, "Hey," and then I regretted my very existence as I realized what was coming: he spit out the window. Did I think for a moment that someone was flirting with me? And if I elicited that kind of response from boys then, why would I expect anything different now?

Bringing myself back to reality, I grabbed the next rung on the dome and looked around at the scene below me.

I had been so immersed in my current open-minded community of artists, dancers, and lovers, that I forgot there's a culture that finds this guy's kind of behavior acceptable, and the slur cut deep. What did I do wrong? Why was he so rude? I began to question whether I was meant to perform outside of the safety of my own community, which respects women, artists, and people at large.

Rosie was successfully convincing people to step inside the middle of the dome, where she continued to dance with them. Morgan and Rhiannon were in their own worlds as well. It looked like they had everything under control, and so I made my way back down. I had to get to the restroom, where I could just have a quiet minute to think, to be *off*.

Once in the ladies' room I started fiddling with my hair. As I leaned toward the mirror to wipe some eyeliner that had smeared in the corner of my eye, the bathroom door swung open, bringing with it a momentary burst of house music and the two girls from earlier. *Oh, look,* I thought involuntarily. *It's bob and braid.* They saw me and seemed embarrassed.

"That dude is a dick," said the woman with the bob.

"It happens," I said, trying to maintain a professional attitude and keep my cool in front of these strangers. I had to be on again, after all.

"No, he is a dick," she repeated. The woman with the braid nodded her head as she opened a piece of gum that had come from our goody bags. "He was being creepy to us before you even came over. Trust me, he was just pissed because he was trying to get laid."

"I didn't mean to interrupt," I said apologetically, looking at the door. I was ready to get out of there.

"You don't need to apologize," she said, shifting her weight to one hip. "Let's get real. Calling a woman a 'ho' is insulting to all women. It's even insulting to men. He's a jerk. Period." Her friend was still nodding her head but had begun playing with her hair as she primped in the mirror. "Kudos to you for going out there and doing your thing."

"Thank you," I told her, appreciating her support but feeling awkward about the pep talk. "Well, I should get back out there. Have a great time tonight." I walked out of the bathroom and back into the bar scene, tucking away my emotions.

It was difficult for me to tell my friends about the insult because I was embarrassed. I was afraid that they would consider me a weak link, I suppose, if they found out that a patron had talked to me like that. Like I didn't deserve to be respected. I wished more than anything that I could just go home—not to my apartment but to my parent's house, where in any other situation I could find comfort. I knew they wouldn't understand, and I wasn't looking for a lecture. Instead, as soon as we were back in Cincinnati I called my mentor, Miranda, one of the first women who taught me at Dance Mecca. Miranda would walk around anywhere she pleased with ankle bells that made nearby people look and listen, when most of the time women are taught to be silent. Those bells alone gave me so much confidence. Once on the phone with her, I tearfully explained what had happened. The burden lightened only slightly as I confided in Miranda, who offered me strength.

"You don't seem like the type to let something like this hurt you so much," she said. "Look deep and tell me, why are you letting him have this effect on you? You're giving him power."

"This is hard, but I guess I know where it comes from, Miranda." I took a deep breath, ready to let some of my past go. "Not that long ago, when I was in high school, other kids made fun of me because of my complexion. And when I say 'made fun of,' I mean they were downright hateful. I thought I was away from all that, but I guess not."

"Sometimes it's easy to forget what the rest of the world is like beyond the safety of our community. Would you like to tell me more about it? Sometimes it helps to talk. You can't keep things like that bottled up. It's not good for you."

I sighed deeply. Those who knew me in high school were aware of the bullying, but I rarely talked about it. It was just always there. "I don't know what to tell you. It was hard. One day I just couldn't take it anymore." Miranda was silent, so I continued. "I tried to cut my wrists, to end everything. My dad found me. He and my mom took me to the hospital. I went to therapy. Dance became my church, my salvation. It was all I had to express my love, my hate, my depression."

"And you pulled through, and here you are," she said. "Summer, as a dancer, and especially as a fire dancer, you will have to be careful about who you share your energy with. It's very powerful and can evoke varying reactions from people who don't know how to interact with it. Not everyone is equipped to deal with the pure beauty of creativity and innocence that art inspires." And so my lesson was learned. I kept these words close to my heart, humbled by the enlightenment that I held a special flame of energy that I could protect and share as I chose.

The easy thing for me to do would have been to write this guy off as a dickhead, but part of me considered feeling sympathy for him. What in his life made him feel so insecure that he had to insult a stranger, a performing artist, no less? Did he get so little love that he was incredibly desperate for the attention of the two girls he was flirting with? Who knows. But I knew that it was not my burden to bear, and this made it easier to move on, and to dance with confidence. I deserved to share my art.

By the time the next Noir meeting rolled around, I felt like I could talk about it again. Morgan happened to be sitting on the cabin porch having a cigarette when I pulled up.

"So what did you think about the show last weekend?" She asked before I had a chance to start a conversation about anything else.

"The show was great. I loved the other acts, and we had a great time," I said. "I could've lived without some of the testosterone-filled dickheads that were there, though."

"Dickheads? I've yet to hear you call anyone a name. What gives?"

I relayed the story, trying not to sound as victimized as I felt. I thought I would be able to do so without breaking into tears again, but damned if I could not stop them. The pain was still too fresh. Morgan was more indifferent than Miranda had been.

"I hate to say it, but you have to expect stuff like that to a certain extent," she said as she put her arm around my shoulders. "I mean, it was a bar. And we're not, like, supermodels or anything."

"Bullshit." We had not heard Adrian come up behind us on the porch. Rhiannon was still getting her fire gear out of the trunk of her car. "If I'd have been there, I would've let his face walk into my fist."

"That's very kind of you, Adrian," I told him. I abhorred violence, but it did feel good to know that he would have stood up for me. The idea of him punching someone in the face for calling me a name was flattering. I wiped away the last tear and shook my head, smiling through the hurt.

"Besides," Adrian added, "even if you were a ho, you'd be our ho. Now, it's time to practice. Let's see you fire dance."

Chapter 19

NOIR ARTS OF THE APOCALYPSE

In addition to Robert Downey Junior, Rosie loved zombies. Obsessed, even, as she had a burning desire to create a zombie choreography, inspired by a Halloween-themed striptease she had performed back in the day. She easily convinced us to play along. "Noir Arts of the Apocalypse," as it came to be known, was an intricate story about a gravedigger (Adrian, the group unanimously decided) who buried the body of someone (yours truly) who rose as a zombie. We were to enter the stage with Adrian dragging my limp body, which was hidden under a sheet. After Adrian laid me down on the ground, he would sneakily lift the sheet a bit and steal a "valuable" ring from my finger and then exit the stage, where I and the other zombies (Rosie, Morgan, and Rhiannon) would then finish the story through a performance.

We spent weeks writing the piece, rehearsing, designing the costuming, and rehearsing some more, until our group was ready to perform for an audience just north of Indianapolis at a variety show.

On the night of the gig, I waited patiently backstage with just enough butterflies in my stomach to remind me how exciting it was to perform. The number that preceded ours was a comedy routine by a local act. I could hear their off-color sex jokes from behind the stage curtain, and I giggled to myself along with the audience, who warmly responded on cue with each joke. The comedian wrapped up her set, bowed, and left the stage as the audience applauded loudly.

The house lights dropped and raised, cuing the zombie piece to begin. In character, Adrian dragged my lifeless body to center stage. When the music cued me, I rose slowly and performed as a zombie (in torn and bloody clothing, my dreaded hair a mess), as Adrian got spooked and ran off stage. Just a minute or so into the part of the music where I was dancing a solo with jerky, zombie-esque movements, Morgan, Rosie, and Rhiannon suddenly climbed out of somewhat-hidden boxes that we had made, which were flush with the raised stage floor. They, too, were zombies, complete with white contact lenses that made their eyes look unnatural. At that point, the four of us danced together and performed some acts of minor contortion, such as dramatic backbends, until Adrian returned to the stage to try and kill us. He swung a shovel, we ducked quickly, and then we attacked him, eating his "guts," which included grotesque varieties of candy-shaped organs. Fortunately, since it was October when we did this show, it was just in time to catch a ton of Halloween props on store shelves that we could use. After the gruesome feast, we exited the stage, leaving him lying in a heap before the audience. Just after we were behind the curtain, Adrian raised his upper body slowly, confirming what we all know happens when you get eaten by a zombie: you become a zombie yourself.

It was a masterpiece. The music was perfect, the costuming, the elements of surprise and disgust—it all came together, mostly thanks to Rosie's perfectionist-style management of the project. After our zombie number was completed, I had to change into my next costume. The girls were out front at the bar, and Adrian was still backstage removing his candy guts.

"Hey, Adrian," I said. "Can you help me with this? I can't reach the back of my top. Can you tie a knot with these straps?"

"This goes against every instinct that I have, you know," he said.

"Good grief." I laughed. "Just tie it."

"I can't help it! It's completely unnatural for me to be putting clothes on a woman," he said, letting his fingers trace down my spine. I just rolled my eyes, suppressing the shivers he caused.

Dressed and ready for my next set, I followed Adrian to the second floor of the venue where we found Rosie, who had performed a sexy number earlier in the show, plus Rhiannon and Morgan, all watching the rest of the evening's entertainment. Even Phoenix had come along for the ride, although fire arts were prohibited inside the venue. I was scheduled to go back on stage and spin glow-in-the-dark poi while my friend, another soloist, sang a gothic tune in celebration of the holiday. I hated to perform with poi sans fire, but sometimes the venue simply was not conducive to fire arts, and that is when glow poi had to do.

One of the numbers in between these two included a full-blown burlesque strip-tease act. She was great. *More power to all women who take this on,* I thought. However, I felt embarrassed to go on stage right after her, regardless of the fact that I had performed on the same stage as burlesque dancers in the past. For example, some of my earliest gigs along the way included "adult variety shows" at a lesbian bar for tips, stage experience, and because I just had to say yes to something that sounded so bizarre. At the time I didn't think anything about it and just went with the flow of the group. I was excited to be on stage and didn't care when or where. But there was something different about this show. Maybe it seemed more professional. Maybe I had matured as a performer and was more conscientious about my surroundings. My fear was that the audience would be bored with little ol' me, spinning only LED-lighted poi, fully clothed with no hope of losing my top and revealing pasties or showing my ass. I was worried that my talent would not be able to compete with nudity, and so I braced myself to be booed offstage.

Of course, that didn't happen. I went on, rocked it out with the singer, and no one so much as threw a tomato at me. But I realized that night that I was uncomfortable being on the same stage as a naked person—following her act, anyway. It set different standards and expectations by telling the audience that any other performer they saw in the same show may get naked. That, and the whole time I danced with my glow poi on that particular night, I felt like I should have been much "sexier"—like I should have worn scanty costuming, teased the audience with glimpses of my skin, or used a romantic song. But none of that is me, and my stage personality had become essentially the authentic me, times ten.

After my last number, our group began to make plans to leave for the evening. I assumed that we were going to get a hotel room together and crash in Indianapolis, then head home first thing in the morning, but everyone in the group scattered in different directions, except for Adrian and me. Even Rhiannon rode back to Cincinnati with Rosie because she had to work early in the morning, and Rosie had to study. Neither Adrian nor I were up to driving all the way back home that late at night, as we ended up staying at the club until it closed, well after midnight, maybe two a.m., maybe three a.m.; it was *late* . . . so we agreed to get a room on our way home.

Although I had changed out of my ripped-up zombie costuming, I still had some of the fake blood and red makeup on my clothes and skin. I intentionally left it on—it was Halloween weekend after all—and in hindsight, I realized that it was much more professional to remove all stage makeup once a show was over. But this was my life, and the makeup was realistic enough that I wanted to "enjoy" it longer before I washed it away forever. I sort of wanted it to last, like a memory.

And so we drove, with me in zombie makeup, looking for a place to crash for the night. I was so tired that I had little to say, and enjoyed listening to the car radio with Adrian next to me, my mind playing out the most fun little scenes of what I would do with him, if he were single.

Just south of Indianapolis, we saw a motel sign from the highway, so we took the next exit. Suddenly red and blue lights fired up behind us. "I wonder who's getting pulled over," Adrian said as he drove into the parking lot of the motel to get out of the way of the police car.

We were both surprised when the cop pulled up behind us as we parked. The first officer approached Adrian's window and asked, "Do you know why we stopped you?"

"No, what did I do?"

"You were speeding," he said. "Going sixty in a fifty-five. Have you been drinking?"

"I had a beer several hours ago, but I'm fine," Adrian answered. Upon request, he handed over his license and registration. About that time, another officer walked up to my side of the van, where I sat politely, waiting out the scene, silently fuming about getting pulled over for going just five miles over the speed limit. He shined his flashlight on me, and noticed the stage blood. "Are you all right, ma'am?"

"Yes, I'm fine . . . oh! This—"

"She wouldn't shut up, so I punched the bitch in the face!" Adrian interrupted sarcastically. At first I was stunned. The police looked at Adrian in horror, until he and I burst out laughing at his less-than-politically-correct joke. The cops quickly understood that his comment was in jest, and Adrian continued to fill them in on our earlier performance. Thank goodness he was able to break the ice with these guys, because they seemed hungry to write a ticket. They went on their way, and Adrian and I went inside the motel to book a room.

When we got to the front desk, Adrian asked about a room.

"Do you have anything available for one night? We're looking for a double."

The clerk looked at us as if he was thinking, *I've seen it all now*, typed something into his computer, then said, "The only room we have open right now has a single, queen-size bed."

"We'll take it," Adrian said. I inhaled sharply, wanting to oppose, to ask if there was another nearby hotel, and yet wanting to stay. He took care of the rest before I could argue, and when the clerk handed us the keycard, we went back outside to find our room.

Someone on the sidewalk approached us, saying, "Hey, man, you got any weed?" Adrian said no as he opened our room door, which we quickly discovered had a broken deadbolt, although the lock on the doorknob worked.

The inside of the room had a torn lampshade, carpet that was dark enough to hide anything, and a sink stained from a leaky faucet. This was easy to overlook, however, because all I could sense was the bed. It was the elephant in the room, imposing its presence, impossible to be ignored.

"We are not going to take a shower together," was his humorous mantra as we got cleaned up from the performance.

"Hardy har har," I smirked as I closed the bathroom door. After I took a hot shower and scrubbed all the makeup from my face, I stepped out of the bathroom and grabbed my overnight bag. "Damn. I didn't bring pajamas," I muttered. I slipped my jeans off and folded them next to the bed, pulling the hem of my T-shirt down.

"Oh, isn't that convenient!" Adrian laughed. I rolled my eyes as he rolled a joint. We sighed as we looked at each other, alone in a different city, without any signs of our normal lives and, most notably, without Rhiannon. I wanted this evening to go somewhere; I wanted Adrian to lean over and kiss me through the haze, yet I knew that no kiss was worth losing what we had built with our tribe. It was a delicate balance of personalities, and I owed so much of what my life had become to Rhiannon, a girl who had grown to be one of my best friends.

It was a moment that lasted long enough for the smoke to clear, and I broke both the silence and our eye contact by saying, "It's late."

"You ready for bed?"

"Sure," I said. "Which side do you want?"

"I'll take the side closest to the door if it would make you feel safer."

"That's kind of you. And it works for me."

We folded back the covers and sat down on either side.

"We didn't take a shower together!" I said jokingly, trying to make it less awkward. "And now, we're not going to make out." I looked at him and saw he was making a puppy-eyes expression. "We're not going to make out," I repeated, grabbing the remote control from the nightstand and turning on the television. I left it on the first channel that came on, which was airing a rerun of *Judge Judy*.

"Listen, I know you and Rhiannon are close," he said. "Has she ever told you that we're in an open relationship? We see other people, but we don't make a big deal out of it, so not a lot of people know."

I didn't know this, at least intellectually. It could have changed everything at that moment. I could have simply said "cool" and then hopped on top of him and ripped off his shirt like I wanted to. Somewhere in my clouded mind, I recalled talking with Rhiannon at Cincinnati Burns, and the words she quoted from Adrian: "Everyone is free."

I maintained restraint, and I was too stoned to move very fast anyway. "I didn't realize that," I said slowly, pronouncing every syllable. If I was sober, I would truly have known better than to take this slippery road, but my current state kept me planted where I was, my mind slowly turning over this new enlightenment.

"So, it's cool, you know, if we kissed, or something. She would be cool with it," he told me.

"It's late," was all I could say. Why had Rhiannon never mentioned this? How had I never noticed? I was slightly mad at myself for being so naive, and for not sensing that theirs was an open relationship. Was that why Adrian didn't seem to have a problem sending unspoken messages? Had I unknowingly been sending my own? Was what he just said even true? I felt like I needed to at least have a conversation with Rhiannon about their relationship, so that I could better understand it and what my place within it could be, if anywhere. And a part of me said, "Fuck all that," because even though I was single, I didn't want to share a lover with someone else. But maybe . . .

Adrian took my cue and lay down, facing away from me. I looked at him lying there—his hair, his shoulders, the shape of his body as he lay on his side. Feeling bold, I reached over and touched the back of his neck, playing with his hair. His breath changed, his chest expanding as I ran my fingers along the collar of his T-shirt. Without looking at me, he sat up just enough to pull his shirt over his head and tossed it to the floor, revealing more tattoos that I had not yet seen. He lay down on his back and watched me as I looked at his ink, thinking about his path to piercings and tattoos. He had nipple piercings, which I should have guessed but was still surprised to see.

"I could give you some of these, too, if you want," he said.

Shocked, I let out a giggle. "I bet you'd love to."

"They don't hurt as bad as you'd think."

"Can I touch one?"

He took my hand and placed it on his chest so I could feel the jewelry, so I could feel him. Going against my better judgment, I leaned forward and put my face just above his. I stayed, my lips just a breath away from his, and waited for him to raise his head to meet me in a kiss. He did, just as I expected, and I closed my eyes, enveloped in emotion. He put his arms around my waist and, in one swift movement, pulled me on top of him. I let my legs fall to his sides as we continued to kiss.

He started to reach his hands up my shirt, and I put my hands on his wrists, guiding him. We continued to kiss, and between the buzz and the anticipation of being with Adrian, I took off my shirt and threw it to the floor next to his. We made out through two more episodes of *Judge Judy*, oblivious to the court proceedings as we explored each other with our hands and mouths.

"I should tell you, I don't have any protection," Adrian said, as I was about to pull off his boxers.

"Oh. Okay. Right. No problem," I said. "We'll just, have to stop. That's all. It's cool."

"It's ironic, I know," he said. "All this time I've been dying to be with you, and yet I wasn't sure if I'd ever get to. I didn't think we'd be in this situation, as much as I've fantasized that we would."

I smiled at him. "Really, it's fine." My breath was still shallow. "It was fun while it lasted, right?"

"God, yes."

"Why don't you toss me my shirt so you're not as tempted to get frisky again," I said.

He did, and after I put my shirt back on, I reached for the cheap lamp next to our bed and turned it out as I lay back down, my mind racing, knowing that sleep would elude me.

"Good night, Summer."

"G'night, Adrian."

Chapter 20

INDIA

Adrian and I were able to continue as friends after we all returned home, and yet I realized that there was no turning back. Did I want to pursue this? Our relationship had become stronger only because of Adrian's constant presence at the gigs and rehearsals, and yet he had never become a "just a friend" type of guy. I was attracted to him, and it was more than a minor crush. But what about Rhiannon? What about the tribe?

Learning to manipulate fire had taught me several things about life and had strengthened my belief that you must seize the day. Life was too short to not become who you were meant to be. After all, I had blossomed into this creative and free spirit who just a few years prior had hit rock bottom and was ready to put an end to everything that I knew—when ironically, I knew very little.

The strong friendships I had developed with others gave me the strength and understanding that we were all in this together—however it was that each one of us defined "this." We literally entrusted our lives to each other when we fire danced.

Because of my insecurity as a teen, I had never had a real boyfriend. In college I flirted with guys here and there, but I was still healing from the pain of the verbal abuse I had suffered. Embarrassingly, I still had moments when I felt so ugly—more on the outside than the inside—that I found it hard to believe that anyone would take an interest in me. All these things I thought about as I drove to the next meeting that we were to have at Rosie's house. Driving and listening to music, I considered that because I was no longer around people who made me feel ugly—or whom I allowed to make me feel ugly, as my therapist had taught me, like a good therapist would—that I could let that go. My dreadlocks, tattoos, piercings, and my tribal belly dance were all things that made me feel physically attractive, and I knew inherently that I had a good soul. Only fairly recently did others begin to see and recognize it. Adrian was the first guy that I felt a physical connection to, yet it seemed to me that he was unavailable.

As I wondered what it might be like to join this nontraditional relationship, I also wondered who else was involved that I didn't know about. I needed to talk to Rhiannon about it and just get everything out in the open, to know if Adrian truly was available, and if so, to what extent. Would we be able to go on dates with each other? Where would the relationship go? I had so many questions, but I wasn't sure if I was ready for the answers.

I was the first to arrive at Rosie's, and I walked in the front door as she was watching the last few minutes of *The Avengers*.

"Get yourself a glass of wine. This is almost over and then I can talk," Rosie said from the living room. I obeyed, pouring a glass and then standing in the kitchen for a few moments alone, still contemplating my thoughts from the car ride there.

"A genius billionaire playboy philanthropist," Rosie quoted from the movie. "Damn, I could use one of those myself."

"Speaking of playboys, can I ask you something in confidence?"

"Sure, babe; what's up?" Rosie poured more wine into her own glass.

"I'm not sure how to say this, and we might not have much time before everyone else gets here . . . ," I began.

"It should be fine. Rhiannon and Adrian are running late because they got stuck in a drive-through, Morgan had to work overtime, and I'm still not sure if Phoenix is even coming tonight. You know how it goes with schedules and all that happy horseshit."

"Well, that's helpful. Nice to know that I could've taken more time, but at least it gives us a minute to talk."

"Talk then!" Rosie smiled at me.

"Have you heard that Adrian and Rhiannon are in an open relationship?" I couldn't believe I was saying this out loud, and also didn't want to do so in a way that would be considered talking about them behind their backs. I was curious and wanted to know more before I actually talked to Rhiannon about it. I was afraid that it might be a delicate topic and wanted to handle it the best way that I could.

"I knew. It just wasn't my place to tell you. I found out when I ran into Rhiannon one night and I thought she was alone until this guy came up with a drink for her and started rubbing her back. I was like, what's up? But I didn't say anything. I guess she could read my mind because she made an excuse for the two of us to talk in private, and then she told me all about it. They were on a 'date night.' It was shocking at first, considering how serious she and Adrian have always been, but what the hell? If it works for them, I don't give a damn."

"Right," I said as I took a drink. I didn't know what else to say, but I had to agree. They weren't hurting anyone, and everything was out on the table. They were being completely honest with each other, at least— perhaps more honest than I was being. But did I want to be a part of that equation?

Just then, Rhiannon and Adrian walked in the front door. I finished my glass and poured another as Rhiannon announced, "I'm going to India!"

Rosie and I both tilted our heads at the same time, not very different from two pups that may have seen a reflection move across a wall simultaneously. Adrian looked indifferent . . . or maybe he was just high. I couldn't tell, but I sensed that perhaps he had found out fairly recently himself, perhaps even en route to the meeting.

"What?! India, huh? That's exciting!" Rosie finally responded. "What made you want to go? And when? And can you fit me in your suitcase? Pretty please?!"

Rhiannon smiled. "Well, do you remember a woman named Priyam from Dance Mecca? She's been hanging around a lot. Miranda had studied classical Indian dance with her, on the side. They were talking about co-teaching a session in it, but it just wasn't in the stars. Miranda might actually still do something with it because she wants to share it. Anyway, the three of us went to lunch yesterday to talk about teaching and to compare notes, and one thing led to another! Priyam is returning to India in a few weeks and has welcomed me to join her there for six months while I study dance and nanny for her family as needed. Can you believe it? She'll take care of my room and board, and I get to experience India!"

Adrian finally appeared to become present in the room as Rhiannon shared her exciting news. I was thrilled for my friend and jealous at the same time. *Damn,* I thought. "I want to go to India and study dance," I continued my thoughts out loud, hugging Rhiannon with love and good hopes for her.

"We'll miss you," I said, sad that it would be a while before we went on any more festival trips together. I stole a glance at Adrian to try to better gauge his reaction, then casually said, "You're not going along?"

He made eye contact with me briefly, perhaps out of respect for Rhiannon, and answered, "No. I think I'll stick around the Queen City for a while. Besides, I'm not allowed to leave the country ever since my incident at the Canadian border."

"Shut your mouth, smartass," Rhiannon said as she gently shoved his shoulder. "You've never had an incident at the border." Rosie and I rolled our eyes at each other and I giggled, slightly excited at the thought of having him—dare I think it—to myself in the States.

Being the den mother of our tribe, though, my mind quickly went to business. "This is exciting news and all, but we should also talk about some logistics within our group while we're here tonight. Are you going to be around for the next gigs that we have lined up? You might need the time to pack and get your things together."

"I need to figure all that out. I'd like to say that I'll still commit to the Club Nocturne gig, but I might need to ask you to cover for me." Similar to our arrangement at Chez Es Saada, Club Nocturne was a new, regularly occurring gig that I had booked for us when a talent agency contacted me looking for entertainment to add ambiance to the club scene. We were to begin working for the club within a couple of weeks.

"No worries if you can't, doll," I assured her. "You'll have a lot going on, so just let me know when it gets closer."

"Let me know, too, Summer, so I can request off work as soon as possible," said Morgan. "That's great news, Rhiannon. I can't wait to see what you pick up. You'll have to teach us everything you learn!"

"I absolutely will. I'll even take my camera so I can record moves and stuff. Summer, what's the next date again for the club? I'll check my calendar now so that you guys can make plans to be there if you have to."

"It's the twenty-second, the Saturday before Thanksgiving."

Rhiannon fumbled through her purse and pulled out a small calendar that was stuffed with notes. "I might leave that weekend," she frowned. "I'll ask Priyam for sure and get back to you on that. But in the meantime, let's celebrate!" It was true that celebrations were to be had, because this was such an exciting new endeavor for Rhiannon. I knew how much I would miss her, but I was grateful that I still had the rest of the group. And a part of me that I was not ready to acknowledge yet was relieved that Adrian was staying in the Queen City.

The following weekend, our tribe was booked for another tribal belly dance hafla. Kyle and Edward had organized an evening of improvisational Middle Eastern-inspired music and had asked us to be the hosts. We had also invited others from the community to come and simply enjoy the exotic music and movements. It was a typical hafla and was held at Dance Mecca, where incense burned inside, vegetarian snacks were spread out on a table, and smiling, friendly faces abounded. We went with the flow of the evening and had time for open dancing—where all performers and guests were able to dance freely. Noir performed a few fire numbers in the studio's backyard area, which was often used for smoking and enjoying small campfires when the weather allowed it.

"Summer, you want to spin fire poi now?" Kyle asked.

"Always," I joked. "I'll soak my poi and let you know when I'm ready." I walked outside to get my props. Adrian came up behind me.

"Can't wait to see you spin," he said.

"Oh, thanks," I replied. "So, Rhiannon really is going to India, huh? I can't get over it." We had reached my gear bag, where I took out my fire poi and began to soak the wicks in the fuel can.

"Indeed. It'll be good for her. She's always wanted to see the world, especially India. She's talked about going for as long as I've known her. Wants to experience the entire culture, ya know? It'll be hard, but I can't hold her back. There's no point in even thinking about stopping her, although I've told her how much I'll miss her while she's gone. Who knows—she might not even come back, if I know her at all. She'll probably end up roaming the country, then either stay there or find a way to travel to another exotic location. I mean, who would want to come back to Cincinnati after all of that?"

I took my poi out of the fuel and began spinning them in tight circles inside of a bucket, to catch the extra fuel that was flying off. "Couldn't tell ya. I don't know if I would, either, to be honest. Without any firm ties here, like kids or a mortgage, it would be hard to come back once you start experiencing the world. But then again, my roots run deep here. Born and bred not very far from this space where we stand now."

"And here we are now. I'm glad that our paths have crossed, Summer."

I stopped spinning the poi and looked into Adrian's eyes. I was so close, within almost touchable reach of kissing him like I wanted to . . . especially since I knew that I could soon take our friendship to a different level, once Rhiannon's plane left American soil.

"Me, too, Adrian. Me, too." He took a step toward me and I put the poi down on the ground for a moment to let him hug me, putting both of my arms around him. We had shared hugs before, to be sure, but this time we held each other tight as the music continued to play through the open studio door. Folks from inside began to trickle outdoors to watch the fire spinning.

We let go of each other, and with new energy, I picked up my poi as Kyle and Edward walked outside, still playing their instruments and bringing a parade of people behind them. Lit paper lanterns were strewn around the outdoor area, casting a soft glow on the faces of everyone, who parted to the sides of the space when they saw me enter the center of the yard with my poi. I raised an eyebrow at Morgan, who faithfully held a lighter—one of mine—to one of my poi to ignite the flame. Then, I danced. I swung the fire in large, slow arcs, like planets rotating around the sun. The fire was loud enough to compete with the music, and I used it to my advantage, for every time that I "stalled" the poi by stopping them dead in their paths, they were silenced. I paused the poi in the same quiet moments that I anticipated the music to have. Because everyone there knew of the improvisational and unrehearsed nature of the music and the fire spinning, it was magical. I danced for Adrian.

Chapter 21

SAYING GOOD-BYE

"I can't imagine what our tribe will be like without Rhiannon." Rosie had called me the day after the hafla. "We should do something special for her before she leaves, like have a little going-away party."

"That's a good idea. How about if we have one last dinner together? My place, Sunday evening, seven o'clock?"

"Works for me! I'll get in touch with everyone and see what we can do."

And so she did. The next night, Rosie, Morgan, Phoenix, Adrian, and Rhiannon gathered at my apartment to eat and drink, as we shared one last evening together as a complete tribe. In addition to remembering the shows, rehearsals, and fiascos, we had business to address, like the upcoming gig at Club Nocturne. It was a high-profile opportunity, since it was recurring and paid well. We agreed that it would be best for Morgan and me to make the first appearance there, as the others either already had plans for the night or had to work at their "day" jobs.

"I guess this is it," Rhiannon said as we wrapped up the details. "We've come so far from the beginning of all of this. I love you all."

"We love you, too, Rhiannon," I responded when everyone had fallen silent, not sure how to say good-bye. "I'm a different person, a better

person, because of you. You taught me how to eat fire, and you introduced me to so much. I would be nowhere without this tribe. I'd have
a normal job, live in a normal apartment, and life would be boring. But
now, I have a normal job, a normal apartment, and an amazing life, not to
mention amazing friends. And you'll be amazing in India."

"Let's put on some music and dance, the four us, one more time," said
Rosie. "Something that'll hold us over until Rhiannon returns."

"I would so love that," Rhiannon said.

"I'll find us a song," Morgan said as she dug out her MP3 player.

"I'll just be outside. You girls have fun," Adrian said.

Phoenix stood from where he was seated, and said, "I'm going to head
out and meet up with some other friends. Rhiannon, it's been real." He
gave her a hug and they embraced for a moment. "Safe travels."

"Thanks, Phoenix. I won't forget you," Rhiannon said to him as he
waved good-bye and left my apartment. "Adrian, thank you."

"How did you originally meet Phoenix?" I asked her.

"At a festival, of course," she said.

"He's a good one," Morgan said. "And easy on the eyes, too."

"But not on the nose," Rosie said under her breath, making a waving
gesture with her hand in front of her face.

"Rosie!" Rhiannon exclaimed.

"Sorry. I had to say it. Anyway, moving on! Morgan, is that song ready
yet?"

"Yeah. Just had to turn on the Bluetooth and fiddle with the volume.
We're good to go."

The music was turned up, but it was a soft-toned song. A mellow beat
filled the room as we fell into a circle, leaving the last words of conversation to float away in the atmosphere. We swayed our hips in perfect time,
as we always had and I hoped we always would. We spun and paused in
sync, like quintuplets that intuitively knew each other's movements without having to look.

As the song came to its end, we bent our knees, dropping slowly to the floor in unison, until we were sitting together in our circle. It felt like an ancient dance ritual, even in this modern apartment setting.

I was the first to break the silence. "Will you return?"

"I intend to," Rhiannon said.

"We'll wait for you," Rosie said. "Just be safe."

"I will," Rhiannon answered.

We took each other's hands for a moment in our circle, then let go and stood up, the magic having come and gone as it had during so many of our enchanted evenings.

We each hugged Rhiannon and then hugged each other just for good measure. One by one, everyone said their good-byes to her and left, until it was only Rhiannon and me. I had a hard time making eye contact with her as we cleaned up in the kitchen, but she finally said, "I'm going to miss you, too, ya know."

I looked up. "I wouldn't be who I am today if we hadn't met," I said. "I wouldn't be living the life I'm living." My chest felt tight.

"I think you would have, at least eventually. This was meant to be. You found yourself, and I just happened to have helped. You've inspired me, too, Summer. Not to mention Adrian. Have fun with him." With a the hint of a bittersweet expression, she winked at me, and I knew that Adrian had told the truth. "Now it's time to spread my wings."

What could I say? I put my arms around her one more time and held on tight, grateful that she had come into my life.

Chapter 22

A CASUAL MEETING AT THE BEANERY

And just like that, Rhiannon was gone, likely settled in India, and I was alone in my apartment. It was a bright fall day, cold and crisp outside. I lit a candle on my living room table and allowed the sun to come in through my windows, providing all the light I needed. I streamed music through my laptop, set on a mellow trance station, while I played around with my hoop, dancing. I stopped every so often to watch a YouTube video of my favorite hoopers for inspiration, made notes in my journal, and referred to the list of moves that I was working on so that I would remember everything that I had picked up along the way. Then I danced again. The practice was a teeter-totter of movements that ranged from technical to unstructured. I loved to flow with any prop I was using, but to do so with skill, I also needed to understand the tricks of the trade and be able to nail them. It was a delicate balance. I wanted to know the rules so that I could break them, to combine hoop tricks with ballet technique, to combine fire spinning with modern dance.

It was during these moments when I found Zen. All I had was music and dance, which resulted in a love for humanity that I had difficulty expressing in words. During these sessions in private, in the studio, or on stage, I saw everyone as my sister or brother. Dancing brought out my best side, as well as the beauty that I found in others. This love made me want to shout from the rooftops that everyone should dance, or at least find the one thing that makes them want to shout from the rooftops themselves. It was bliss.

I was spinning in circles with my hoop, almost to the point of becoming dizzy, when my phone beeped with a text message. It was Adrian.

S'up?

Dancing. What's up with you?

Heard that Kyle and Edward are playing music at the Beanery tonight, like in an hour. Meet me there?

Kewl.

This gave me time to brush my hair, put on some makeup, and stretch out my muscles, coming down from the high I experienced during my impromptu sessions. I started to change out of my tie-dyed, bell-bottomed yoga pants and tank top, but thought, *fuck it,* because I knew I would fit right in at the Beanery, which welcomed a variety of clientele, from artistic college students to poets to people who simply didn't have anywhere else to be. I put on my boots and a jacket, grabbed my purse and a book about creativity to read for a bit as I waited for Adrian to show up, and headed out.

The sun was starting to set by the time Adrian walked through the door and spotted me sitting at a two-top table. I saw him through the window and tilted my face down as I turned a page in the book I was reading. Kyle and Edward were already set up and had begun playing music. From the corner of my eye I watched them acknowledge Adrian with friendly nods, and he smiled back at them, lifting his hand in a casual wave.

He stood at the entrance and watched me for a moment. Although I felt his presence, I stayed in my seat. I picked up a spoon and slowly stirred my coffee, then set the spoon down, took a small sip, and licked my lips. I was having fun flirting with him in this subtle way. I had a feeling that he did the same thing with me, such as one time when he came up and said hello to me by putting a hand on my waist and bringing me to him for a hug that no one else would think to question.

"It's not a real hug unless our privates touch," he had said.

"Keep it in your pants." I laughed.

I could not believe how inappropriate he could be, but he had what it took to always get away with it. We got along well, despite the fact that, for the most part, I kept my distance up until now because I was afraid I would fall for him too hard. With Rhiannon in the picture, that thought carried too much emotional energy that I wasn't ready to invest. But now Adrian was free, and so I was free to explore the possibilities of a relationship with him.

In an attempt to be sultry, I slowly closed my eyes and then opened them again, lifting my head until I was looking at Adrian, who had only then started to make his way to my table. I stood up and we hugged and said our hellos, then sat back down.

The waitress came by and asked Adrian, "Whatcha havin', doll? Coffee, tea, chai, bourbon, whisky, mai tai, hummus, soup, ham on rye?"

Adrian was surprised by her poetic and rhythmic question and ordered a Blue Moon.

"So here we are," I began. I wasn't sure where the conversation would go or if we needed to talk much. Just being in that space, in that moment, was good enough for me.

"I'm glad you could make it. I thought maybe you would be busy or something."

"Well, I'm always busy or something, but this is better than sitting at my place by myself. Good music, good company. Shitty coffee, but two out of three's not bad."

Our attention turned to the music for a moment, and the waitress returned with Adrian's beer. Our drinks slowly disappeared as we sipped and shared a conversation that began with small talk, carried into work and tribe gossip, and then evolved to the real deal.

"There's nothing to stop us from giving this a go if you want to." Adrian finally said out loud the thoughts that had been streaming through my mind for the past couple of weeks. But I wasn't sure what the next step would be . . . would this mean we would start dating? Exclusively? The look on my face must have expressed that I was interested in pursuing something.

Just then Kyle walked up to our table. Stuck in the moment, I hadn't noticed that they stopped playing music to take a break. "You going to dance for us at all this evening?" he asked me.

"Not tonight." I smiled, flattered that he had asked even though I was obviously wearing street clothes, as opposed to anything even remotely resembling costuming.

"Next time, then, next time," he said. "How's that Blue Moon? Need a fresh one, on me?" he asked Adrian.

"Nah, I'm good. Thanks."

"Right on. Well, our break's only a few minutes long, so I'm gonna grab a drink and hit the men's room. See you guys later. Thanks for coming out!"

We waved a casual good-bye to Kyle, and just as we made eye contact with each other again, Edward came up. "Hey guys! It's so great to see you here! What's up?"

"Not a whole lot," I replied with an inaudible sigh.

"Where's the rest of your group? I'm not used to seeing just the two of you out and about."

"Well, Rhiannon is on the other side of the world, in India," I began. "I'm not sure what the rest of our partners in crime are doing tonight. We just thought we'd grab a drink and—"

"India?!" He took a step backward in shock. "How amazing is that! What's she doing there?"

"Nannying, studying dance, eating naan, you know, the usual," I replied, wondering what she was doing at that moment. "She'll be gone for several months, we think."

"God, that's gotta be hard for you, Adrian."

"It's cool. I miss her, but everything'll be fine. I'll stay busy here in the States." His tone was light.

"Good, good, then," Edward said. "It's good to see you guys. I hope you can stick around for the next set."

Adrian and I looked at each other. We had been there for a while, and I, at least, was ready for a change of scenery. "We might be heading out soon, but we'll catch up. Great to see you, dear," I told our friend. Edward then went up to the counter to order a drink, leaving Adrian and I alone once again.

"I think I'm going to call it a night," I announced. "Walk me home?"

"Of course."

It had gotten chilly outside with the setting of the sun, and we walked closely together until we reached my building.

"Thanks for texting me earlier. It was such a pleasant surprise," I told him.

"I'm glad you were free. This was fun," he said. Not sure what else to do, I put my arms around his neck and he pulled me close for a hug good-night. "You're so beautiful," he told me.

I only blushed, wishing I could see myself as he saw me. When we pulled back from each other, we smiled for a moment. "Adrian," I began, "things are different now. This, whatever it is, does it mean we're, like, dating?"

"You can call it whatever you want," he said, running his hand over my dreads.

"I've had this thing for you since we met. I can't believe we can finally be together."

"I've been wanting it for a long time myself," he said. "I'm glad you finally came around."

"Well, it was weird before."

"I happen to like weird." He leaned in and kissed me, and when we parted he raised his eyebrows. "It's one of the reasons I like you."

"Lucky me," I said, lowering my hands from around his neck to his waist as we stood, still so close. Images from the motel room came back to my mind as I remembered what he looked like undressed. But one thing I wanted to forget was the open nature of his relationship with Rhiannon. I didn't want to ask him if we would only see each other, because I feared his answer would be no, or worse, a roundabout way of no that left me wondering what his actual answer was. But I had to know.

"Are you seeing anyone else right now?"

"I'm only seeing you right now," he answered.

"Literally, yes, but . . ."

"I'm not seeing anyone else," he said, adding as he looked around, "right now."

"Be serious!" He was still making me laugh. That's one of the things I liked about him. He was a relentless flirt and a smartass. I decided to let it go for the night and trust that he would be honest with me if he was dating anyone else. I didn't want to ruin this before it started. "Adrian," I said.

"Summer," he said my name so perfect.

"I have to get up early for work. Thank you, for tonight."

"Summer," he said it again. "Good night." Then we leaned forward again and kissed. He left, leaving me wanting more.

Chapter 23

CLUB NOCTURNE

Back in my apartment the next day after work, I streamed music from my laptop again and sat down to work on my dreadlocks. Rhiannon had done an amazing job to help me get them going, but I found that they needed a lot of maintenance, which I actually enjoyed. It involved twisting and backcombing my hair, separating the narrow dreads that were trying to combine into fatter ones, and using a little hook-like tool to weave loose hairs back into the nearest lock. It was calming, and I felt like I was crafting, to a certain extent.

With my laptop open, I checked it every few minutes to see the name of the song or band that was playing, making mental notes about future gig music. While reading the current song title, an e-mail popped up. It was from the talent agency that had booked our group for Club Nocturne.

> From: Mona, We Find Talent
> Dear Summer,
> This is a friendly reminder about your upcoming performance at Club Nocturne. You and your partner are welcome to hula-hoop, eat fire (on the outside deck), and dance with or without props as you like throughout the evening. Your schedule is from

9pm to 2am, and you may take a 15-minute break each hour. You can interact with the patrons as much or as little as you like. There is to be no smoking in public and no drinking while on the clock. Your first night is November 22nd, and if the club likes what you have to offer, we'll hire you back and will discuss a contract, possibly for the last Saturday of the month moving forward. Every weekend has a theme, and the first Saturday that we're booking you for is '80s night. If you have any questions, please let me know.

We're always looking for girls to be a part of this great opportunity, so you're welcome to share referrals. Also, please review, sign, and return the attached contract.

Best regards,
Mona

I read the e-mail as I finished working on a single dread, then let go of my hair and wrote Mona back.

Dear Mona,
Thank you for your message. This all sounds perfect. Morgan will perform with me on the 22nd, and we're looking forward to it.
Thank you for your time,
Summer

Next, I forwarded Mona's message to the tribe so that everyone was on the same page. The only thing left to do was finish my dreads.

The date came, and Morgan and I got ready together at my apartment. Morgan teased her hair as big as she safely could (keeping in mind that she would be swinging fire around her head), and we both wore loud cotton stretch pants and layered neon tank tops. With bright-red lipstick and big hoop earrings, we may have looked more like hookers, but at least we looked like hookers from the '80s. The club was standard fare—loud, dark, and smoky. There were go-go dancers on the mini-stages as we walked in with our fire props.

Before we began "working," Morgan turned to me and said, "Summer, I don't know what you've gotten us into here, but I want you to know how glad I am that you brought me into all of this with you. Noir, I mean."

"Are you kidding me?" I responded, my hoop resting on my shoulder. "It wouldn't be the same without you. Did you ever imagine when we were in college that we'd end up doing this?"

"Never in a million years, chica," she said. "I just wish I had more time to devote to it. But work's work."

"Yes, indeed," I said. "And speaking of which, let's get started."

Before I could begin, my phone beeped with a text from Adrian.

Hope you guys have fun tonight!

Oh yeah, big hair, all '80s music. This totally fits in with what we do. NOT. But at least it puts food on the table.

I put my phone back in my purse and surveyed the scene, reminded of my philosophies about performing. When I had realized that there was crossover for some dancers between belly dancing, burlesque, and even stripping, I knew that I needed to draw a line somewhere for myself. I was tempted at times to be more risqué, but I wanted to keep my personal boundaries in check. To do so, I decided that I would never do anything that I wouldn't want my parents to see me doing. It kept things very clear for me, and for those in the community who knew me. But this was a different world. The other dancers at this club wore supersexy outfits with their cheeks showing—and not the cheeks on their faces. Their outfits were incredible, though, and I found out that they had an enormous costuming department at their disposal. The DJs and bartenders were friendly enough to Morgan and me, but the rest of the dancers were in a tight clique.

It was obvious that we were misfits among them, but I thought that maybe that could change. I hoped that this gig would be more than temporary, that I would eventually fit in, or at least that the others would come to accept me. It was a lot of fun to get paid to hoop in a club, even though it wasn't my normal scene. The bar was dark except for the strobe lights, and the music was so loud that I was able to get lost in it as I danced around. I used a hoop that, like my glow-in-the-dark poi, had LED lights strung throughout the inside of the plastic. It was magnificent. As I spun it around, it changed colors, leaving bright rainbow tracers in the smoky air. To get the effect, I actually didn't have to work too hard with it, but dancing is where I was free, so I took advantage of it and let loose, performing each hoop trick that I knew I could nail, flirting with the patrons, and stopping to pose for pictures when asked. Morgan owned the floor as well, and we ended up skipping some of our breaks because we were having so much fun.

The fire set went well, too, with us safetying for each other as we spun fire poi, ate fire, and used other various fire props on the club's large patio. By the end of the night, I left feeling like I had worked hard and entertained a ton of people who were already happily buzzed, and it made me feel desirable to have the attention of the patrons. It was a different world from my fire dancing within the belly dance community.

Morgan felt differently. "God, all these girls do on their breaks is talk about each other behind their backs," she said as we left for the night. "Do you have a light?"

"Yeah," I said, digging into my purse. "But who knows how their lives are entangled beyond this club," I said, handing her my lighter.

"Still, I feel like we're getting paid to dance for a bunch of drunk-heads who are wondering why we're wearing so many clothes," she said.

"It's not so bad, though," I said. "You can't beat the money, especially for what we're doing. We could live off this kind of cash, for a while at least. Who knows? Maybe I could even quit my job at the library, if I can pick up more shifts here on the weekends."

"You just keep telling yourself that," Morgan said as she gave me a hug. "Keep your feet on the ground, okay, Summer?" She started to walk toward her car as she raised one hand in a peace sign.

"Thanks for dancing with me tonight!"

"Please. Any day of the week, girl." The air outside felt so fresh against my skin; my clothes were still damp with sweat from dancing in the club all night, and I couldn't wait to get home to change and take off my makeup. When I got to my car, I pulled off some of my jewelry and kicked my shoes off. I checked my phone and saw that I had another text from Adrian.

Did you break a leg, big hair?

LOL. I guess so. The crowd was pumped. There's a lot of testosterone. It's kind of a meat market, but Morgan and I held our own. We put on our happy faces and danced.

Cool. Wish I could've been there.

Nothing's stopping you, but you'd probably hate it. Beer is $6 a bottle.

Oh. Fuck that.

LOL . . . good night, Adrian. (hugs)

I knew that the banter could potentially go on all night, and as much as I liked the idea of that, it was late. Then my phone beeped again.

Hey – it doesn't have to be good night. Want me to come over?

I considered. Did I? Yes. But tonight? I was a sweaty mess, and exhausted. I wrote back.

Come over tomorrow night, before the Dance Mecca hafla.

I put my phone back into my purse and drove home with '80s music stuck in my head, considering when I would be able to come back to Nocturne again.

The next night before the hafla, I began to put on my makeup in front of the bathroom mirror at my apartment. I ran black eyeliner around my lower and upper eyelids, carefully glued on false eyelashes, and as that dried, I applied foundation, a light blush, and lipstick. I added eye shadow and then drew a small and delicate tribal design around the outside corner of each of my eyes with black liquid eyeliner. Lastly, I applied a single bindi to my forehead, just above my eyebrow line.

I felt like a warrior dressing for battle. Trip hop music played in the other room as I continued to get ready. I put a few beads in my dreadlocks and then went to the closet to choose my costuming for my solo debut: ankle bells, dark harem pants, twenty-five-yard black skirt, coin belt, and a camel belt, which is a beautifully colorful and decorated piece of fabric art that dancers in this community would wrap around their waists. Mine had tassels hanging from it for an extra dynamic visual. It went over the top of the skirt, and then an intricate belt lay over it. My bottom half was ready. Then I chose a coin bra that matched my belts, and paused for just a moment as I pulled several heavy bracelets over my hands and to my wrists. I added a couple of bigger bracelets that slid all the way up to my narrow biceps, added a heavily jeweled necklace, large earrings that were lighter than they looked, and lastly, a few rings.

Then I had to go to the bathroom. *Damn it,* I thought. Normally I would go before even attempting to get ready, then fast from drinking anything until the performance was over so that I wouldn't have to go again in the meantime. I went back into the bathroom, pulled the low-hanging belts above my waist, hiked up the skirt, and pulled down the pants. As I sat and tried to keep the tassels on my camel belt from getting rained on, there was a knock on the door. "Really?" I said softly. I sighed and called to the door, "Who is it?" I would have said to come in, but living alone, it wasn't uncommon for me to leave the bathroom door wide open when I was in there. The guest knocked again as I called out and pulled my costume together once again. I washed my hands as I hollered, "Be right there!"

By the time my shenanigans were over and I opened my apartment door, Adrian was starting to leave the building. Against my conscious-ness, my heartbeat sped up slightly and my legs began to tingle. As I got ready for the hafla, I tried to mentally prepare myself to perform, to breathe deep, and to find my stage presence, but his arrival offered me a respite from belly dance costuming hell.

"Hey," I called to him from the doorway.

"Hey, you," he said, turning and coming back up the stairs toward me.

Moments later I let him walk into the apartment. When he saw me, he stopped for a moment and just watched me. There was something about it that made me feel so attractive. I could feel it in his presence and in the way he looked at me. He had seen me dressed in full performance wear before, so it wasn't like it was the first time. But whatever the reason, I liked it. I offered him a cup of coffee. Before he even answered, he closed the door behind him, then playfully pulled me toward him for a kiss. He smelled so good. *Why does he smell so good?* I thought. It was a mixture of patchouli and pot smoke. I could feel his chest through the T-shirt he wore under his unzipped coat, which I slipped off his shoulders and let fall to the floor as I disregarded my better judgment.

"What are we doing?" I said to him in between our kisses.

"I don't know. Let's just go with it."

"You do have protection this time, right?"

"I am prepared. For anything."

"Do we have time? I'm about to leave, and I've got all this stuff on . . ."

"I think I can find my way . . . ouch."

"Sorry! I think my coin bra scratched you."

"That's what I get for interrupting a belly dancer when she's getting ready to perform," he said.

I laughed as he lifted his shirt to see how bad the scratch was. There was a thin red line that marked his smooth skin. "Looks like I'll be late," I said as he undid all my costuming work. My only regret was the logistic reality that I would have to get ready all over again, but I accepted that. The sun began to set and soft light came through the windows as our clothes piled up in a heap on the floor, as if two strange creatures had been standing there and then disappeared, leaving only their earthly belongings.

The practical side of me worried about my coin belt and ankle bells becoming knotted together. I quickly let that thought go, along with the subconscious voice in my head that said that to push him onto the couch and wrap my legs around his waist was a bad idea. The flutters I felt in my stomach said otherwise as he ran his hands over my tattooed skin.

"You're glowing." Rosie's was the first familiar face that I saw when I got to the hafla. "Really, you're, like, glowing. What's up?"

"I'm not sure," I responded. But when I made eye contact with Rosie, I knew that wasn't cutting it. "You don't want to know."

"Did you just have sex? Oh my God, you just had sex."

Just then Adrian walked in and said hello to Rosie.

"Are you kidding me? Really?" She looked from one of us to the other in disbelief. She knew that it was hard for any woman to resist Adrian, but from what I could tell, she was peeved that I gave in to him.

"What? Everybody needs love," I told her as I tried to laugh it off so that there wouldn't be any awkwardness. I wanted the evening to go smoothly and certainly didn't want it to start off with Rosie upset with me for sleeping with Adrian. I enjoyed the impromptu visit, regardless of the surrounding politics.

"I got your 'love' right here," Rosie said sarcastically. "Listen, don't fuck this up, Summer. You're playing with fire."

Trying to make her less aggravated, I retorted, "I'm always playing with fire." For a moment she looked like she wanted to slap me in the face, but it didn't last.

"It's not just him, even though he's not worth it. I worry. If shit goes wrong, it could ruin everything we've built. It could break up the tribe."

Her words made my chest ache with pain. "I would never let that happen," I said, wanting to believe it.

"I've come a long way from where I used to be. I've worked with a lot of people in this business, and it's the same across the board. But this, us, it's different. This is more than business, and you guys are like my family." She then said lightly, "This is like incest."

"Ewww," I said. "It is not. Besides, it wasn't a problem with Rhiannon, so why would it be a problem with me?"

"I never said it wasn't a problem with Rhiannon. It may have been fine, but who knows how long it would've lasted. He could leave any day and nothing would really change. But now, it's not just him and Rhiannon, it's him and Rhiannon and you. And that's a smokeless fire."

Chapter 24

BUZZKILL

It all seemed glamorous somehow—the shows, the attention, the praise—even though in the end, I was still hiking up a twenty-five-yard skirt to squat in a porta-potty or, more recently, dressing in '80s clothes to share my talent with a tipsy bar crowd. Looking around at my fire-dancing cohorts who were local, national, and international, I began to realize that not even the best belly dancer or fire artist on the planet had any kind of mainstream reputation. Very, very few could make a decent, steady, reliable living by teaching and performing. Maybe fame was part of what I wanted. Is that what anyone who gets up on a stage for any reason desires? Having a day job made it okay for me to "play" on the side. The extra money was decent, as it sometimes was enough to cover my gas money and pay for a meal. Maybe I could just work harder to make it happen.

I questioned if I could go full-time with it. Would I ever be able to afford a house? Or vacations? And even if so, how long could it possibly last? I was in my midtwenties, and yet I felt that there was an expiration date on my belly dancing days. I could foresee the day when I would no longer be able to get the detailed black liquid eyeliner to hold a delicate tribal shape around the inevitable soft wrinkles that would form around the corners of my eyes. And I knew that when someone contacted us to hire a belly dancer, they would not be expecting a group of middle-aged women who would need to call it a night early so we could get up at eight a.m. to go into the office the next day. The general public has a preconceived notion of what a belly dancer is, and there was little in my power to change that except to continue to perform and educate them by way of example.

It was a conundrum, but I chose to simply put it out of my mind for as long as I could, and continue to ride the wave of momentum that I was on. It was as these thoughts streamed through my mind over breakfast one morning that I received an e-mail notice on my phone. It was another gig opportunity. This time it was for a private party.

> From: Chris Schmidt
> Subject: birthday party
>
> Hello,
> I saw your group when you did the Cincinnati Sadistic Ladeez halftime show a while back, and I'm interested in having a belly dancer and/or fire dancer show up at a birthday party I'm throwing for my son, who's turning 16. Are you available on December 5? I'm not sure how long you perform, or what you charge; please let me know more details.
> Thanks,
> Chris

At least one person didn't notice our snafu with the wax on the Roller Derby floor, I thought. I checked my calendar, and the date was open for me, so next I texted Rosie, Morgan, and Phoenix. I put in Rhiannon's phone number out of habit and then frowned when I remembered that she was so far away. I texted our group:

Birthday party gig 12/5. In?

Rosie texted me back right away with a negative, because she had already registered for a live "Robert Downey Junior Answers Fan Questions" webinar. I rolled my eyes with a smile as I responded to her text: *Dork*.

Phoenix texted me back and said he would be out of town for a fitness training retreat.

Morgan had not yet responded, so I put the phone down and went to the bathroom. When I checked it again, there was still no response. Next I went to my kitchen to clean my breakfast dishes and make a cup of Earl Grey tea. As it steeped, I heard my phone beep with a text alert. It was Morgan:

In! Woot!

Cool. Will let you know more details asap.

I grabbed my tea and sat down at my laptop to reply to Chris.

> Dear Chris,
> Thank you for contacting me regarding your son's birthday party. I'm happy to let you know that I have two dancers available. We can provide a mixed show of belly dance and fire arts, for twenty minutes total, for $750. We'll bring one fire safety and a PA for our music, and will arrive around 9:00 p.m. (the darker, the better, for fire arts). I've attached a contract for your review; please sign and return to me at your earliest convenience.
> We're looking forward to providing the entertainment at your party!
> Sincerely,
> Summer

Next, I texted Adrian:

> You free on 12/5?

He responded within just a few sips of tea.

> Yep. S'up? You finally going to go on a real date with me? ;)

> Uhhhh . . . actually, I wanted to see if you'd safety for me and Morgan at a gig. Lol. And yes.

> Sure, and cool.

> There's a party at my friend's place later on tonight. Pick me up at 9:00?

> Mmmmhhhmmm.

I smiled. He was so cute. I finished my tea and then made another cup to drink while I sat next to the living room window and watched inspiring fire arts videos for a while. I eventually went to the store to buy some groceries, stopped at the bank to make a deposit, and swung by the post office to get some stamps. It was the kind of uneventful afternoon that made me crave the rush I felt with our gigs. Once at home, I did some laundry and light cleaning to pass the time. Before I knew it, it was 8:50. I was almost, but not quite, ready for the party. I put on a pair of jeans and a T-shirt and pulled my dreads back into two ponytails for fun. I applied just a little makeup that I considered mandatory for leaving my apartment: eyeliner and some lip gloss. As I dabbed a touch of scented oils on my wrists and behind my ears, Adrian knocked on the door and then turned the handle to walk in.

"Hey, lover," he said as I walked toward him. We embraced, and he softly inhaled my perfume. "I could eat that."

"Ermergerd, stop it." I laughed. He laughed, too, at my silly response, and I started to take his hand as we left the apartment, then changed my mind. That's something that boyfriends and girlfriends do, and it still felt like we weren't quite there. Yet.

The car ride to the party was relatively quiet as we listened to a CD of Kyle and Edward's music. We chatted about who we could expect to see at the party, how our day was—nothing serious. I was beginning to wonder if Adrian ever got into deep conversations. Whenever we did talk, he was pretty brief, but I just considered him to be concise. He joked a lot, so maybe he was more comfortable keeping things light. *I can stay light,* I told myself, ignoring the thought that maybe he wasn't mature enough for serious *anything.* When we arrived at the party we barely found a place to park because there were so many cars lining the driveway. We found a spot on the street, got out of the car, and walked toward the house, where there was a sign that said, WELCOME HOME. COME AROUND TO THE BACK, HIPPIES! Kyle was standing nearby talking with someone.

"We were just listening to your beats in the car," Adrian said to him.

"Cool. Which CD was it?" Kyle asked.

"Does it matter?" Adrian said, smiling. "Actually, I really have no idea. Summer put it on."

"And how's Summer tonight?" Kyle said as he turned to me.

"I'm well. Good to see you, as always."

"Likewise," he said, bowing slightly as Adrian and I continued on toward the rest of the party.

It was dark, and the path was lit with torches. We could hear voices and music, and as we walked around the corner into the backyard we found about thirty friends—and friends of friends—sitting, standing, and dancing around a large bonfire. Someone played an acoustic guitar, and a couple of guys were laying down beats on hand drums. Once again,

I was in my element. Everyone welcomed us with hugs and hellos, and we found a spot on a fallen tree trunk that was used as a bench.

"Hey." A young woman I didn't recognize gently poked Adrian in the arm. "You want some of this?" He accepted the joint from her, took a toke from it, then continued passing it around the fire circle. "Follow me," she said to him.

He looked at me and shrugged, so I returned his shrug and watched the fire as it flicked into the air, lighting the faces of our friends.

"Did you bring your fire poi?" a friend named Collin asked me.

"Do bears shit in the woods?" I laughed as I nodded. I rarely went anywhere without my fire gear, especially if there was even a remote possibility that I would be able to dance with it.

"All right!" Collin responded. Everyone was always stoked to see me and the tribe come to a party because it meant an extra dose of entertainment. The fire dancing, coupled with the music our friends played, the stars, the bonfire—it was a recipe for magic. As the joint made its way back around the circle, I told my friends to call me "Skip" because it is much easier (and safer) to manipulate a fire prop when sober, for me anyway. They continued to pass it along, and I sat contentedly taking in the scene.

The music continued as some of our friends began to dance around the fire. I gazed around and felt so much gratitude for this life that I was living. I was thankful to be under the stars enjoying the space, these wonderful people, and the organic music, and knowing that Adrian was near. I had become more attracted to him with each moment we shared. Every time I performed when he was there, I added an extra touch of sensuality. I made sure that I would catch his eye as I danced for myself, and for him. And now there were no barriers. Not seeing him, but assuming he was mingling nearby somewhere, I stood up and walked away to get my fire gear. The tribal music was right and the setting was perfect. Unlike when I performed at gigs, I felt like I could truly just be myself. This was about being creative, about expressing myself through movement, about sharing the experience with friends, who were there to do the same.

I took off my jacket, which had a tag that labeled it 95 percent nylon, 5 percent cotton—in other words, flammable—and laid it aside as I prepared my fire poi.

"You look ready to go," Kyle said to me.

"Kyle! I didn't see you there," I said to him as I gathered my gear. "I think I am ready, but I don't know where Adrian wandered off to," I said. "I'd like to go ahead and light up now, so that I can have a drink. Will you safety for me?"

"Happy to oblige," he said.

I thanked him as I handed him my duvetyne, the flame-resistant material that I always kept on hand. It was a special fabric that could smother the flames on fire props or people. With my poi soaked in fuel, I gently put them inside of my spin-off bottle to collect the excess fuel. This prevented me from throwing lit fuel into the crowd and saved a few cents, since I could pour it back into my dip can and reuse it.

I stepped into the circle of our friends around the bonfire, which was within a large circle of sand. Everyone shifted back to clear a space for me as I gently swung one of the poi wicks into the flames. It caught immediately, and I used it to light the other poi in my hand and began to move in circles. The music began to change, to mimic my own movements, and together, the musicians and I created an ephemeral art that would never be repeated again in exactly the same way. I felt that this moment in time was recognized by the others who were there, who came to the party with great expectations of magical, artistic marriages of music and dance.

What I didn't expect was an accident.

As I danced, spinning the two balls of flame around my body, my footing faltered. While I normally had an excellent sense of balance from my years of training, not to mention the many times I had performed on uneven surfaces at numerous gigs, I wasn't able to recover quickly enough. I tried to stay upright, not fall into anyone else or the fire, and keep out of the way of the fire poi swinging from my hands. I succeeded at all but one. One of the chains that had so many times moved with me, parallel to my arms, now found its way around my elbow, wrapped as snugly as though it were a boa constrictor taking its prey.

I felt the burn immediately as the hot metal seared into my skin. I immediately steadied my balance and swung my arm in the opposite direction of the chain so that it would unwind from my arm. My friends sat in shock and confusion. The music stopped, and Kyle ran up to me with the duvetyne in his hands. I dropped the fire poi to the ground where they lay quietly burning the last of the fuel that was left in their wicks. At this point the duvetyne itself was useless.

"Fu-huck," I moaned as I looked for the damage on my arm.

"What can I do?" Kyle was desperate to help as quickly as he could and handed me a clear plastic bottle. "Here's some water." I slowly poured the water over my arm, on which was forming a red tattoo of chain marks spiraling around it. I wanted to cry, but two things stopped me: One was thankfulness that I wasn't hurt even worse. I knew that the fire could just as easily have hit me in the face and even landed in my eyes. Or I could have lost my equilibrium all together and landed in the bonfire itself or taken someone with me. The other thing that stopped me from crying was pride. I was too embarrassed to admit just how badly it hurt, and I didn't want to call any more attention to myself for this fire faux pas. To escape the scene, I said to Kyle, "Let's go over there by the lights, where we can see better. I have some ointment I can use right now."

He followed me and carried my gear bag. Inside of it, I found a bottle of burn cream that I always carried, just in case, and a standard first aid kit. Kyle helped me tend to the burn as I caught my breath and began to calm down from the scare.

"That was a buzzkill." I looked up and saw Adrian, wondering what in the hell kind of thing that was to say in this moment. I had enough to deal with, from the discomfort of the burn and the frustrating reality that I would have to re-enter the party and be cool. I wished that I had an announcer to protect me: *Nothing to see folks. Move along.* I was so mad at myself. I had never tangled my fire poi before, and I hated to admit that I did just then. "Are you okay?" Kyle offered, looking from my arm to my eyes.

"I will be. Thanks for helping me out there, and back here. I'm shaken up still. It just happened so quickly. What the hell?"

"I'm so sorry. Do you know what happened? I was watching you, and it looked like you might've tripped on something."

"Speaking of tripping . . . ," Adrian interrupted.

"I didn't trip on anything; I just lost my balance or something. Maybe I was spinning around too much. I don't know. I'm just glad that it's not worse," I said to Kyle. Then I turned to Adrian and said, "Are you okay to drive? Give me your keys. I'll take the wheel tonight."

Kyle ignored Adrian and said, "Do you need to go to the hospital? It looks pretty bad."

"No, really. I'll be fine. I don't think it's as bad as it could've been, and this cream works well. It just hurts. I don't want to go back out there yet, either. I feel like a jackass."

"You're so *not* a jackass. You're a badass. I bet everyone's worried. We should get back to the bonfire and at least let 'em know you're okay."

"Can I just sit here for a minute?"

"I'll sit with you," Adrian said. Kyle looked at me for approval, and I nodded my head.

"You do that," Kyle said. "I'll be over there if you need anything, Summer."

Adrian sat on the ground up against the house and motioned for me to join him. I felt like I needed to be in my own headspace, so instead of sitting next to him, I stood, leaning on the wall, even though I craved the comfort. After all, he wasn't there for me when I needed him a few minutes ago, so why should I need him now? He didn't seem to notice. The music began again, and we quietly listened to our friends mingle, play, and laugh as they were before. I heard footsteps, then saw Chloe, an acquaintance I knew from Dance Mecca, come around the corner of the house.

"There you are! Are you okay? What happened? Everyone's worried, but we didn't want to bombard you."

"Hey, Chloe. I'm fine. I'll be fine. Don't worry," I responded. I thought that was sweet. It took some of the sting out of the burn.

"Oh my God, that was scary, though. I wanted to run back here with you, but I didn't think there was anything I could do to help, and I knew that Kyle was with you. You sure you're all right?"

"Yes, dear. It didn't burn too much. It'll probably just be red for a while. I put some ointment on it, and a bandage that I had in my first aid kit." I smiled at her to reassure her that I was honestly okay.

"Hmmm, if you say so. Would a drink make it any better?" She offered me a bottle of beer.

"I think I'll pass. After this, I'm just not in the mood, but thanks."

"Well, you know where it is if you change your mind, honey. I'll catch you guys back by the bonfire."

"Thanks," Adrian replied. As Chloe left, we sat listening to the party for a few minutes. I was lost in my own thoughts about my arm and what had happened when Adrian asked me, "You ready to head back now?"

"That sounds good. Since things have returned to normal out there, I won't feel so weird making an entrance." I smiled again and we stood together, Adrian kindly trying to help me even though I didn't need his assistance. Back at the bonfire, the music continued as my friends checked on me here and there. I enjoyed the rest of the evening with Adrian's arm protectively resting around me, and I contentedly accepted his affection. At one point, I turned my head to look at him, and he tilted his head to kiss me. My senses heightened and my frustration with him softened. I closed my eyes and felt like I could hear each musical note and each pop of the bonfire amid the murmur and laughter of conversations. I felt the warmth of the fire, Adrian's arm still around my shoulder, my feet on the soft ground, and his lips connecting me to him. All of this made it easier for me to ignore the bad taste left in my mouth from a single word that I couldn't quite let go: *buzzkill*.

Chapter 25

FEAR

My neighborhood was as quiet as a cloud that night. Adrian brought me home and we said good night to each other with our typical hug and then one more kiss. Once inside I left my laptop closed and instead chose to sit by the living room window and listen to the crickets through the thin windowpane as I drank a cup of tea to wind down from the evening.

I was glad that Adrian was there with me at the party. That single word that he uttered, *buzzkill*, still rang in my ears. It told me everything I needed to know, and yet I wanted to remain naive. Adrian was so easy on the eyes, and he made my heart flutter when he was near. Part of me wanted to think that there was something about his just being there, and coming to help Kyle help me so quickly when the accident happened. But then I knew that if he was really into me, that it would've been *him* instead of Kyle who was by my side to begin with. I was glad that I had asked Kyle to be my fire safety since Adrian wasn't around, but before this happened I had only come close to having any kind of a problem, the first time I lit up. Other than that I only needed a safety for putting out the poi flames when I was finished with them. This was because sometimes I finished dancing with them before the flames died down on their own from the fuel evaporating. I wanted Adrian before, but I had *needed* him that night. A voice in the back of mind kept whispering, *He wasn't there*, and it was layered on top of another voice, that of Rosie's, telling me that I should just stay away from him. But that was when Rhiannon was in the picture, and things were different now. But were they different for Adrian? Perhaps. I didn't want to go out of my way to ruin a good thing, and I had other things, more important things, to consider, I told myself.

As far as the burn, I played it all much cooler than I truly felt, for in reality, I was very scared. I was afraid to look under the bandage because I knew my stomach wouldn't be able to handle it if there was any serious damage, so I tried to ignore the discomfort and just relax. The bigger problem was fear. In the back of my mind, I could feel it wrapping its fingers around my love of fire arts and planting seeds of doubt about whether I should continue fire dancing after this. My next performance was the following weekend, at Club Nocturne. I would be expected not only to eat fire, which was relatively safe as far as tools were concerned, but also to spin fire poi and use my fire hoop. The hoop was notorious for the closeness of its flame—and not just one, but five wicks, spinning around my waist, and even my neck, when I felt bold enough to do so.

To be honest, the doubt and the fear that skimmed the waters of my mind when I first began dancing in public had never truly disappeared. I simply kept them well at bay. I knew that fear would mean the death of my passion for performing, especially with fire, which was the pulse of my existence. It made my blood flow through my veins, made me feel alive, made me want to live. Who was I, if not a fire dancer? And the more I sat and drank my tea and thought about all of these things, the more terrified I became of the thought of lighting up my fire tools again, especially so soon after this scare. I had to keep my momentum going and either stop thinking about the burn or accept it. The possibility of a burn was always there, and statistically, it was amazing that I never slipped up before this incident. I remembered Leslie's first lessons about fire arts, and the sage advice that she shared about getting burned: *It's not if—it's when, and how bad.* But as many fire artists as I had met at various parties, performances, and festivals, I never heard of anyone simply stopping because they got hurt once, or twice for that matter. It was just part of the deal, and perhaps part of the thrill.

From the audience's perspective it was certainly part of the excitement. If it was completely safe, anyone would do it, and it wouldn't be so freakishly beautiful in its own right. And that's another reason that I loved it so. I didn't want to be just a dancer of ballet or jazz. I wanted to push my limits. Perhaps, although I never admitted it out loud, I still felt the deeply rooted insults of my teen years as well, which told me that I was too plain, too ugly even, to continue dancing anywhere other than the sheltered boundaries of my own living room. The burn seemed to have gone beneath the skin to my ego somehow, and I needed to suffocate these negative thoughts. It was getting late, so I decided to sleep it off, as a tired mind tends to welcome irrational ideas.

When I stood up to take my teacup into the kitchen, my phone beeped with a text message from Adrian:

Just checking on you; you okay?

I just looked at it for a moment, not sure if I was okay, but I knew that I would be before too long. I kept it positive:

Yes. Going to sleep now. Good night. See you soon?

I hope. Wish you weren't sleeping alone.

I raised an eyebrow. He was such a flirt. I gave it right back, just for fun.

There's always next time . . .

Sweet.

Good night, Adrian.

Good night, lover.

He called me lover, I thought. It was flattering, and I began to have second thoughts about going straight to bed. Suddenly I remembered his flirting at Cincinnati Burns, and those thoughts led to Nailface Nina, and how inspired I was by her sideshow performance. I never did follow up with her about how to learn human blockhead. Maybe now was the time to try it.

Forgoing the idea of going to sleep, I reached up into my closet and pulled down my little toolbox. It didn't contain much because I didn't need much in the way of handyman tools, just a small hammer, a measuring tape, a flashlight, and a few different types of nails. I picked up the nails and fingered through them in my palm. There were corkscrews, pin-like nails, and three-inch nails that were smooth, although sharp. I took one of these and placed the rest back into the toolbox.

Inspecting the nail, I pushed it into the skin of my index finger to see just how sharp it was. It left a perfect pinpoint dot pushed into the small pad of my finger, reminding me of the night in high school when I took a blade to my own wrist. *At least there's an art to it this time,* I thought, hoping that if my parents ever saw me perform this, they wouldn't be forced into remembering that horrible night of my most selfish act. But they wouldn't see the behind-the-scenes trials and errors that I might experience. I hoped I wouldn't have any errors, at least, as I studied the nail.

I sat down in front of my makeup mirror, where normally I spent time putting on eye shadow and mascara, making myself prettier for the stage and in a somewhat-traditional sense. But maybe putting a nail into my face was a beautiful act. As I leaned forward and held it close to my nose, I felt again like I was pushing against the boundaries that kept me from being as colorful or unique—whatever you want to call it—as I was meant to be, or as I was.

The nail felt cold inside my nostril, and my eyes watered as I gently, slowly pushed it inside. It actually tickled, and when I felt a sneeze coming on, I had to quickly pull the nail out before I jerked my head from the reaction of it. I wiped the nail with a washcloth, looked at myself in the mirror and knew that I had better try again before I began to think too much about what I was doing.

The second try was just as slow, but I kept the nail straight and convinced myself that it didn't tickle. It couldn't tickle. I had to do this. I kept watching my progress in the mirror as I worked its way in a little deeper than the first time. For some reason I felt like I needed to avoid eye contact with myself, at least while I was trying this. It felt so strange, but strange was my normal, so it felt instinctual. It felt human—more real than anything I could've been doing with my cell phone or computer.

With my eyes watering too much to see, I removed the nail and wiped it on the towel again. *Third time's the charm,* I thought, leaning forward once more and pushing the nail into my face—yes, I was pushing the nail into my face—until it was two inches in, and only one inch remained visible. I let go.

I let go.

I let go.

I can do anything.

Chapter 26

PRETTY GIRLS WHO CAN DANCE

A week passed and gave me enough time to heal both physically and emotionally from the burn I got at the party. I found that my mind drifted to Adrian more and more, and although I wanted to see him every day, I didn't want to rush things or do anything that would change the nature of our relationship too quickly. Dance was the only other thing on my mind, and I looked forward to performing with Morgan at Club Nocturne that evening, where the theme was "White Wedding." We were expected to wear white costuming for our appearance. With this being our second time at the club, I knew we needed to make a lasting impression and put our best show on, so we could continue the run. *This may be our big break,* I thought. As I listened to the rain tap my bathroom window while I applied my false eyelashes, I got a text from my partner for the gig.

Would you hate me if I had to back out of tonight's gig?

Damn it, I thought, staring at the phone in my hand. In my mind, the show must go on. Period. I put on my diplomacy hat and responded with understanding—at least, what could pass as understanding in a text message. Maybe.

Can I ask why?

Had a hell of a week at work. I feel horrible and just really need some downtime.

Hope you feel better soon! I'll figure something out.

Thank you! I'm so sorry to leave you hanging. Don't hate me?

Of course not. Take care!

I felt the need to vent to someone, so I called Adrian. I paced around my apartment as the phone rang until he answered. "Can I bitch for just a minute?" I asked when he answered the phone.

"Yeah. Go ahead. What's wrong?"

"Morgan bailed on our Nocturne gig for tonight. Rosie was already busy, which means that I'll have to go by myself, carry the act through the whole night, and I still need a fire safety." Even as the last words came out of my mouth, I realized that I could ask Adrian to come along to safety for me while I was fire dancing.

"That sucks," he said. "I'm actually free tonight. Do you want me to safety for you?"

"Great minds think alike," I told him. "Let's meet at the club by 8:45. Cool?"

"Sounds good. See you then, babe."

"Adrian, thank you."

"Happy to help."

With this minor catastrophe solved for the time being, I continued getting ready for the gig and sent an e-mail to Mona to make sure she knew that we would have only one fire dancer for the evening. False lashes in place, it was time to go to work on my dreadlocks.

Once at Club Nocturne, I took my place on one of the raised platforms as Adrian went to the bar for a club soda. I looked out over the dance floor, which was relatively empty compared to how it had been the last time I was there. "Where is everybody?" I asked the DJ, who looked at the monitors with a bored expression.

"Saturdays are usually our busiest night. It might be the weather. People freak out when it rains for some reason. It might pick up later, though."

I nodded and continued on, although it was more difficult than last time. It was one thing to dance and get into the party mood when I was surrounded by a hundred or so others who were already having a good time, but it was another thing entirely to have to be the only one living it up on the floor. I knew that I was basically bait for the patrons. People are more likely to start dancing if there is already someone else who is out there with them. I also felt "off" because I hadn't lit up any of my fire tools since the previous weekend, and although I was fighting it tooth and nail, I felt gun-shy about using my fire poi and hoop. Fortunately, the rain was still steadily falling, and this gave me a solid excuse not to use them. Part of me hoped that it would continue to rain hard enough that no one would want to go outside to the patio and fire dancing area, but a stronger part wanted to battle the demons of my fear, and I wished that the clouds would move along and allow me to come to peace with fire dancing.

As I danced alone on the platform, Betty, the club manager who was also my agent's contact, approached me. "Summer, you can go home now."

I was surprised. The night was young, and I didn't realize that it would be a possibility that I could be sent home early. "Is it because the crowd is so light?"

"Yes. I think I'll just have the servers handle it for tonight, since we're so dead."

I stepped off the platform and went to get Adrian and my things. "We're going home," I told him.

"Really? Well, it's pretty shitty out. I guess it's not worth it to pay for the entertainment when so few people are here."

"Well, they're going to pay me, because my contract says so." On our way out the door I had Betty sign my work voucher and confirm in writing that the club would pay me in full.

"So what now?" Adrian asked once we were outside, walking toward our cars. "Want to hang out still? Go to my place, or yours?"

"That sounds good," I said. "Doesn't matter to me where."

"Follow me, then. We'll go to my apartment and we can watch a movie or something."

"Or something," I replied. We smiled at each other and waved as we got into our respective cars.

On the drive over my thoughts drifted to the evening at the club. It seemed strange that they would have sent me home so early, and I was bummed out that I went through so much trouble to get there. I did my stage makeup and came up with white costuming pieces for practically nothing. But business was business, and I figured that it shouldn't matter too much, since I got paid either way. I was glad, though, that Morgan hadn't wasted her time and effort, and that Adrian had been free to spend the evening with me. Not to mention that I was all dressed up with nowhere else to go but home with him. I made a mental note to contact the agency to find out when they would book me and/or the girls again. Hopefully we would get it every month, because it paid well and would look good on our collective resume.

Once at Adrian's apartment, I left my fire gear in the car and walked up the steps, where he waited for me on the front porch. I started to say something, some sort of small talk about the rain or the drive over, when he pulled me close and kissed me on the mouth. I was still and let him, forgetting any doubts I had. It was just what I needed after the letdown of not performing that night, and especially after not reconciling my relationship with my fire poi. The rain fell just beyond the porch. When the wind began to blow it toward us, Adrian opened the door, and we went inside. There, we silently undressed each other in the dark. He spoke first and said, "I will probably go to hell for the things I want to do to you right now."

I shook my head and giggled in spite of myself. "Way to be romantic," I half joked.

"I can't help it," he said. "I hope you know how beautiful you are. Temptress."

"Oh," I said, blushing. No one had ever called me that before. I felt like a queen. *A dirty queen.* I laughed to myself.

"What?"

"Nothing," I said. "Keep going."

And he did, until I left Adrian's place late that night.

A few days later, I was lounging around my apartment, fresh out of a hot shower, sipping a cup of coffee as I checked my e-mail. There was a message from Rosie asking how Saturday night had gone and another from Morgan saying that she felt better. I read a follow-up e-mail from Chris about the birthday party for his son, who was "grounded indefinitely"— for what, I could only guess. I imagined this teen who was well-off enough that his parents would hire entertainers for his sweet sixteen, and what he possibly could have done to upset them. I stopped snickering when I read that Chris regretfully canceled the party. Lastly, there was an e-mail from the talent agency.

> Dear Summer,
> Betty from Club Nocturne contacted me last night regarding our arrangement. Unfortunately, they are not interested in booking you for the future, but I wanted to let you know right away so that you could book other gigs if possible. Thank you for your time. Your check is in the mail.
> Best regards,
> Mona

Confused, I finished my coffee as I scanned the e-mail over a few more times, trying to read into the problem. I decided to call Mona.

"Mona here, can I help you?"

"Hi, Mona. This is Summer. I read your message and thought it'd be best to call you to talk about it. Can I ask why this isn't working out? My other dancer was sick last night, and I hope that didn't cause too big of a problem for the club."

"It wasn't that, although we do hate to send only one person when they're expecting two," she said and then paused for a moment to cough. "I hate to tell you this, honey, but since you called me, I might as well be honest. Betty told me that you're just not what they're looking for."

"Oh." I expected to negotiate, to have a discussion, but not to be flat out told "no."

"She said that they're looking for pretty girls who can dance."

Now this cut even deeper. Although I didn't even know how to respond, I knew that I didn't want to burn any bridges. I quietly thanked Mona for her time and hung up the phone. And then I cried.

Pain is a funny thing that can have two faces. It is physical and emotional. It is buried and yet it isn't so far below the surface. Sometimes it can make an appearance when summoned by unwanted memories. I *knew* that I was pretty. I *knew* that I was a wonderful dancer. But I knew these things only because it's what others told me with their specific words and showed through their sincere actions. Just about every time I performed, I landed a contract for another gig, and there was not a time that went by without at least one guy—and hell, sometimes even a girl here or there—flirting with me relentlessly when I danced. Even Adrian, whom I felt attracted to from the beginning, always complimented me either with words or with his eyes. And I, like a mirror, reflected these things until I became them. But Betty's words, repeated so harshly by Mona, wounded me more than the recent burn that was just another distant memory now. I was shocked that Betty was so rude to have said that, and also that Mona didn't have the common decency to at least edit the comment that was directed so personally at another woman.

I couldn't stop crying. My eyes were swollen and red, and my hair hung down in my face. I lay down on the floor and heaved sobs, while emotions from as far back as my high school years bubbled up . . . painful and insulting words and phrases from that time echoed in the sound of Mona's voice. I cried long enough to begin thinking rationally, and tried to turn the negative thoughts around. I guess in my heart I knew from the beginning that Club Nocturne wasn't the place for me to be sharing my dance, but I wanted it to be. The allure of being desired by a talent agency inflated my ego just enough to convince me to ignore my intuition. I was in denial about the fit, even when I compared myself to the other go-go dancers and servers, who were dressed more scantily than I would ever have been at a club or anywhere else. I didn't want the kind of attention that I would have gotten if I continued working at Nocturne. These thoughts became my mantra as I washed my face with a cold towel and pushed my shoulders back to stand straight again.

It seemed like between the burn at the party and this burn of an insult, I would need to do something drastic to keep my head above water if I wanted to continue on this path. I needed to clear my head, so I took a walk to figure out how I would protect my tribal sisters from the possibility of experiencing the same hurtful interactions. I wanted to save them the pain that I felt now, in case Betty would say the same thing about my amazing friends whose talents were beyond that of the thumping night-club with indiscriminate drunks. I would have to tell the rest of the tribe that this gig was canceled. Stepping outside, the crisp air felt good against my face, and I welcomed the cool breeze that seemed to brush the negativity out of my spirit as I walked, searching for internal harmony.

Chapter 27

TWO TEARS IN A BUCKET

At the next practice, I was tempted to tell my friends about what happened, but I couldn't bear to do it. Several days had passed, enough time to begin to heal from the insult and to push forward, once again not letting fears and reservations hold me back. I had no choice but to conquer them. Once everyone arrived at Rosie's and settled in, I took a drink from my glass of wine and announced with my best poker face that the Club Nocturne gig was over. Morgan was the first to speak.

"Oh no," she gasped, holding her hand up to her mouth in shock. "It wasn't because of me, was it?"

"No. Don't worry. It wasn't you," I said.

"Good," she said, although her brow was still furrowed.

I went on to explain with the white lie I had finally decided to come up with. "It was a combination of their budget and their insurance company freaking out about the fire. They said they already had enough regular dancers there and only needed us because we brought fire to the club."

"Who the hell do they think they are?" asked Rosie. "First they book us; then they dump us. I bet we could bring in tons of extra money for them. People drive all the way from Columbus to see us."

"Please, just let it go," I said, not wanting her to raise too much hell about it. I was afraid that if she pushed too much, I would break down and tell them the horrifying truth.

"Two tears in a bucket. It's not like we won't have other gigs come up," Morgan said optimistically. "There's always something, and this way we won't be locked down to just one place. It'll give us more flexibility."

"I'm so glad you understand," I said. "Rosie, you cool?"

"Not really, but it's not like I can do anything about this one, I guess. Fuck 'em."

I looked at Adrian, who smiled and winked at me. I wanted to tell him the truth, but it hurt so bad, and some irrational part of me was afraid that if he heard what the agent said, then he might agree with her. Perhaps if I hadn't been bullied when I was younger, I wouldn't have had this self-doubt. But still, the insult cut me deeply.

Having jumped the hurdle of announcing the end of this gig, we moved on to talk about other troupe-related things, like costuming, the possibility of choreographing dances together with fire, and music choices that would be good for future gigs. It was all so normal and familiar; I was able to relax. I knew that I could have talked to any of them about what happened, but I was so embarrassed that I couldn't bring myself to tell anyone.

"The paperwork's all done, so now all I need to do is wait," Rosie was saying. I had zoned out of the conversation, lost in my thoughts. "I need to buy my textbooks, too, though. But I'm just about ready."

"I think I tranced out," I admitted. "What did I just miss?"

"Rosie's going back to school, for real," Morgan answered. "Getting her degree, like a grown-up or something." She reached over the coffee table and jokingly pinched Rosie on the leg.

"Gotta do it sometime, I guess," Rosie said. "I've thought about it for too long. I'm not fucking around with my life anymore. I'll go to school and work during the week, we'll have our gigs on the weekends, and it'll all work out."

"That sounds like a lot," Adrian said. "It might be harder than you think, especially with homework and everything. Not that that should stop you, but it's something you might want to consider."

"I'll deal with it when I need to," she said. "Just do my best. I don't really have any other choice. I want a better job, ya know?"

"We understand," I answered. "I'm happy for you, and proud of you! Just let me know if there's anything I can do to make your life easier. Got it?"

"Watch what you say . . . I might take you up on that and ask you to cook dinner for me once in a while."

"Name the date!" Everything was going to be okay, I knew. I stood up and stretched, then went to Rosie's kitchen to put my wine glass in the sink. When I returned to the living room, Rosie was telling Morgan about how she thought that Robert Downey Junior looked "so freaking fantastic" both with and without facial hair, and she just couldn't decide which she preferred. Morgan patiently listened, since it was all she could do. I contemplated the same conundrum, for just a moment (without facial hair, I thought), then announced that I was ready to head out for the night. I waved good-bye to everyone and Adrian stood to walk me outside to my car.

"Everything okay? You seemed just off tonight, or something," he said to me. I wasn't sure if it was because of remnants from the Club Nocturne fiasco, so I played it cool.

"Yeah, everything's fine. Thanks for asking, though." He leaned in and kissed me, and I immediately forgot about both issues that just moments ago had plagued my mind. Why did he smell so good all the time? He apparently knew that taking a moment to dab on a drop of scented oils would be worth the effort. Appreciating the attention, and the confirmation that I was attractive and desirable, I lifted my hands and rested them on his cheeks as he put his hands on my waist and held me close. It was just what I needed.

"You okay to drive?" He still held me as he asked.

"I'm fine, thanks. I only had one glass. I'm just tired and ready to go home."

"What really happened, with the club? Did I miss something that night?"

I paused before answering. For me, the truth was never more than a blink away, and even white lies came to light sooner rather than later. "I suck at lying," I said.

He waited, the silence giving me a moment to come up with the words.

"I was fired. Not what they're looking for. They don't want us back." Like a bandage. Feel the sting.

"I guess I'm not shocked."

"Really." It was a statement rather than a question.

"I mean, they are looking for a certain, well, look," he said. If he felt sympathetic in any way, it wasn't showing.

"There ya go, then. I don't have *that* look."

"No, but, you can't blame them. Aw shit," he said when he saw my reaction. "Fuck it."

"Yeah, fuck it. Thanks for the wonderful pep talk and inspiring words. Much appreciated."

"You know what I mean, Summer."

"Adrian, I don't want to be a *buzzkill*, but I think we're—this—is done. Over. It was good while it lasted." I was furious. Rosie had warned me. The fire accident warned me. And now this. Not here for me when I need him. Again.

He stepped away from me and put his hands in his pockets. He let out a laugh, short and sharp, and tilted his head back in what I could only interpret as complete arrogance. "So that's the way it's going to be. Can I still pull your hair once in a while?"

"You wish." I got into my car, regretting that I had told him anything, and began to drive home, reliving the argument but also all our moments together that were good, and sexy, and . . . exaggerated? Had I made it more than it was?

Once at my apartment, I gave in to the tears that had threatened to drop, no matter how much I tried to ignore them and not give in to the emotions. By crying, I was admitting to myself that I cared about him and that somewhere in my mind at least, we had a potential future. As I let go, I refused to think about the surrounding issues and how all of this was going to affect the tribe. I sat with my knees up to my chest, softly rocking to try to soothe myself back to a calm state, and to try to stop giving so much of a fuck about Adrian.

I took off my necklace, earrings, rings, and bracelets, pulled my dreads back into a low ponytail, and got into my flannel, tie-dyed pajamas. I flipped on the television to watch a DVR'd episode of *Austin City Limits*, and hit "Play" when it highlighted Alison Kraus as the performer. *Something to soothe the soul,* I thought. As I tucked my feet under me on the couch, my mind meandered to thoughts of Adrian.

I wondered why I thought that things could or would work out so well with him. I knew, in the back of my mind, that it couldn't possibly end like a fairy tale. There was the complication of him probably expecting some kind of open relationship, plus how weird things could get in our troupe if it went downhill with him. He was one of our safeties, after all. As much as I wanted him, things just weren't clicking. Maybe it was because that now that I could have him, I no longer wanted him. Maybe it was the chase I was in love with. *Why did it have to be so complicated?* I thought.

I also couldn't help but wonder if he was thinking the same thing the agent said, that I wasn't pretty enough. I took a deep breath and let it out along with an intentional release of any anger I felt.

Emotionally exhausted, I resigned to the bliss of sleep, where I would be confronted with neither the events from the evening nor the previous weekend.

Chapter 28

SHE CALLS IT LIKE SHE SEES IT

All week, the private online group was relatively quiet. Generally there was a healthy amount of banter among us members. Rosie normally posted belly dance articles that she had come across as well as pictures that she would find of a shirtless Robert Downey Junior. Morgan often shared how her day went and asked others the same. I usually sent updates about gig details. Phoenix became increasingly absent from the online conversations, and I felt him start to drift away. Part of me was bitter that he remained silent in the group conversations, but I knew that change was inevitable. Nothing stays the same, and that includes circles of friends and fire arts ensembles. I sensed that Phoenix would not be around much longer, but I hesitated to specifically point it out to anyone else.

Although Adrian was a member of the online group, he rarely responded to the posts because they often didn't affect him directly. I guess that if someone had asked him, he might admit that he enjoyed being a silent part of the conversation. He had an exclusive window into what us girls talked about, and fairly often it got personal or downright sexy. For example, Rosie always let us know if Victoria's Secret had a sale on panties or bras, including links to her favorite styles. We felt no need to censor ourselves within this private group. It didn't bother me that

Adrian was relatively quiet, but I liked that he was included in the discussions because it meant that he was aware of all the gig details, or group gossip, for that matter.

I had few updates to write about, as our schedule was clear at the time. While fall was usually busy, our schedule would open up quite a bit because of the chilly Cincinnati weather. We would get some indoor tribal belly dance gigs at haflas but, in general, nothing that we would have to rehearse for. I guessed that Rosie was starting to think more about school than tribe affairs and that Morgan was probably busy with work. Rhiannon was halfway around the world, probably learning how to meditate or something. I missed her company.

When the following Thursday rolled around and it was time for the meeting to begin, I asked the group, "Is there anything we need to discuss tonight?"

"I have some news!" Rosie exclaimed. "Rhiannon is en route to come back home!"

"That's awesome," Morgan said as she took a seat in a chair. "Did you hear from her? What else did she say?"

"Well, that's about all she told me in this postcard she sent me. Said she was surprisingly homesick, and missed us more than anything, even though she has had a great time in India. I wanted to tell you girls in person. She said she has to catch a couple of flights with layovers and stuff like that, but she'll be making her way back within a week."

"It'll be nice to have the four of us back together again," I said, feeling like I needed to say something to hide the thoughts that were turning in my mind. In a way, I was relieved because maybe things could just go back to normal. At least, normal in the sense that I had become so comfortable performing as a fire eater with a tribe of belly dancers. It was my reality. "Does Adrian know? I wonder if he's coming tonight."

"I don't think he has a reason to show up here tonight, other than to try to get some," Morgan said.

"Damn, girl. What's in your craw?" Rosie got straight to the point.

"I call it like I see it, love. Sorry, Summer. I know you guys are sort of dating, or whatever, but he seems like the kind of guy who's only interested in one thing, and it ain't tribal belly dance. Just don't get hurt, okay?"

I was surprised by this turn in the conversation. Although our "meetings" were often casual and personal—it's what had made us such dear friends—I didn't realize that Morgan was aware of how our relationship had developed, or that Adrian's affection was even on her radar.

"Thanks, babe. I'm really not sure what to say, though. We'd been hanging around each other a lot lately. But we never talked much about what we're doing together, or where it was going. I think it's over, anyway."

"Over before it started, huh?" Morgan said.

"Details. Now," Rosie interrupted in a faux-firm voice.

"I like him. I *liked* him. I thought he liked me. But we started getting into, I don't know, a relationship, I guess you'd say. But if felt so . . . shallow. He was like candy. Tempting and sweet to taste, but empty when it came to sustenance. I need vegetables." I looked at them to see if they followed me, and they were both nodding. They got it. They always got me. "I should've seen it coming. He's always been so flirty, even when Rhiannon was here. I don't know what I was thinking."

"You weren't," Morgan responded. Rosie shot her a look. "What? I call it like I see it," she reiterated. One of Rosie's eyebrows went up in a subtle look of agreement.

"Here," Rosie said as she handed me a glass of wine. "I'm sure Rhiannon sent him a postcard, too, to let him know she's on her way back. So what's his place in Noir now, after this thing between you two? Actually, you three, since it just got interesting."

"The same," I said. "It doesn't have to change. He and Rhiannon can even get back together for all I care. Adrian and I can be mature about it, I'm sure. I hope."

Chapter 29

THE CHANCE OF A LIFETIME

Anticipating Rhiannon's return, I was feeling a mix of emotions, including happiness to see her again, reservations about how she'd feel about me and Adrian, and curiosity to hear about her adventure. I also felt single and lonely, so I opened my laptop to check to see if I had any e-mails. There were none. Next, I checked my social media accounts. One retweet of one of the tribe images that I shared the night before. *That's nice,* I thought. Another site greeted me with several notifications, most of which I ignored, except for one in particular. Audrey from Hypnosis had sent me an invite to an event. It was an audition they were holding for new performers to join their ensemble. I read it twice and then responded with a "maybe" until I could consider it further. I had always admired this tribe. They were sexy, talented, and always landed respectable gigs that also paid well. Their musicians were dedicated to the dancers, and I loved how they all worked together to create choreographies and experiences that left me wanting even more. But they didn't do any fire. *Yet?* I wondered, *Maybe I could bring the fire.*

If there was one thing I had learned during my time as a fire artist, it was to always accept and go after new opportunities. It was the only way to keep pushing forward, to learn, grow, and improve as a performing artist and even as a person in general. I felt a thrill. A new challenge was ahead of me, and it might just be the thing to take my mind off Adrian.

The sound of someone knocking on my door brought me back to the moment. It was my neighbor from across the hall. A peppy girl, she was always friendly enough, although we never really hung out.

"Hey," she said to me, distractedly looking at a few envelopes in her hand, "the mail just came, and this accidentally got mixed up with mine. It's for you."

"Thanks," I said, accepting a letter and then closing the door behind her as she went toward her own apartment.

Not used to receiving handwritten letters, I opened the small envelope and began reading.

Dearest Summer,

I hope you don't mind that I'm writing, instead of calling or waiting to see you. I have a lot to say, and sometimes, I've found, this way is best. It lets me organize my thoughts and get everything out without interruption or distraction.

First, I want you to know that I thought of you often while I was in India. I wished you could have gone with me, and hoped that that could have happened one day. The colors, the smells, the flavors were unlike anything I've experienced here at home, although, home is home and I did miss it and everyone there.

This was the chance of a lifetime, and I realize it more now than ever. Before I left, the world felt small. But even as I flew across continents I had time to distance myself from my life and begin to detach, to see it for what it was. I hope you can experience this, too, one day. You see how amazing everything is, from the technology of simply being able to fly across the world to the smallest, kindest gestures you'll experience from strangers on your journey. I know you would, too, because you're that type of person.

I danced my heart out while there, learning new styles and forms of dance that I didn't know existed before, and yet, they felt so familiar to my body.

I expected to return home to find things were the same, but I know now that that was wishful thinking. Time and distance can pull people together and equally push them apart. I know that I gave you my "blessing" to see Adrian when I was gone and I regret that decision now, even though it likely would have made little difference. I don't hold a grudge against you for this. I belonged to no one, and neither did he, and whether you realize it or not yet, neither do you. We are all alone.

Adrian told me everything. Honesty was one of the few things that we had agreed from the beginning would help us maintain our relationships, with each other and with others. I did everything I could to make it work, except allow jealousy to enter my mind.

I know that the two of you aren't seeing each other any more. It's irrelevant to me, if you continue a relationship, as I'm going to treat myself to new beginnings in love and dance. They're almost interchangeable, aren't they?

If our paths cross, which they likely will, I won't be mean or rude. You know that's not in my nature. But please understand if I'm distant and respect that. One day, who knows, maybe things will come full circle and we could be closer than ever. But my heart can't go there. Not yet.

As you may have guessed, I'm leaving Noir. Rosie knows, and I'm sure she'll tell Phoenix and Morgan as well.

India is to thank for opening my eyes about Adrian, but so are you. For this, I'm grateful. Who knows what life will lead me to next?

Peace, love, and fire,
Rhiannon

As these words sunk in, my stomach turned to knots in a mixture of guilt, anger, and sorrow. *Good one, Summer,* I thought. *Way to ruin everything.* But I knew that this wasn't what Rhiannon wanted me to feel, and I did want to respect her feelings. They weren't aimed at me in a way that did anything other than express what she was experiencing. *If it wasn't me with Adrian, it probably would've been someone else,* I told myself. In the end, of course acting on my crush wasn't worth the damage it did, but how could I have known? Besides, the heart can drive all reason from one's mind.

I had already said good-bye to Rhiannon when she left for India, and she was gone for so long that I could look at this as just an extension of that trip until we both healed our friendship. At least, that's what I was trying to make myself think.

Chapter 30

ENJOY THE MUSIC

S ometimes, I've learned, it's easier to think about things by not thinking about them. To put them in the back of my mind and let the gears
turn on their own while the conscious part of my brain can catch up to
the unconscious, or maybe vice versa.

And so I practiced tribal belly dance movements, did yoga, and
enjoyed my quiet, creative space. It was healthy. This time gave me what
I needed to express my frustrations through dance, and before I knew it, I
turned the music on my stereo as loud as I could and swirled through the
entire apartment as if no one was watching, because no one was. By the
time the third song finished, I realized that I was being "that" obnoxious
neighbor. I turned the music down to a level that would be considered
tolerable for the other inhabitants of the building and began to get ready
to leave for the coffee shop to meet Morgan and Rosie, having gotten my
dose of therapy for the day.

Once at the Beanery, I saw my girlfriends sitting at a high-top table.
Kyle and Edward were there, as usual, playing music for a small crowd.
"Why do you come here so much, Summer?" Rosie asked. "This coffee is
so strong it tastes like tar. No wonder they have fifty different kinds of
everything but a cup of joe."

"I told you, you should've ordered the tea," Morgan said.

"Thanks for coming, guys. I'll get a cup of coffee, or tea, or something, and then we can talk about a few things." I couldn't resist smiling at Rosie's sarcasm over the coffee.

By the time I ordered a drink (tea, please, thank you very much), the music had stopped playing. Kyle approached the table. He was wearing cut-off shorts and a button-up shirt that said "Plant Food Not Bombs."

"Did you guys hear the news?" he asked us. We looked to each other with negative reactions as I wondered what he was talking about. "Hypnosis asked me to help them spread the word. They're holding open auditions for one or two more dancers to grow their tribe. I thought one of you might know someone who'd be interested." As the glazed look melted off our faces, he said, "What?"

"That's exciting, about the audition," Morgan said casually. "Do you have any more details?"

"Yeah, they gave me a couple of flyers to hand out. They're next to my drum kit by the stage, so I'll drop one off to you, or you can grab it from me later."

We looked to each other again as he left our table, leaving me to wonder who was going to bring up Adrian and Rhiannon first.

"So, I'll say it." Rosie seemed to have read my mind. "What about the group now? We've lost Rhiannon. Adrian probably has one foot out the door, not that we couldn't keep going without him, but still. I wish you would've listened to me, Summer."

Before I could respond, Morgan spoke up. "Rosie, you can't blame her. It's part Adrian's fault, too, ya know. And who's to say what would've happened in other circumstances? Rhiannon was gone. They were dating other people. Well, he was at least, but I'm sure she could have, too."

"That's not the point. Summer shouldn't have dated him or slept with him, or whatever they ended up doing, because she should've known it could fuck up the tribe."

Sick to my stomach, I finally responded. "I had no idea it could have fucked up the tribe. I thought I was in the clear when Rhiannon left. I'm sorry. I'm so sorry. But Morgan's right, too. Rhiannon came back, and she's different now. It was sort of inevitable, for her to travel and see a whole new part of the world and then come back and things change. It's how life happens. It would be boring if it didn't. And yeah, you were right about staying away from the whole thing with Adrian, but I thought I loved him. I was wrong. I've been through a lot, and I can't lose you, too."

Rosie sat, staring into her coffee mug and tapping her fingernail against the porcelain handle. She finally looked up at me and said, "I'm sorry, Summer. There are enough catfights in this world already, and I don't want to make an enemy, or even upset you, for that matter. We've just worked so hard to build Noir. I feel it slipping out of my grasp. Is it enough to just have three of us?" She was quiet for a moment. "To be honest, I'm starting to worry about school. I got the syllabi from my professors for my first classes, and it looks like this semester is going to be more intense than I expected. What are you thinking, Morgan? Think we can hold it together?"

"I don't know. Phoenix seems to have gone AWOL, too, and I don't know what's up with him. Let's just stop talking about it for a while and enjoy the music together, can we?" Morgan looked sullen. I could tell that the thought of the tribe falling apart hurt her, too. So the three of us sat, drinking "tar" and tea, quietly listening to the music that we had performed to together so many times, as I wondered how much longer Noir would last.

"Well, fuckin' A!" While it wasn't a surprise to see Rosie's name show up on my cell phone as it rang, the last thing I expected was to answer to this.

"Um . . . what?" Was all I could muster.

"I take it you didn't hear the new news yet."

"Doesn't seem like it."

"Phoenix is leaving the group, too."

I felt my eyes roll back, hearing Rosie and Morgan's original warnings about this happening, while I was happily in denial about the possibility. I groaned, "What happened?"

"He said it's time for him to move on. Said that he didn't think it'd be possible to just leave the group because we had become like family, but since Rhiannon did, it made it easier. I just wished Phoenix the best. Told him to try to keep in touch."

"I feel so bad about this," I said. "It's all my fault, isn't it?"

"Don't blame yourself for this, too. Phoenix has always been flaky. I think he was getting bored anyway. He's a wanderer, that one is."

"You're right. You usually are." I was trying to feel better. Everything I had built was crumbling, and Audrey's invitation to the audition began to feel serendipitous. With Noir's members dropping like flies, I realized that joining Hypnosis might be my only option, if I wanted to continue with this way of life.

"Usually, right?" Rosie snapped me out of my thoughts.

"Ugh! Damn, I'll admit it. You're *always* right. It's why I love you so much."

"I love you, too, sister friend. Now stop worrying and go spin some shit or something."

Chapter 31

THE AUDITION

Hint, hint. You know, the auditions are coming up.

Audrey had texted me just a few days before the actual event.

I know ... I just might be there. :)

I choreographed a number for the audition, and I chose obscure music that I was confident would be unique for the tryouts that day. I wanted to use something that no other dancer was likely to play. I decided that I would wear simple clothing that wouldn't distract from my actual movements. While my usual costuming included tassels, flowers, feathers, and scarves, for this, a close-fitting top, tights, and a ballet skirt would do just fine.

By this time, I had become dear friends with the ladies in Hypnosis, and Audrey in particular had hinted around about how I should try out and join their tribe.

I didn't want to completely give it away and say that I was going to try out, but I felt destined to be a part of their group. Whenever our gigs aligned and we had the chance to share a song, Audrey and I danced together like we were made to be partners. I remembered a conversation that we once had, when I hinted to Audrey that I was interested in being a part of their tribe as well, but that I would only be able to commit to one rehearsal a week. Hypnosis practiced three times every week, and my unpredictable library schedule just wouldn't allow me to add this to my already busy life, with work and my own tribe. But I was thirsty to perform as much as possible.

I wondered how so many people in this group (there were about fifteen performers, between the musicians and the dancers) were able to give this much time to a hobby, as each of them had full lives as well, with families, jobs, and multiple bands. Not to mention that Hypnosis arranged performances that included heavy promoting, staging, and cleanup. I never felt like my time was more important than anyone else's, but I wanted to be realistic about what I could offer. Yet, I also felt confident enough in my abilities to know that I could learn the moves and would practice them at home on my own time, because I lived to dance. I had created and developed my stage presence, and had a high level of dedication to my art. I always made time to rehearse, create, practice, and study it.

I wanted to at least let my tribe mates know that I was interested in joining an additional group, so I posted a message online to let them know that I was going to attend, and that any of them were welcome to join me. All responded with support, but none were going to the audition. This didn't surprise me, since it felt like Noir Arts was slowly deteriorating as it were, due to everyone's commitments, for better or for worse. Even Morgan seemed to be getting more and more caught up with her work, despite the fact that she loathed it. Knowing how many hours she was putting in already, I didn't press the issue with her, or anyone else.

When the day of the tryouts came, I walked into Dance Mecca. The location was a benefit for me, as this space had become like a home. It had a strong energy of empowerment and sisterhood, which had developed from the bonding that took place during the many haflas, classes, and workshops in the sacred space. There was a blackboard sign at the entryway that said AUDITIONS and had a fancy arrow that pointed to the sanctuary.

Once inside, I found Chloe, the girl who had checked on me after the incident at the party. Chloe was helping to run the auditions, and after we said our hellos, she had me sign in on a sheet of paper. "It's really great to see you here! How's your burn healing?" she asked, stealing a glance at my arms.

I set my purse down next to my feet and slipped off the light jacket I was wearing, revealing a pale stretch of arm that only hinted of the memory. "It's doing well; thanks for asking. You know what they say," I said, trying to keep it real, "it's not if, it's when." There's nothing like burning yourself with your own fire prop to make you feel humble.

"Yeah, that's why I stick to glow-in-the-dark props, I guess," she said. "But I love to watch the fire. Your burn's hardly even noticeable now, though. That's great," she added. "Good luck."

I smiled a thank-you in response and added my name to the list of hopefuls. In the room were a handful of girls who stretched and primped, also there for a shot to join Cincinnati's best tribal dance and music ensemble. I was surprised by a couple of people there that I knew. They didn't have nearly as much experience as I did, and when I was saying hello to one in particular, the girl said flatly, "I know I don't have a chance, but I'm trying to push myself to do more, to put myself out there and try some new things, take a risk now and then." I respected her for this. I was nervous but felt that because of my experience and relationship with the people in Hypnosis, I would be a shoo-in.

"Summer." I heard Chloe call my name across the bare floors; the moment I looked up, I saw another dancer walking into the room. It was Rhiannon.

"Summer, it's your turn." Chloe repeated herself as Rhiannon noticed me. I turned my head to avoid making eye contact with her, unsure of how she'd react.

I ceased stretching my hips to go into the actual audition room, walking past Rhiannon with an inclination to reach out and pull her to me in a hug, in a gesture of peace and of asking forgiveness. Instead, I kept my arms to myself and acknowledged her with only a slight nod. This was my moment.

This was the space where Hypnosis often performed, and where I had been a part of their shows with Noir Arts. Although it was a familiar space, it felt different when I entered. My friends, my partners, my tribal sisters—the girls in Hypnosis—sat in chairs in a semicircle in front of the stage, and although they welcomed me to come in, they didn't portray the normal warmth that I felt when we saw each other. They were cool and distant, playing the part of judges instead of friends. *That's all right,* I told myself. *This is business.*

I suddenly decided to scrap the choreography I had intended to use for this moment, as I felt the need to improvise and give them my self, a physical presentation of my love and talent, rather than planned steps and movements. I handed one of the judges my MP3 player and asked her to play a song at random, leaving my musical fate to chance. Moving to the middle of the space, which felt enormously empty with only my body to fill it, I made a sudden turn toward the wall, spontaneously grabbing a high-backed bar stool that had been pushed aside with several others. As the judges silently watched, I carried it with me back to the middle of the floor, the boards creaking here and there, making the only sound in the room. Once in place, I adjusted my body: shoulders back, chest up, bottom tucked, knees slightly bent, and lastly, chin slightly raised.

As the music began to play, I stopped thinking with my mind and let my arms, hands, legs, and feet take over. Muscle memory from my days in ballet classes made my body move with a fluidity that only comes from the type of training that I had both received and taught. For my dance, I began to portray a ballerina who was in a class, practicing *tendus* and *plies*. As the song continued, my character ventured out to move freely in a belly dance-esque style, demonstrating muscular isolations, belly rolls, and hip drops, only to return back to the *barre* toward the end of the song to complete the ballet exercises. *And point, and point, and point,* I remembered my own teachers saying on beat with the piano music throughout my formative years. During these few moments, the judges of Hypnosis were able to see a glimpse of me that I only revealed when I performed.

I felt solid about the audition. My technique was spot-on, and I had given them emotion, story, and passion, all at the drop of a hat.

As I caught my breath and the room returned to silence, I looked up at the panel of judges. They had been reserved throughout my piece, and although I felt them there, I couldn't interpret what they were thinking. It's funny how an audience provides another essential dimension of a performance. Without them, my dance would have lacked the depth of feeling that I was able to give to it, to give to them. They began asking me standard audition/interview questions, which went just fine.

"Why do you want to be a part of Hypnosis?"

"Are you going to be able to commit to our rehearsal and performance schedule?"

"Tell us something about you that we don't know." And so on.

They thanked me for my time, and I was kindly and politely excused from the room, left with only my emotions and contemplations.

I needed this. I needed a win. I could feel Noir slipping through my hands, and I knew there would come a day when I would no longer have this tribe to perform with, collaborate with, dance with. If I lost them at this point, I would lose everything I loved.

A couple of weeks later, I received a painfully formal e-mail from Audrey, letting me know that I wasn't chosen. It was a hard pill for me to swallow, but I responded to the message with equal professionalism and then searched online to see if I could figure out who had made the cut. I was surprised with the results. They chose not one, but two dancers, one of whom had considerably fewer hours in classes, workshops, and on stage than I—and the other was Rhiannon.

Chapter 32

SOMETHING TO MAKE MY ADRENALINE PUMP

With my tribe on the verge of disbanding, and with the rejection from Hypnosis, I felt lost. I knew that there was no way to try to continue to hold my own tribe together. We all began to drift in different directions, on different paths, with different intentions. I loved Morgan and Rosie still, so dearly. I missed Rhiannon. I missed Adrian, and I felt a sting about Phoenix leaving as well. But this was life. Fire had brought us together and had held us close, but it alone was not enough to keep us joined. Like all things in life, the ensemble had to evolve somehow—or, at least, *I* had to. I looked back at the many months that were marked with classes and practices, with meeting other fire dancers, doing shows, and immersing myself in what had become my life. Practically every mile on my car's odometer was there from driving to something that involved the tribe, and I was still driven. I felt like a freight train, and I didn't want to stop performing just because everyone else seemed destined to drift away from our shared life. I had a sense that I owed it to myself—and even to society at large, because we were sharing magical, ephemeral dances that most people may only hear stories about.

When I performed, someone would almost always approach me with praise for the fact that I was doing something that I was so passionate about. It inspired others to do the same, and this humbled me. I loved not only to entertain but also to encourage those I met to find what sparked life for them, and to chase after it. Tribal belly dance alone had empowered me so much from the very beginning. It taught me how to appreciate my healthy, strong body; how to stop trying to hide my soft belly by "sucking it in" American-style; and how to look at other women with respect and love, rather than with judgment or jealousy. All of this, in addition to the actual, physical moves that I used to express myself on stage, made me who I had become. They helped push me through the insecurities that I had developed when I was in the hell of high school, and to discover that there was a life—a *happy* life—out there in the world.

If I stopped now, what would I have? My day job. That was it. I feared the boredom that would come. I imagined working all day, to come home to my empty apartment, and then do what? Watch television? Waste my time away browsing the web? I needed something that would make my adrenaline pump, that would make my heart beat out of my chest at the thought of it. Fire was the only answer. I could continue to teach, which also satisfied this need. I thrived when I shared skills and watched others learn and grow, not to mention that I loved to watch my students discover their own love of spinning poi or dancing. I had made a lot of friends this way, as well. But there was something about performing that I had become addicted to. I would feel a slight burst of excitement when I had the first contact with someone booking the group. It was both frustrating and fun to organize our shows and practice for them. Then, just as relevant, I would feel relaxed when I got into makeup and costuming for the gig while I burned incense and listened to music. I also thrived on the show itself and the butterflies that accompanied it, not to mention the appreciative audiences afterward. Finally, saying good night to my dear tribe members, complete with hugs, made for one hell of an evening. Every time we performed together, I was honored to be a part of something so special. They were each so talented.

I wasn't ready to give it all up, and although I was naive about where my path would take me, I knew that the destination was at least somewhat within my control.

Chapter 33

EVERYBODY NEEDS LOVE

"I hope you don't mind my asking, but would you be interested in performing for a hafla next month?" Audrey's voice came through my phone in a message a couple of weeks after I had received the rejection. "Hypnosis is hosting it at Dance Mecca, and we were looking for an act that's . . . different. You could hoop, either with fire outside or with a glow hoop inside. You could spin or eat fire. You could even do the crazy trick you told me about, where you put the nail in your face. Ooh! I can barely even say that. We'd just love to have you be a part of the show, even if you choose to do a tribal fusion number. So, think about it, and call me back, okay? Bye!"

Although they didn't accept me as a tribe member, they apparently thought I was talented enough to invite me to be an act in their show. *That's cool, at least,* I thought. Of course I would love to be a part of it. But it would be the first time that I would be booked as a soloist, without even the possibility of my tribal sisters joining me. I thought about Miranda, my first mentor who ran Mecca, in all her wisdom and experience, and considered what she would do. I decided that Miranda would probably go for it. I rarely ever regretted taking an opportunity to perform. My gears turned as I thought about whether I wanted to hoop, or do the nail-in-the-face trick I learned from Nailface Nina, or both, or something completely different. Even a tribal fusion solo might be fun, as I could take qualities from genres like contemporary dance and weave them within the belly dance movements. I had limited time to work out the details either way, so I called Audrey back.

"Hey, Audrey, this is Summer," I said into her voice mail when she didn't answer the phone. "Thanks for the invite, and yes, I'd be happy to. Just let me know the details. What time does the show start, how many songs do I have, how much time should I fill, are there any special costuming things I should know about? You know the drill. Thanks again, babe; talk to you soon." Once I clicked the "End Call" button on the phone, I sat down next to a window, opened my laptop, and began browsing my hard drive for music files to see if anything yelled out to be used for this next show. My choices were endless—fast, slow, happy, sad—and I had no one to check with, no one to agree or approve or dispute the choice, as would have been the case if I had to run it by the tribe. It was a strange feeling: slightly liberating, slightly unnerving. Not wrong, but different. It was something I could get used to.

Several e-mails and a couple of phone calls with Audrey later, I had everything I needed to know about the hafla. She confirmed that my options were completely open. I could either break tradition and hoop in a way that was wildly unique and unexpected for those who knew me, or I could go old school and pay homage to Miranda and Audrey, and share the original tribal belly dance style that I initially fell in love with. After I let Morgan and Rosie know about the gig, I found that I had their complete support. Of course I would. They were cherished friends who wanted nothing but the best for me, as I did for them. I never knew that I could love other women like I did Morgan and Rosie, but if I had been born with a sister I would have understood how possible it is.

I snapped out of my daydreaming when my phone rang. When I answered on the second ring, Kyle's voice came through. "Hey! Just wanted to call and tell you that I'm glad to hear you'll be performing at the hafla!"

"Aw, thanks. I'm looking forward to it. A little nervous, since it's my first official solo gig, but at least I'll have a lot of friends there."

"Yeah, definitely. I'll be there, cheering you on. I'm bringing a dish, too. I made up a recipe for vegan chili that I'm dying to share with everyone. It's actually called 'The Best Vegan Chili You'll Ever Eat.'"

"You made it up, and it's the best in the world? Well, we'll just have to see about that," I teased him. "See you soon, dear."

After a pause, Kyle answered, "See you later then."

"What time do you go on?" Morgan was at Dance Mecca, waiting for the show to begin.

"There you are!" Audrey came up behind me and pinched my hip before I could answer. "You're almost up! I was starting to freak out that you wouldn't be here!"

"I'm here. I've just been floating around saying hello to everyone," I replied nervously. I was as nervous as I was excited about performing.

"Be on standby. Rhiannon's about to go on, and then you're after her. Come with me."

"Oh!" I felt a pang of surprise and, if I had to admit it under oath, jealousy as well. I walked with her as I said, "How's that going?"

"She's doing great," Audrey said out loud, but her eyes and her tone said more: *I'm sorry.*

"Good! I can't wait to see her dance with the group," I said, taking off my coat.

"It was a little early to have her and the other new girl perform in the same numbers with us, so they're each doing a solo number. I don't really know what to expect, even. They were given the same direction as you, to come up with anything they'd like to share. Tonight's about expression."

As we settled in next to the stage, I set down my purse and coat and quickly began to stretch as the band finished their song.

"Well, here we are," Audrey said. "I need to go make sure that the dancer following you is going to be ready. Break a leg!"

I looked out over the audience and saw Morgan and Rosie, then noticed Kyle. Despite our earlier phone conversation, I thought that it was unusual to see him there. He performed so often that he rarely came to events where he wasn't actually booked. He considered those evenings his "off work" nights and would do things with his other friends and family. I subtly waved to him from next to the stage, and he waved back with a warm smile.

Kyle looked exceptionally attractive this evening, not unlike the first time I met him when I "zillgamsed" during the call-and-response game he and I played with my zills and his drum. I had always thought of him as a distant friend, someone who played music for our ensemble, and nothing more. But I didn't have time to consider it any further, as I was distracted from my thoughts by Rhiannon taking the stage.

She was using recorded music that was upbeat and filled with the melodies of bells and flutes.

She wore grass-green silky pants, layered under a beautiful, loose-fitting bright pink skirt that came to her knees. Her midriff showed beneath a top that was a combination of the same green and pink shades, with sequins sewn along the seams of the entire outfit. Her hair was pulled back into a bun, from which hung several earring-like pieces of jewelry that were tucked throughout her dreads. Even her makeup was brighter than usual. I was used to seeing her in neutral tones, but tonight her lips were pink, and she even wore blush on her cheeks. She smiled so big throughout her dance, but I could see a touch of sadness beyond her false eyelashes.

Right away I could see how much she had learned in India. Before, I could've predicted her next dance movement because we had been so close, had mirrored each other at classes, at rehearsals, and on stage for countless hours. I knew her body language almost as well as my own. But now, her movements were foreign to me, such as the intricate way she used her eyes and fingers as she seemed to tell a story. It was a new dance vocabulary, and it made me feel even further away from my old friend.

I remembered the times that we would try out new dance combinations together, and how we would laugh with each other when one of us would mess up a move. I remembered the very dreads that now hung from my head, and how she helped me change my hair into something that expressed who I was so clearly. And I wondered, maybe, just maybe, if we could put Adrian behind us and be closer than ever. We would have one more thing in common, after all.

The song came to an abrupt end that left the audience in a silent shock for just a second, until they broke out into applause and Rhiannon bowed graciously and left the stage. As she passed by me, our eyes met briefly, but long enough for us both to acknowledge each other, and our pain. I missed her, and yet she was so close.

"Everyone give a round of applause for Rhiannon!" Audrey said into the microphone as I forced myself to focus on my own performance. "Ladies and gentlemen, it's turning out to be quite the chilly winter, and so we're going to heat it up in here. We're pleased to bring you Summer!" The audience applauded, yelled, and whistled as I blushed with the unexpected announcement. As much as I would love to heat things up, that wasn't the angle I was going with at the moment, but I quickly let it go and fell into my stage character as the music started. It was so soft at first that the audience quickly realized that there could be no chatter if they wanted to hear it. They quieted down as I took the first few steps across the stage and swayed my hips while I kept the rest of my body still until I was in the center of the stage. I stopped there on cue with a pause in the music, and began to perform the tribal dance that so many there were familiar with, yet I did so with my own flavor of movements. It was more sensual, bolder, than they were used to seeing from me. My eyes probably held the same distant sadness as Rhiannon's. It was like I could feel her energy still present on the stage where I danced.

As the song ended, I slowed my movements to almost a complete stop and drew my arm through the air one last time, as slowly and gracefully as though I were waving it through water. No one moved. It was so quiet that as I came out of the trance from the movement, music, and space, I started to fear that those in the front row could hear my breathing. By the time these silly thoughts made their way through my mind, the crowd burst into an applause that was by far more enthusiastic than what they had greeted me with.

Honored with their response, I stepped down from the stage as the band returned and began their next set. I started to grab my coat to step outside for a quick breath of fresh air when Kyle came up to me.

"That was amazing. Did you audition? I've been wondering if you went for it," he said.

"Hey! Um, yeah, I did, but I wasn't accepted," I answered. He had a questioning look on his face, so I continued, "Rhiannon was there, though, and she actually got in."

"You're kidding."

"I'm not," I said, half laughing to hide my disappointment. "But it's all good. I was able to be a part of this tonight, right? I'll keep dancing, always."

"As you should," he said, and I knew that he was someone I needed to keep close to me. A proponent, an ally that would hold me accountable and not let me let go of what I so love.

"Well done, love, well done." Morgan had come up to Kyle and me. "I'm so proud of you. You got up there and you did it. How do you feel?"

I started to talk, but tears came to my eyes instead. I was feeling so many emotions. The rush of performing, the complex feelings for Rhiannon, even standing with Kyle suddenly had me feeling . . . something. Instead of answering, I hugged Morgan, knowing that I wouldn't have to talk about any of it, not at that moment anyway. When we pulled away from each other, she changed the subject.

"So, Rosie's over there talking with Rhiannon. She seems to be doing okay, considering that, you know, she came home a single woman without a tribe."

I winced with guilt.

"Do you think we'll be okay?" I asked.

"Yes, I do, at least eventually. She's not the kind of person to hold a grudge, and it's not like you did anything deceitful. You were just living life, and so was Adrian, and it is what it is. Can't go back."

"Right. Can't go back."

"Can only go forward," Morgan added.

"And outside," Kyle said. Morgan and I looked at him with questioning expressions. "We can go outside. You can fill me in on what the hell you're all talking about."

"Oh God, you don't know," I said, regretting that Morgan and I had this conversation in front of him.

"When Rhiannon went to India," Morgan began, "Summer and Adrian started seeing other, then Rhiannon came home . . ." She continued as I raised a weak wave to them both and took Kyle's suggestion by walking outside for some fresh air.

I was outside standing around and taking in the stars, in the same space where I had lit up with my fire tools for other haflas, when Kyle came out and invited me to sit down on a bench in front of the blazing campfire. A few other people were outside, too, mostly other dancers and acquaintances whom I knew from mutual friends. The music from inside drifted out through the door, which constantly opened and closed as folks wandered around and mingled with friends.

All of my emotions from the evening boiled up into tears that threatened to fall from my eyes as we sat watching the fire. I was a hot mess, at least on the inside.

Kyle was next to me, and it felt so good to have him there, quietly waiting for me, just being a presence. Blinking back the tears, I sighed. "I'll be fine."

"I know you will. I can see it in your eyes," he said. I turned to face him, listening. "The way you dance . . . you can't see it, but there's a spark there. It radiates from you. Not everybody has that kind of energy. You know?"

I did, now. I thought about everything I had been through, and how I had kept going despite people trying to hold me back.

"I was blind to it," I said modestly as I picked up a stick and poked absentmindedly at the embers in the fire. "This is sacred. This—our friends, our experiences—they mean something. And things keep changing, but they're not really changing. It's more like they're evolving."

Kyle leaned forward, putting his elbows on his knees. "I get it. I think all of us want it to be perfect, and it nearly is, but it takes a lot of work, and it takes understanding from each other, and it takes friends being there for each other. No matter what." He sat up again and said, "The trick is to focus on your own essence. Your path. Who you are, who you want to be. You may not be able to deny your past, but it's part of who you are today, now, in this moment. And I can tell you that I'm grateful for that. I'm sorry that you had to go through pain, with Adrian or Rhiannon, or anytime in your life, but maybe if it wasn't for that, you wouldn't be who you are now. I like who you are now."

His flattery had quite the effect on me, and I suddenly realized how warm my cheeks felt.

"We've been friends for a long time now," he continued. I immediately had a sense of where this was going, and I liked it. I had been so preoccupied with Adrian that I had overlooked Kyle. I saw him for the first time, not as if we had been partners in a performing arts ensemble, but as a man who I knew was a talented musician and a caring person. Not to mention that he was easy on the eyes.

I'd never really looked at his arms since we first met, for example, or noticed how his shirt hugged his biceps, or that his cheekbones were so defined, or, for that matter, how piercingly emerald his eyes were.

"We've had a chance to be together quite a bit," he said, "but not really get to know each other. I'd like to get to know you better, as a person and not just as a dancer."

I unconsciously licked my lips and looked at the fire for a moment before turning to face him. "I think I'd like that, too."

He smiled shyly at me. "I don't want to come off too forward too fast, but I've liked you for a long time. I want to be closer with you." He reached into his pocket and held out something that was in his hand in a gesture of giving. I opened the palm of my hand to receive a small, polished stone that I immediately recognized.

"It's the rose quartz," I said, closing my fingers around it. Then I held it up to the fire in front of us, letting the light dance off its polished surface. "To new possibilities."

"To new possibilities."

Chapter 34

CHILLS

"It wasn't completely my decision," Audrey said. She had invited me to meet at the Beanery to talk about the audition.

"It doesn't matter, though, does it?" I wasn't going to hold on to any grudges or waste too much time trying to figure out if there were other reasons why they hadn't chosen me to join their ensemble.

"I know what a great dancer you are. Everybody knows it. But others in the group felt like you were so committed to Noir that we would get the short end of the stick. We all work our asses off, and I know that you know that, and I know that you would've been able to pull it off because you already practically know our choreography."

It was true. I had been to almost every Hypnosis gig from the first time I saw them. I would watch, entranced, as they performed their various complex routines countless times over the previous couple of years at different events. I knew the music as well. By this time I was already practically a member of their group, considering how much time we had spent together at the gigs, parties, and festivals we had worked at or attended together, which gave us plenty of time to bond over music and dance.

"What do you want me to say?" I asked gently. I wasn't sure where this conversation was going or what her intentions were.

"First, I just want to make sure that we're okay as friends. Everything seemed fine at the hafla and all, but I just wanted some one-on-one time with you to make sure there were no hard feelings about the audition. Cool?"

"Yes, of course. I wouldn't let that come between us, anyway. If I had even thought that it might, I wouldn't have auditioned to begin with."

"I thought so, but it's good to hear. Let me ask you this, then. I heard that Noir Arts was sort of splitting up. Is that right?"

"It is, but I didn't realize word was getting out to everyone already. How did you hear about that?" Even as I asked, I realized that I knew the answer.

"At the hafla. Morgan had mentioned it to someone, and it got back to me. She wasn't saying anything bad. I think she's just bummed about the whole thing."

"You mean Rhiannon didn't say anything about it?"

"Well, she's pretty quiet. Hasn't said much about Noir, but she's sort of one of the reasons I wanted to meet up with you."

"Oh, okay. Well, as far as Noir goes, Rosie's going back to school, Morgan has had to work a lot of overtime, Adrian . . . well, that's complicated. And there's Phoenix. He straight up quit the tribe." I paused to let it all sink in for Audrey. "But I'm not ready to stop. That's why it felt so good when you asked me to dance at the hafla. It gave me a chance to realize that I don't have to stop performing, even though the tribe might be falling apart. I was surprised to see Rhiannon at the audition, but I guess I should've seen it coming."

Audrey nodded her head. "Perform with Hypnosis then. Join our tribe. Rhiannon is returning to India, so we have an opening."

"What do you mean, she's returning to India?"

"She said that after coming home, she realized that she should have stayed there."

"Oh," I said simply. "If that's what she wants."

"I'm sorry. I assumed you'd know."

"Well, like you said, Rhiannon can be quiet. I'll miss her, that's all. I guess that's what she and Rosie were talking about so seriously at the hafla," I said, remembering how distant they both seemed, wrapped up in their conversation. "Okay, so everyone else in Hypnosis is cool with me joining?"

"It wasn't super easy to get you in, to be honest, but when the rest of our group found out that Noir is disbanding, they were completely on board with you joining. You'll be able to eat fire and stuff like that for our shows, as you'll be the only fire dancer in our tribe."

I looked up from my tea and blinked slowly. I took a sip, tilted my head to the side, and looked Audrey in the eyes to see if I could read further into this. It seemed pure. No hidden motives, no agenda.

"I just got chills up my legs."

"Is that a yes?" Audrey raised her eyebrows with a hopeful smile.

I answered with a nod, and an invisible shiver of giddiness ran up my back.

My first date with Kyle was a breath of fresh air. We didn't go to a bonfire party, didn't have tar coffee at the Beanery, and didn't do anything that was in the norm for us as performers. Instead, he took me out to dinner at a nearby cafe that had folk musicians playing acoustic melodies on a small stage in the corner. "This is quaint," I told him.

"Isn't it? I've been coming here for years. They have the best grilled cheese sandwich this side of the Mason-Dixon."

I laughed. "Grilled cheese? Isn't that something that you make at home when you have nothing else in the kitchen?"

"It sounds basic, but I'm telling you. You gotta try it," he said.

"Okay, I'm convinced. Grilled cheese. Split a bowl of tomato soup for dipping?"

"I don't know about that . . . you might get my cooties if we double dip."

"Or even worse, you could get mine!" We laughed together, both with a look in our eyes that made me wonder why we had never done something like this before. Breaking our stare, the waitress came to our table to take our drink orders.

"You look so familiar to me," the waitress said, tapping her pen against her cheek. She added, "Have you been in here before?"

"Who, me?" I asked. "I haven't, but my friend here has."

"No, no, it's you, I mean. I love your hair by the way. I'd love to do that myself, but I don't have the guts."

"You should just do it then. What's the worst thing that can happen?"

"Um, I'd have to shave my head when I got to the point where I didn't want them anymore. Don't think that'd go over too well with management, if you know what I mean. I just have to live through my customers. Speaking of which, wait a minute . . . it's coming to me now . . . you're that fire eater who belly dances, aren't you?"

"Probably," I said, smiling modestly.

"That's cool shit. I saw you at a faerie festival downtown last May. You do have guts." She tucked a stray hair behind her ear and clicked her pen so she could write our order. "So what'll it be? Grilled cheese?" On a dime, she switched her focus from me to Kyle, and he commenced ordering two grilled cheese sandwiches and one bowl of tomato soup. The waitress left our table, and Kyle looked at me.

"Do you get that a lot?"

"What, about the dreads or the fire?"

"Either. Both."

"Probably just as much as you do, for being a musician who plays out all the time." I realized the truth of it, and the fact that this was yet another thing that we had in common. I also noticed the way the waitress's gaze had lingered on him while she was at our table, and it confirmed that I wasn't the only one who thought that Kyle was the hottest thing in the cafe. I wasn't jealous, but I liked the fact that someone else noticed how dreamy my date was.

"Do you mind if I ask you something? You probably get this all the time, too," he said.

"What is it?"

"What's it feel like, to eat fire? Do you ever get scared?"

"It's a little scary. Just scary enough to make it exciting. If there wasn't any danger, I wouldn't get any adrenaline out of it, you know? For me, it would just be another job that I did on the weekends or something. But it doesn't hurt. I mean, sometimes my lips get a little chapped, and once in a while I can taste the fumes, but the act itself is magical. I feel like I'm tapping into a practice that's been done across time and cultures. I feel close to my human roots, if that makes sense."

"It does," he said. "It's like me with my drum. When I play, it's like a heartbeat. It's essential. Rhythm is everywhere around us, but most people are oblivious to it. The drum brings it out, makes it more accessible."

"Like fire," I said.

"Like fire," he repeated.

Our dinner arrived and we devoured the sandwiches while sharing the soup. Long after the bowl was empty, we stayed at our table to drink and talk about our shared experiences.

"Remember that time that I had the 'wardrobe malfunction' at the Moroccan restaurant?" I laughed.

"How could I forget? We booked like twelve gigs from that performance!"

"I thought I was going to die when Edward fluttered his flute when my pants tore. It was bad enough that they ripped like that, but his sound effects pushed me over the edge."

"It was hilarious. I'm just glad that you didn't trip over them. It looked like your foot had gotten caught up in the fabric. Only in the life of a belly dancer." We continued to commiserate together over drinks until the waitress returned with the bill. She laid it on the table and Kyle picked it up to pay.

"So when's your next show? I'd love to see that again," she asked before walking away.

"I don't really have anything lined up right now," I told her. "It's sort of our slow season, with the weather and the holidays and everything, you know?" I looked away briefly, realizing that "our" would mean something completely different moving forward. For so long, it meant "Noir Arts of the Queen City," and it would mean "Hypnosis" from now on. This would take some getting used to.

"That makes sense. Do you teach classes? Where did you learn? How do you even get into something like that?"

"Well, yes, I do teach, but it's a long story as far as how I came into all of this. Here's my number." I jotted it down on a napkin and handed it to her. "You can call me about classes when you have a chance. I do private lessons and workshops, too."

"Hell yeah. This is so cool. Thank you! I'll give you a ring sometime."

As Kyle paid for dinner, we waved good-bye to the waitress and left the cafe. "So what now?" he asked. "We could catch a late movie, or there might be a party going on somewhere."

"I'm not into movies, to be honest, and a party would be fun, but I kind of like just hanging out with you right now. It's nice. It's like we're getting to know each other for the first time." I looked down bashfully, hoping that he would agree.

"How about if we go downtown and walk around Fountain Square? I think they have live music there tonight. We can grab a coffee and just sit at the fountain if you want to."

And I did want to.

Chapter 35

TO DO THINGS LIKE NORMAL PEOPLE

Despite the looming breakup of the tribe, things looked good. I had an opportunity to perform with Hypnosis on a regular basis, and my new relationship with Kyle had me feeling optimistic. I had renewed hope that the end of Noir was not the death of my creative outlet. Dance and the fire arts had helped to keep me sane, particularly since my attempted suicide. And my new friendships had made it all a less painful memory. I felt less alone, and my attempt at self-mutilation had less power over me. I was more free.

Without fire and dance, however, I knew my life would be a series of monotonous daily tasks. It was a week before Christmas, and the remaining members of Noir Arts agreed to meet for our rehearsal to exchange small gifts and talk shop if needed.

I arrived at Rosie's place with tokens of handmade goat soap that I had bought at the local market. Rosie welcomed me into her home and poured me a glass of wine. As we were catching up with each other, Morgan showed up with a couple of gift bags, and we each hugged our hellos. I could feel the love that we shared as we embraced.

After we had gotten comfortable in Rosie's living room, I looked around and remembered all the times we had gathered here in this space, and the friends who had been a part of our tribe who were no longer there: Phoenix, Adrian, and of course Rhiannon . . . "Has anyone heard from Rhiannon?" I asked.

"Not very recently," Rosie said. "She told me about returning to India, and I guess she's been busy getting ready to leave again."

"I'm happy for her," Morgan said. "It's not every day you get to go to India, ya know?"

"I'm sure it'll be good for her," I said. "Maybe she'll find the peace she's looking for."

"Yeah," Rosie said. "Sometimes it takes a trip like that to help you see the light. I think it did for her the first time, but, I don't know. Maybe it was all too painful. I really thought that dancing with Hypnosis would bring her happiness."

"It has to come from inside, the happiness," I said, knowing how true this is. "And you know, she is a wanderlust queen."

"True, true," said Rosie. "So what else is up with you two, anyway?"

"Freaking work," Morgan said. "I hate it. I'm so done. I can't believe I was even able to make it here tonight because they were pushing so hard for me to stay, but I told them I had to leave. I already put in ten hours today, and anything they needed me to do at that point could wait until tomorrow. Assholes."

"That sucks," I said with empathy. I hated to see her have to work so many hours at a job that she hated. Although I wasn't madly in love with my own job, at least it was tolerable and flexible. "I guess I have some news, on a couple of different fronts. You know the night of the last Hypnosis hafla? Kyle, our drummer Kyle, actually asked me out. I said yes."

"Aw, that's sweet," said Rosie. "He's so cute. I'm kind of surprised that he waited this long. He's been eyeing you for a long time now."

"Really? I guess I hadn't noticed."

"Seriously, Summer. You were so preoccupied with Adrian. It's hard to be open to someone new when you have horse blinders on," Morgan said. When I gave her a mildly offended look, she added, "Just keeping it real."

"I wouldn't say I had horse blinders on," I retorted. "I mean, I've been busy. I just didn't pick up any vibes from him until recently."

"Well, I'm glad that you finally did. He's a good guy," Rosie said. "He'll treat you right, and he's not a pothead."

"Who's a pothead?" I asked.

"We're all potheads." Rosie laughed, partly because we all knew it was such an exaggeration. Although we did all partake once in a while, I never considered any of us to be burnouts. But, it was nice to know that Kyle rarely smoked. This somehow made him even more attractive, now that I thought about it. He wasn't wasting his time and money getting high, as can so often happen when social sharing turns into a daily habit. He was either playing music, teaching, or working on his gardens for his farming business.

"He's a catch. We'll see where it goes, though. It's still early, and I don't want to jinx anything. Like the Grateful Dead said, 'sometimes you get shown the light in the strangest of places if you look at it right.'"

"I'll toast to that," said Rosie.

"A toast!" said Morgan.

"To seeing the light!" I added, and we toasted.

"You said you had two bits of news," Rosie said as she gently dabbed her mouth with a napkin. "What else is going on?"

"Audrey invited me to join Hypnosis."

"Even after they turned you down from the audition?" Morgan asked.

"Well, yeah. I hate to admit it, but when I consider the direction that our tribe is headed in, things look kind of grim. We have to be honest here. As much as we truly want to hold it together, life is happening, and it's changing priorities for us, as individuals and as a group. This is a new opportunity for me, and I don't want to pass it up. I hope you both understand."

"Do we have a choice?" Morgan asked sullenly. "You're going to do what you want to do."

"Yes, you do, but consider what kind of a choice I have. I don't want to stop dancing, and I don't really want to become a soloist. Part of the reason I love all of this so much is being a part of a tight, collaborative group. I know that we'll continue to be friends, and there's no doubt in my mind about that. But I don't know how much longer we're going to be able to continue as a professional ensemble. You have to admit this," I said. "And I believe that our friendship is strong enough to last even if we're not bound to meeting once a week."

"That's true," Morgan said, looking me in the eyes. "It just bums me out. It's, like, real now. We're actually breaking up. It's the end. We've just been through so much."

"And we'll still go through so much together," Rosie interjected. "Like Summer said, even though we're not performing together, we can still hang out. Maybe we'll do things like normal people, like go shopping together and stuff."

And just like that, we had broken through the denial we had all been living in, as well as the pain of realizing that it was time to let go of the past, and even the present, and move forward with our own lives. It felt good to say it out loud, considering that it had been lingering on my mind through the recent months. I was relieved, knowing that it could have gotten nasty if either of the girls had felt bitterness or jealousy over my joining Hypnosis. Although they were usually cool as cucumbers, I knew that one can never predict how another person will react to news of change.

The evening came to an end. With the presents exchanged and the wine glasses emptied, we hugged good-bye and Morgan headed out to leave. I walked out to my car and sat in the driver's seat for a moment, watching her car disappear down the street. I turned the key just far enough so that the radio would come on, started to put on my seatbelt, and then paused to look at Rosie's house. I had spent so many evenings there with laughter, tears, fire, and dance. My memories of this place would forever be fond ones. As I looked back, I felt incredibly happy. I had come so far on this unexpected path. I stared off as I thought about who I was at the beginning of this adventure, and whom I had become.

Rosie's front door opened, and she walked down her porch steps. She was saying something, but my window blocked her words. As she approached my car, I rolled down the window and said, "Come again?"

"I said, make sure you 'ROCO.' With Hypnosis, I mean."

I laughed, fondly remembering our code. "It's not going to be the same, dancing without you."

"I'll be around," she said, putting her hand on the car. "You just keep going—for me, for Noir, for you."

ABOUT THE AUTHOR

Cherie Dawn Haas is a writer and a dancer who loves all things that involve creativity. She has taught and/or performed tribal belly dance, poi spinning, fire eating, and hula hooping, and continues to attend classes in movement arts and occasionally perform. She lives with her husband and two sons in Kentucky, where they manage a small vineyard and take care of their two dogs, Rusty and Hazel.

54558485R00143

Made in the USA
Lexington, KY
20 August 2016